Get a Proper Job

By

Keith Armstrong

Copyright © Keith Armstrong 2017

First published in Ireland, in 2017,
By
Fairbairn Publishing, Fairbairn House,
Drumgora, Stradone, County Cavan,
Republic of Ireland
www.keith-armstrong.com

All rights reserved. No part of this publication, may be reproduced, stored in a retrieval system, or transmitted, in any form or by any means, electronic, mechanical, photocopying, recording or otherwise, without the prior permission of the publishers.

This novel is entirely a work of fiction. The names, characters and incidents portrayed in it are the work of the author's imagination. Any resemblance to actual persons, living or dead, events or localities is entirely coincidental.

Keith Armstrong asserts the moral right to be identified as the author of this work.

Other novels by Keith Armstrong

A Day at the Races

Sand Dollar Logistics

Colonel Smythe's Daughter

The Hunt For Larry Roberts Master Forger

The Cruise Family Connection

To
My Family

About the Author

Keith Armstrong was born in Lancashire, England, and emigrated to Ireland in 1967. He lives with his wife Rosemary in Drumgora, County Cavan. Since his semi-retirement from international textile design and engraving, he has devoted a lot more time to writing. 'A Day at the Races' was his first novel published in March 2013. His second novel 'Sand Dollar Logistics' was published in December 2013. His third novel 'Colonel Smythe's Daughter' was published in December 2014. 'The Hunt For Larry Roberts, Master Forger' was published in July 2015. His fifth novel 'The Cruise Family Connection' was published in 2016.

His sixth novel 'Get a Proper Job' was published in 2017.

Chapter One

To all you aspiring comedians, who are thinking of making it your full time profession, forget it, because it is a lonely place standing in front of people trying to extract a laugh. I've been booed out of working men's clubs, more times than you've had chicken in a basket. As my dad used to say, 'Tha needs to get a proper job son, like a rag mans trumpet tester or a fat rustler in a corned-beef factory.'

You don't know what those jobs are, do you? I've got news for you; neither do I. Just a couple of the insane comments he used to come out with. My dad should have been the one on the stage not me. He was a bus conductor on the route from Ramsbottom to Bury in Lancashire. In the evening when he came home we would get a one-hour monologue of the day's events, from dealing with fare dodgers to unruly kids on their way to and from school. Some of the stories he told us had my mother and I in hysterics. One day this young lady got on to his bus, she was in her mid twenties, blond and drop dead gorgeous anyway, she did just that, dropped down dead. When he came downstairs from collecting fares on the upper deck, he found her lying spark out in the aisle. Dad immediately sprang into action to use his training and give her CPR. He opened her shirt and placed his hand on her chest searching for a heartbeat, well you would, wouldn't you? Then he proceeded to give her mouth-to mouth-resuscitation; well you would, wouldn't you? Anyway, after several minutes the poor girl came around. When she opened her eyes she found my dad lying on top her kissing her or so she thought, she went absolutely hysterical, screaming 'rape...rape' before kneeing him in the balls as hard as she could. When she calmed down and realised that he had saved her life she apologized for her reaction. Several of the passengers attended to dad who had won second prize in this altercation and the emergency services were called. The ambulance arrived and took dad away to Fairfield Hospital to reposition his Crown Jewels from his Adam's apple to south of the equator. He vowed never to save another life again; in future he'd 'just bloody leave em there, then drag em off at the next bus stop.

One day a week mum would let him go down to the pub for a few pints, it was always on a Sunday from noon until mid afternoon when he and his mates played dominos, as well as sinking a few beers. He would come home three sheets to the wind, on a few occasions he was found spark out on the kitchen floor. When mum accused him of being drunk he would open his eyes and say, 'He is not drunk who from the floor can raise his head and ask for more.' I used to practice my gags in my bedroom, honing my delivery skills, practicing my timing, visualising lots of laughter before I hit them with another gag. Then I'd realise dad was standing there, listening to my rehearsal.

"Well, what do you think?"

"Tha can't polish a turd son...tha can't polish a turd."

That's what I wanted to hear, encouragement. Comedy had always interested me, at school I was described as the class clown, or at least that's what it said on my report. Later, I came to realise that it was a criticism and not a form of accomplishment. After leaving school I had four jobs in quick succession, at that rate by the time I was twenty I would have exhausted every position in the job centre, so I decided to become a full time comic. A couple of people told me if I was serious about pursuing a comedy career, I needed a good manager who would secure regular bookings for me. Fat Albert, who owned Bonetti Entertainment was recommended and approached, and after listening to me perform at the workingmen's club in Ramsbottom, he signed me up. Now, Fat Albert wasn't fat, in fact, I've seen more meat on a butchers apron. He must have weighed about forty kilos wet through and it was probably because he was so thin he got this nickname. His real name was Albert Bonetti, his parents originally came over from Florence and had done very well for themselves, they had built up a string of ice cream parlours and fish and chip shops.

He promised me work on a regular basis and his commission would be twenty-five per cent of any booking fee. I thought this was a bit steep, but if he could get me bookings it would probably be worth it. After signing his contract he proceeded to inform me I would have a travelling companion to some of my gigs, a stripper called, 'Big Rita', and believe me she was big, like a moving mountain. She could not drive so I was to be her transport to the clubs of the north. When she got into the back of my car the front wheels almost rose off the ground, and I soon realised the five quid extra I got for driving this tub of lard around wouldn't cover the wear and tear on my vehicle.

She didn't say much thank god, for the most time she just slept, apart from the odd belch and rasping fart, that was quickly followed by, 'Better out than in.' It soon became apparent that this methane cloud had quite a following, and if she was on the bill the clubs would be full. When she stripped off, her breasts hung down to her waist like a spaniels ears, she could cough and at the same time give herself a round of applause. The wrinkles in her stomach looked like a pile of folded pancakes. And what could I say about her arse? If she were lying on a beach sunbathing they would ask her to move so the tide could come in.

I remember one lunchtime show we did at 'The Stag Room' a popular venue in a place called, Bacup, in the

Rossendale Valley, was a bloody nightmare. After about fifteen minutes into my act the flat cap brigade started getting restless, they started called for Big Rita. I thought this lot would not recognise talent if it bit em in the arse and I was wasting my time trying to extract a laugh out of them. It was times like this I realised my dad was right when he advised me to get a real job, so I cut short my act.

"Ladies and gentlemen, put your hands together for the act you've all been waiting for, all the way from sunny Summerseat, on the banks of the mighty River Irwell, Big Rita."

I strolled off to cheers and applause, for the stripper not for me. She used a beach ball in her act and would throw it out into the audience. By the time it was thrown back she would have removed an item of clothing. However, considering she came on stage looking like a bag lady with more bloody skins than an onion, this took quite a bit of time. Fifteen minutes later she was down to her bra and pants when she tossed the beach ball out into the audience. Unfortunately for her, it was heading straight for a table who's occupants had no interest in her act whatsoever, and didn't realize the missile was heading towards their table that happened to be loaded with booze. Their precious pints exploded, the occupants of that table were beer-sodden and upset to put it mildly. Of course, the rest of the audience thought this was hilarious; some even thought it was part of the act. One of them was so outraged, he raced towards the small stage screaming abuse at Big Rita, but she was ready for him. As he swung a punch at her she ducked, quick as a flash removed her bra and wrapped it around his neck. She flung him to the floor and proceeded to kneel on him squeezing the breath out of him as she twisted the bra like a tourniquet. Luckily, one of the bouncers raced over just in time and stopped her before she severed his head from his body. This was lunchtime

Get a Proper Job

entertainment Bacup style, the audience loved it although it had a profound effect on Big Rita, because, she decided against using the beach ball in future performances.

A few months later she packed it all in, said she had lost the buzz for the business but I suspect she was past her sell by date. At least, I wouldn't have to drive her around after a gig, searching for a chip shop or fast food outlet to get her daily fix of Holland's potato pies and mushy peas a northern delicacy. She used to sit in the back of my car shovelling this shit down, it sounded like a rabid dog worrying a sheep.

At the end of my first year under the guidance of, Fat Albert, I started to move up the bill, this wasn't hard because the venues were hardly the London Palladium. One place billed as the 'Las Vegas of the North' in Oldham, was an old Nissan Hut left over from World War Two that had been converted into a theatre. It had the worst acoustics I had ever heard. When you did a sound check your voice continued to echo as if you where in the Alps. I swear I could hear my voice after I'd walked off the stage and got into my car.

I used to get a lot of my material listening to people in pubs, I would scribble stuff down I heard on beer mats and scraps of paper, then when I got in my car record it onto a Dictaphone. People can be so funny without realising it.

One lunchtime, I was in a pub in Bury, listening to two middle-aged blokes who had been to a funeral that morning.

"Did you see the wife, hardly dressed for a funeral was she, didn't exactly seem that upset either?"

"No, she didn't, rumour has it she's already been seen with Charlie Birtwistle, the landlord from the Eagle and Child, you know, the pub on Essex Street."

"Oh that bastard, he would screw anything as long as it had a pulse. His wife got fed up and left him after she found him in the cellar changing a barrel of beer, or to be more precise, giving one of the barmaids, Amy Turner, a lesson into how to hide the sausage."

Then they returned the conversation back to the funeral.

"Don't like cremations I want to be buried."

"Why, it's a cheaper option than a regular burial, I'm going that route, cardboard coffin the lot but the upgraded version with the tri-wall sides. You can even get an oak wood effect printed on it for a few quid extra. Already looked into it."

"For when?"

"For when I'm dead you pillock."

"You're joking, that's bloody sick."

"I wonder what she did with his false leg?"

"Not sure but they could hardly burn it, could be worth something, all that metal, knowing the wife it's probably up on eBay by now."

I was trying to picture this chap with a metal leg and the wife who sounded like she was a bit of a one.

"Anyway, after seeing a cremation I'm definitely not going down that road."

"How do you know, your Marian, might decide it's a much cheaper option and you'll hardly be in a position to protest."

"She knows my view on what I want, and if she does otherwise I'll come back and haunt her."

"Jesus, Eric, if you don't mind me saying so, she's the one in that relationship that would do the haunting. When you told me you two were getting married I thought you'd lost it, she's not exactly what you would call a looker is she?"

"As the saying goes, beauty is in the eye of the beholder."

There was I conjuring up an image of his other half, one eye in the middle of her forehead and a stoop like Quasimodo.

"Come on Eric, your Marian wouldn't be out of place alongside, Boris Karloff."

"It's a good job you're a friend, I wouldn't let anyone else talk about my missus like that."

"What happens if Marian kicks the bucket before you do?"

"That's hardly going to happen is it, seeing as she's only twenty two?"

This was just too much, I started to crack up, and I had to leave them. I had been visualising some old dear from the blue rinse brigade, not someone so young. Serves me right for eaves dropping.

Fat Albert kept me busy and I was putting serious mileage on my car as I journeyed to various gigs. Motorway cafes became my second home as I pursued my career, although I was still living with my parents. Dad never ceased to offer his advice on getting a proper job.

One morning I was asleep in bed after doing a late gig in Yorkshire, when just after 11:00am my mother woke me to tell me the police were downstairs and wanted to speak with me. What was this all about I wondered, another booking for the policeman's ball, that's a raffle not a dance? I threw on some clothes and went down to see what they wanted.

"Mr. Dean, I'm sorry for dragging you out of bed, I'm DCI Porter, this is my colleague DS Staunton. Can you tell me where you were last night, between the hours of midnight and two this morning?"

The two of them wore suits, and looked more like Jehovah's Witnesses than detectives. Porter was in his mid forties, slim and about one and a half metres tall with slicked back black hair, no shortage of brylcreem there. Staunton was a similar age and build but almost bald, he had puffy face, reminded me of a squirrel with his cheeks stuffed full of nuts.

"I was on stage at the Pickled Parrot in Bradford, I'm

a comedian, or at least I like to think I am. Started my slot just after midnight and finished just before one. As it was my last gig, I stayed on at the club and had a drink with my manager and a chat to a couple of people I know, then left at about two fifteen, got home about three. Why do you ask?"

"We're making enquiries regarding the death of a chap called Markus Stone, a singer."

"Really? I know him, he was on stage just before me last night, what happened?"

"I'm afraid he was murdered, his body was recovered from a disused canal near Shipley, it appears he'd been strangled."

"Murdered, you can't be serious, I know he wasn't the greatest singer, but Jesus, who'd want to kill him?"

"That's what we are trying to establish, this is the third death of an entertainer in the past month. Another cabaret artist was abducted in Bradford as he left a nightclub. He was bundled into a car that was later found burned out near Burnley with his body inside."

"Yes I'm aware about that chap, I've been on the same bill with him a couple of times. I heard it was over a gambling debt."

"Where did you hear that?"

"It's just what people were saying, you know how rumours start?"

"Not sure I do Mr. Dean, people spreading this kind of tittle-tattle can cloud the issue, it makes our job more difficult."

"Hang on a minute, I didn't start the bloody rumour it's only what I heard. The chap was known to be a heavy gambler and would bet on anything. Anyway, you said there have been three murders all together."

"The other incident was a male singer murdered after performing at a club in Manchester and we think they could all be connected."

I had only heard about the guy who'd been

barbecued, not the other deaths. I looked at the two of them who by now thought they had got their man. Porter was standing there with his hands in his pockets wearing a smug grin on his face. His colleague DS Staunton had his foot up resting on a chair, annoyingly flicking a coin repeatedly through his fingers. If my mother had seen him, she would have told him in no uncertain manner to get his feet off the furniture. Why is it when you are placed in this position, they always make you feel guilty of something or other?

"Well it bloody well wasn't me, people can vouch for what time I came off the stage and left the club. In fact my manager Fat Albert was at the club and can confirm I left for home just after two."

"Can anyone vouch for what time you arrived home?"

"Yes, my mother, she always waits up for me until I get home."

"You're a bit old for that aren't you?" he said with a smirk on his face.

What the hell kind of comment is that, the cheeky bastard? "Maybe, but that's the way she is, perhaps your parents didn't care what time you got home or if you got home at all."

"Steady on Mr. Dean, I only passed a comment."

"Well I can do without your smart comments thank you very much, and I don't know anything about this chap's death, go and ask my mother if you don't believe me she'll confirm what time I arrived home."

"Don't worry we will. Did you see Mr. Stone talking to anyone at the club or did you notice anything odd?"

"Can't say I did, I arrived at the club during his act and I followed him on stage as soon as he'd finished his spot. I didn't see him again, but there again I wasn't looking for him. Can I ask why you are focusing your attention on me?"

"A tall blond haired man in his mid twenties with athletic build answering your description was seen in the area of Shipley."

"Wasn't me, after I left the club I came straight home."

"Very well Mr. Dean, thanks for your help, we may want to speak with you again we'll be in touch." said Porter.

I bloody well hope not, you smarmy sod. But Jesus, Stone, dead, literally. Of course, later that day the papers were full of his death and the fact the police had no leads into this callous murder. The press seemed to indicate it was a serial killer with a hatred of cabaret artists. I could relate to that, some of them I'd crossed paths with are pure crap, but I'd stop short of doing them in. I didn't know the chap personally apart from playing at the same clubs on a few occasions. He seemed a nice inoffensive fellow, not the greatest vocalist but by the time he went on stage, most of the audience were too pissed drunk to notice if he struck a bum note.

As soon as the police left, my parents wanted to know why they had called. I played it down otherwise my mother would have been climbing the walls, I told them one of my colleagues had been killed in an accident. No doubt they would hear the truth eventually but mother was a natural born worrier and I didn't want to add to her anxiety.

Chapter Two

Just after 1:30am I was on my way back home from doing a gig at a club in Leeds, in the beautiful county of Yorkshire. The weather was atrocious, strong winds were blowing my car all over the road; it was proving difficult to steer.

Anyway, after half an hour into my journey, I felt unwell. I had an acute pain in my stomach that was now so bad I could hardly drive, so I pulled off the M62 motorway into the Granada service station at Birch. Making my way inside, I was in severe discomfort, I staggered through the entrance, then, as the pain became more and more intense, my legs gave way. I slumped down in a heap and laid there until a young lady spotted me and called for assistance.

The next thing I knew, I was recovering in Fairfield Hospital in Bury, after having a ruptured appendix removed. They told me I was half an hour away from death and they operated on me just in time. Of course, my rise to the top of the comedy ladder was on hold, Fat Albert, had to find a replacement for the next couple of weeks.

I have to tell you, I find it's a humbling experience being in hospital, embarrassing doesn't come close to describing the feeling of having your bits and pieces prodded and the most intimate secrets of your body revealed to all and sundry. Nothing is private; all your bodily functions are recorded in great detail for posterity, like an entry into the Dead Sea Scrolls. Maybe it's just me, but I've always felt conscious about my body, probably because I'm hung like a donkey, only joking, more like a horse. Also, I found getting a decent night's sleep is nigh impossible, because you get disturbed every few hours whilst they give you medication and do physical checks.

There was one particular individual called Staff Nurse Hardman, who looked like the Muppet character Miss Piggy. She strolled the wards like a sergeant major, everyone was terrified of her. Junior nurses would throw themselves on the rat-traps rather than being confronted by her. She was quite tall, weighed about 150 kilos and thought she was gorgeous. She was sure all the doctors had the hots for her. It became apparent this wasn't the case with everyone, when I overheard one junior doctor telling a young nurse.

"That woman is oversexed and needs neutering, she has groped virtually every male doctor in this hospital. Poor Paddy Braithwaite, has put in a request for a transfer after she cornered him in the medical stores, he says its put him off sex for life. He went in for sterile bandages when suddenly the door was slammed shut behind him. When he turned she was standing there butt naked. There was no way out, she grabbed hold of him and said 'you know you want me' but he told her to get off him. He was terrified, she was like a preying mantis and do you know what, he couldn't believe his eyes, he says she had dyed her beaver multi colours?"

"What the hell's a beaver?"

"My god young lady, you are innocent, it's the same as pussy, but I don't mean the four legged kind."

"Oh sweet Jesus, that's so weird," said the young nurse with a look of shock on her face, eventually she asked him, "do you know what colour she dyed it?"

"Yes, red white, and blue, nothing unpatriotic about this nymphomaniac."

"I'd have thought she'd have a black bush."

"No love, you're getting confused, that's the name of an Irish whiskey made by Bushmills."

"I'm finding all this all so unreal, is this true or are you just winding me up?"

Get a Proper Job

"Definitely true, in fact, a couple of chaps are still having counselling after witnessing this colourful display."

The two of them walked off, no doubt the nurse would repeat what she had heard and the story would gain in the telling. By the end of the day, Staff Nurse Hardman, would probably have platted pubic hair down to her knees, with a Union Jack tattooed on her arse.

He mentioned neutering; I would gladly perform that procedure on Miss Piggy with a rusty nail. Just after six one morning, she roused me from my sleep, I was not impressed. As I gathered my thoughts and focused my bleary eyes, she was standing at the foot of my bed examining my chart, I thought in view of her past attitude towards me, that day I would be uncooperative.

"Mr. Dean, have you had a bowel movement today?"

"Do you mean in bed?"

"No you fool, have you been to the toilet?"

"Not sure."

"You either have or you haven't," she snapped.

"Like I said, I'm not sure."

"Good lord man, surely to goodness you know one way or the other."

"Look, I don't consider it of national importance, why are you so concerned whether or not I've had a pony and trap?"

"Part of my job, it's routine."

"Jesus Christ woman, give it a rest."

"I'll ask you again, have you had a bowel movement?"

"Mind your own business."

By now the tension was escalating to boiling point, she was clearly very upset as she walked around to face me, standing there with hands on hips willing me to disobey her. I looked up at her lips; they were reminiscent of a sink plunger, painted bright pink. Her eyes were like pissholes in the snow plus she had a moustache that Hitler would have been proud of. As this vision of beauty lowered her face towards me, my life flashed before me, was this how it was all going to end?

"Yes or no will do, not some smart arse reply."

"Maybe, maybe not, how's that?"

Her face was like a slapped arse and she looked ready to explode.

"They tell me you are a comedian, well, I don't think you're a bit funny, but, I've got a laugh for you, roll over on your stomach I need to give you an injection."

With that she proceeded to waive the biggest syringe I had ever seen in front of my face. The last time I saw anything as big as this, was on a Jurassic movie when they were trying to knock out a dinosaur.

"Keep that bloody thing away from me, you'll do some serious damage with it."

"I'll ask you again, have you had a bowel movement today?"

I wasn't going to be bullied by, Florence Nightingale, who by now was holding the syringe like a bloody javelin. As I looked at the bloke in the next bed, he was enjoying the altercation and gave me the thumbs up.

"Like I said, mind your own business."

"I'll be back."

I hope not, "You mean like, Arnold Schwarzenegger promises...promises."

At that point she realised I wouldn't cooperate so she turned and stormed off. I know she was only doing her job but she was an over zealous cow and I was getting fed up with the cross-examination. I'm not an early morning person, my late night gigs meant I usually slept until lunchtime; this routine was a shock on my system.

Eventually, I was discharged from the asylum; my dad collected me after he had retrieved my car from the service station. Two more weeks of rest at home allowed me to do some new routines, a couple based on my hospital experience. I spoke with my manager and told him I was ready for more gigs, but just a couple a week, and not too far away. Dad agreed to drive me until I felt able and strong enough to do it myself; at least it would give him the opportunity to see my act.

My return to the footlights was at the 123 Club in Rochdale, Lancashire one Saturday evening. It was described as a supper club, their extensive menu consisted of chicken in a basket or scampi in a basket, I've tried them both, I'd recommend the basket.

After partaking in either of these gourmet delights and without going down with instant food poisoning, you could watch the cabaret, which was a loose term for audience participation. A more accurate description would be savaged by a pit bull. I'd played there a couple of times before. It hadn't gone well, the audience had a reputation for letting the acts know if they thought they were rubbish. In fact, it was almost like the management encouraged it. I stood nervously waiting for my slot, and then the MC for the evening introduced me.

"Ladies and gentlemen, put your hands together for a return visit of, Mr. Comedy, himself, Carter Dean."

I strode on to a lukewarm applause, before I'd even opened my mouth the barracking started.

"Get off you puff."

Now the one thing I'm not, is a puff, my dad who was in the audience zoned in on the guy with the big mouth. I spotted this grinning imbecile, about three tables back with four other people in the group, he was small and bald with a fat red face, I needed to go on the attack before my dad sorted him out.

"Well, well we meet again, if it isn't, STD George, has the infection cleared up yet?" There was laughter when I said this, but what I didn't know at that time, his name really was, George. His partner, a huge woman wearing what appeared to be a blond wig was looking daggers, first at him, then at me.

He was thinking of a reply, before he could respond I hit him again.

"Saw George coming out of the clinic yesterday, apparently, he's in there that often he gets loyalty points. Two more visits, he qualifies for a new knob end, because the one he's got has more perforations than a watering can."

There was laughter and applause but George's partner had heard enough, she stormed out of the room, he followed meekly behind her. There was no further barracking for the rest of my act, and I got a huge round of appreciation when I finished.

After my stint I joined dad in the audience for a quick drink before we headed home. Then the MC introduced the next performer, "Ladies and gentlemen, please put your hands together, and give a warm One Two Three welcome to Walter and his Amazing Parrots."

This guy waddled out onto the stage, he was about one metre tall, severely bow legged like an old jockey, he had an awful squint in both eyes, one looked east the other west and he was carrying a cage that contained two parrots.

"Ladies and gentlemen, before I start, could I ask you to please remain quiet during my performance so as not to upset, Polly and Percy?"

What was he on? He was so naive; saying that to this particular crowd was like waiving a red flag to a bull.

"Any sudden loud noise could put them off so please indulge me, and save your applause to the end of our act."

Cocky little fart, assuming he'd get applause in a place that was the graveyard of many cabaret acts.

The first parrot he took out was a clever bugger, it could count up to ten by tipping over plastic cups in sequence that had numbers marked on them. Then he took the second parrot out and it proceeded to stand the cups back up again 1...2...3 and so on, you get the idea? All very entertaining it must have taken an age to perfect. But, it all went south, when a waiter carrying a huge tray of drinks, skidded along the floor, like something, Torvill & Dean, would have dreamed up, before he crashed into a table in an explosion of beer and broken glasses. At the sound of this, Polly & Percy, took to the air squawking in blind panic. Walter, their handler jumped down off the stage and raced after them but they'd had enough, the shit was frightened out of them literally. Several large deposits landed on the table where, STD George, and partner had returned. All very appropriate I thought, after several low level fly-pasts, he was covered in the stuff and looked like, Nelson's, statue in Trafalgar Square. I've never seen so much shit and feathers; the scene was total mayhem as Walter tried unsuccessfully to catch his renegade birds.

Eventually, they were almost like oven ready birds and had lost so many feathers they were having difficulty flying, their activity had been reduced to jumping from table to table, slipping and sliding as they landed in all the spilt beer, and pork scratchings. It was at this point, Walter, was able to retrieve them, but not before they had unloaded at least twenty kilos of shite on the audience. My conclusion was this act would never get to the London Palladium, or if it did, they would need to issue the audience with sou'westers.

The excitement was just too much; I thought my underpants would never dry, so as soon as I got my fee from the manager we left. On the drive home my dad gave me what I considered was his first form of encouragement.

"Tha did well tonight son, you soon shut that stupid bugger up who was barracking you, bet it's a while before he opens his gob again."

High praise indeed. Dad continued to drive me around even though I was now fit enough; I think he enjoyed the experience visiting the various venues. He was even using some of my gags when working as a bus conductor, telling the stories as if they had happened on his route.

High praise indeed.

Fat Albert, called me one day, to say there was a talent show in Manchester to find the best comic in the north. He had entered my name because he was sure I would be in with a good chance of winning it. The first prize was £10,000 with a slot on Granada television in a new show for up and coming comics. Of course, there would be a lot of competition so I needed to tone down the bad language and work on some new material.

The auditions for this show were to be held at the, Blue Garter, a five-hundred seat venue on the outskirts of Manchester. It had been a derelict junior school in a previous life, which had lain redundant and unloved for years, until a property developer saw the potential and converted it into an up-market entertainment centre. I recognised a few of the comics, one particular chap nicknamed, Barry Bullet, had a very severe speech impediment, a cross between Tourette's syndrome and a really bad stammer. If he was drawn before me it could be a long night.

Another comic a female called, Lilly Maverick, told the filthiest jokes, I'm no prude, but this woman had serious issues and made me feel uncomfortable. It would be interesting to see if she modified her language. As I looked around the room, the competition was strong, some of them seasoned pros who'd been doing the comedy circuit for years.

The judging was being done by a panel of four celebrities, none of whom I had ever heard of. It would be even Stevens, they'd never heard of me, and I hadn't a bloody clue who they were. Judging would be done over six nights, the winner from each heat to go into the grand final at the end of the month. The MC for the evening introduced the various acts until it was my turn. "Ladies and gentlemen, put your hands together and give a warm welcome for, Dean Carter."

Get a Proper Job

The prick...he got my name wrong, what was I to do, carry on as if nothing had happened or, correct the mistake? I walked out onto the stage to face the audience, "Actually, it's, Carter Dean, not, Dean Carter. I thought I'd better tell you, it's either that or start telling my jokes backwards, and I'm not sure I'll be able to remember them all."

This got a big laugh and I was under way. I hit them with several quick gags that went down well; even the judges were cracking up.

"What do you do if your mother in-law throws a hand grenade at you? Pull the pin out and throw it back.

"A blond ordered a pizza, she was asked, "Would you like it cut into twelve or six?

"Six please, I'd never eat twelve.

"You hear a lot these days about sex and the high rate of unmarried mothers. Myself, I've always practiced safe sex. I went into my local supermarket the other day to buy some condoms, the guy at the checkout asked me, "Do you need a bag?" I said, "Jesus, she's not that bloody ugly. I'm not a full time comedian; my other job is a wrestling promoter. A few weeks ago a heavyweight wrestler a chap called Tank Jones from America threw out a challenge that we couldn't refuse. His speciality hold was called the Kamikaze Grip, once he had you in this grip there was no way out you had to submit. He challenged the current World champion, the European champion, and my boy the Irish champion to a match, all of them in the one night. How could we turn down a challenge like that?

"The first guy in the ring was the world champion, within thirty seconds Tank had him in the Kamikaze grip and he submitted immediately. The next guy in the ring was the European champion same result, within thirty seconds his arms and legs were tied in a knot, and he submitted.

"Then it was the turn of my boy Paddy, this time Tank

doesn't have it so easy, he tried several times to get Paddy in the grip but he was an awkward customer. They were rolling around on the canvas for five or six minutes neither one had the advantage. Then Paddy looked down at all the arms and legs, in the middle he sees this huge pair of hairy balls so sinks his teeth into them as hard as he can. There is an almighty scream and Tank flies up from the canvas, hits the ceiling before bouncing back into the ring then shoots off into the audience. The crowd go absolutely ballistic, one guy runs over to Paddy.

"That's fantastic Paddy, tell me how did you do it, no one has ever beaten the Kamikaze grip before?"

"Sure it's amazing what energy you generate when you bite your own balls."

Laughter and thunderous applause followed for several minutes, this got me thinking maybe I could chance the odd blue gag. Nobody had said it was taboo at least not for the heats. If I made it to the final on TV, that would be a different matter. So I decided to go for it.

"This elderly couple met at a bridge club and they got on famously, the old guy asked the old dear would she like to come out on his boat the following day. She said she'd love to do, so he collected her and they drove down to his boat dock. Once they were underway they came to a fork in the river. He thought he would give her the option to choose.

"Up or down?" he asked.

"At which point, she took off all her clothes, grabbed hold of him and with a bit of encouragement, they made mad passionate love. The old guy can't believe his luck. They get dressed and continued on their journey until they came to another fork in the river.

"Up or down?"

"Again, she took off all her clothes, again they made passionate love. Once they got back to the dock, the old bloke had enjoyed himself so much he asked her would

Get a Proper Job

she like to come out on the boat again and she said yes. The following day he collected her then they headed down to his boat.

"Once they were underway, they came to a fork in the river, with a smile on his face and anticipation of what was in store for him he asked her.

"Up or down?"

"Down please."

"The old guy can't believe it, but did as she asked and turned down the river. When they came to another fork in the river again he asked.

"Up or down?"

"Up please."

"The old guy can't believe why her attitude had changed and decided to ask her.

"Yesterday, when I asked you up or down, you took off all your clothes and we made passionate love, yet today when I asked you the same question up or down, nothing."

"Yesterday, I didn't have my hearing aid on, I thought my choices were, fuck or drown."

They enjoyed that one.

At that point I was prompted from the wings my ten minutes were up so, I thanked the audience and left the stage to loud applause. After the last act had finished, the judges got into a huddle whilst they debated whom the winner should be.

Surprise surprise, it was me. Fat Albert was delighted and my mum and dad were so proud of me, I'd never felt this good since I won a pot dog in a yodelling competition at Butlins holiday camp.

Two days later, another cabaret singer was murdered after performing at a nightclub in Oldham. An early morning dog walker discovered the body on waste ground, he was identified as Beau Tillord, a singer in his mid thirties, and he'd been strangled. I knew him, had appeared on the same bill a couple of times.

Of course, the press was having a field day they had all kinds of theories as to who was behind it. A couple of people had been taken in for questioning but later released without charge.

What the hell was going on? Some singers were terrified and already started hiring security. Four people, all male singers had been murdered who was the sicko behind this? As a result, booking fees were on the up for singers and the general feeling was it was only a matter of time before it spread to other performers. Fat Albert had about seven vocalists on his books; quite a lot of them were turning down bookings because they were afraid to travel. As a result, he had to provide transport and a minder to the various locations; it was either this or risk being sued for non-performance.

Chapter Three

The heats at the Blue Garter continued, my manager kept a close eye on who was winning each one. After the fourth heat, a female called Ginger Nuts was the clear favourite, according to Fat Albert. I didn't expect to win, but to be in the final was a major accomplishment and my father was telling everyone on his bus route of my achievement.

I tried to keep busy with my mind on other things. One particular booking was a corporate event at a hotel in The Lake District. It was for an electronics firm who were celebrating being in business fifty years. They had booked a weekend for all their staff to celebrate this milestone. I'd done a few corporate gigs before and they had gone very well.

I arrived at this beautiful hotel on the edge of Lake Windermere, just as they finished dinner in the main function room. The MC had introduced the first act for their entertainment, a juggler called; 'The Amazing Philbert' who it turned out was bloody useless. I don't know whether it was nerves or what, but he dropped several of the clubs he was juggling more than once. It went from bad to worse, when one of them hit a spotlight before the club bounced onto a table, breaking several plates and glasses, splattering the remains of someone's desert over a number of people. The natives soon became restless, the insults and comments on the juggler's ability were coming thick and fast. Calls of "He's a tosser" to "Couldn't catch a dose in a brothel" in fact, this guy was so bad he couldn't catch anything. I began to feel sorry for him and was hoping he'd take the hint and sod off, but no, he was the consummate professional. He seemed determined to stick it out to the end of his routine; it was cringe-worthy to see him. Of course, this didn't bode well for me, following this chap wouldn't be easy. It's one thing being first on stage starting from stone cold, but trying to follow someone who's pissed the audience off wouldn't be easy. I could see the events organiser refusing to pay this guy. I decided to give the audience fifteen minutes to calm down before I braved the stage.

"Good evening, hope you're all enjoying yourselves, wasn't he great?" I said in a sarcastic voice, "it's not every day you see a blind juggler."

This got a good laugh and normally I wouldn't criticise another act nor make fun of the blind but, in a moment of panic, it was all I could think of to get them on my side.

"The last time I saw anything as bad as that, was when my mother-in-law was learning to drive. She took her test twenty-seven times, can you believe it? She had four different instructors, two of whom are still having counselling. I wouldn't say she was bad, she was bloody terrible. But at least she kept the panel beaters in business. I always feel sorry when I see an act like that, as the saying goes I'm afraid he died a death. Actually, talking about death, reminds me about a funeral I was at last month for an eminent heart surgeon who was a neighbour of mine. Anyway, the casket was in the church and directly behind it was a large heart made out of what looked like flowers. Following the eulogy, the heart opened, and the casket slid inside. The heart then closed encasing the doctor inside of it forever. The guy next to me broke down laughing. Remember why we are here and show some respect," I said to him.

"Sorry, I can't help it, I'm just thinking about my own funeral."

"Why, what's so funny about that?" I asked him.

"Because I'm a gynaecologist."

Lots of laughter, slowly they were coming around.

"So your company has been in business fifty years, that's no mean achievement. I hear Mr. Barnes your MD has just got hitched, Jesus, he left it long enough, he's seventy two and never been married, still, why should we be the only ones unhappy?"

It always pays to do a bit of background research, especially when it's a corporate event.

"He's seventy two and she's twenty seven, how's that work?"

Mr. Barnes and his new bride, who was a beautiful girl, were sat at their table looking slightly embarrassed, as the rest of his staff was enjoying seeing them squirm.

"Apparently, it was love at first sight, but she's going into hospital next week to get her cataracts removed.

"Did you know he won the lotto, twelve million quid? When Camelot asked him what are you going to do about the begging letters, he said, I'm going to keep sending them?"

I slagged them off for a few more minutes then when I thought the management had suffered enough, I carried on with my normal routine. After sixty minutes I told my last gag and thanked them for being a great audience.

After my stint I was invited to join a table where six women and two men were sat. The women were all in their early thirties a couple of them were beautiful, the men, well quite frankly, they were not my type. After the introductions were made, I got chatting to Cleo Sage who was the image of Sandra Bullock and really gorgeous. She told me she was in charge of all exports, responsible for looking after sales worldwide, she was well travelled and very interesting to talk to, she spoke nine languages fluently, including Chinese and Japanese.

"Do you speak any foreign languages, Carter?"

I puffed out my chest, "Yes, learning English, although what I would call pigeon English, picked it up in some of the northern clubs I've played at. Amazing what people shout at you, things like 'Bugger off you're useless' I think that means they don't like you, to 'You're about as funny as a dose of the pox,' that sounds very sore, oh and 'Get a proper job' that probably means I'm in the wrong profession. I'm slowly increasing my vocabulary, I anticipate after several more months on the club circuit I should be fluent in barracking. I can also count up to ten, which is very useful, because that's what I usually get paid on average for doing gigs like this."

Cleo laughed, "Are you married, Carter?"

"No I'm not, never found the right girl and my job doesn't help, I'm doing the club circuit almost every night, not an ideal situation to get a steady girlfriend. Don't get me wrong, I'd love to find someone, but it's not easy. I live with my mum and dad. How sad is that? Although, I've just put a deposit down on an apartment in Bury, its just being built should be ready in about four months. I thought at twenty-nine, it was time I flew the nest. My mums not happy about it and I will certainly miss her cooking. She's a great cook, makes the best hot pot in Lancashire from a recipe handed down generations; originally it came from Betty Turpin of Coronation Street fame. What about you Cleo, are you married?"

"No I'm not, a bit like you I suppose because of my job, whilst I love it, it's not conducive to a steady relationship, but also like you I'd love to settle down and maybe have a couple of kids eventually. Have you always been a comedian?"

"That's the nicest thing anyone has ever called me."

Cleo laughed, "Well that's what you are, we all enjoyed your act this evening, didn't we girls?" This was met with a chorus of, "Yes, you were brilliant."

"That's very kind of you all, it has been my pleasure entertaining you this evening, however, it's getting late, way past my bedtime and my chariot awaits. Afraid I must make my way back home, my mum will be getting worried. If I don't clock in by three o'clock she'll have Interpol out looking for me. But that's mothers for you."

I stood up and shook everyone's hand; I said my goodbyes to Mr. Barnes, and his new bride. I hoped I hadn't offended them. I thought maybe I would get the offer to share a bed rather than making the long drive home but there were no volunteers. Cleo walked me to my car and said she would like to stay in touch. I was thrilled, it's not everyday I meet a woman as interesting as this. She gave me her card and I gave her mine and we agreed to call one another. With that, she gave me a peck on the cheek and I made the journey home.

The following afternoon, Fat Albert called me to tell me a cruise company was looking for cabaret acts for an upcoming trip around the Mediterranean, and would I be interested.

I hadn't been on a ship since a trip across to the Isle of Man several years before, when I vomited the whole time I was on the boat. There was so much puke the vessel was in danger of sinking, after this I vowed never again to repeat the experience. He had been asked to supply several acts, including dancers, a vocalist, and a comedian and would I be interested. After giving it some thought I quite fancied the idea, so I put my previous maritime experience to the back of my mind and I told him I'd love to go, so I got the booking.

The cruise was for the end of May so he would have time to kick the various acts into shape. Some of the dancers he'd recruited, I had crossed paths with at different cabaret venues, the others were new recruits. He had to supply 12 girls in total and get several dance routines worked out. Florence Patterson who was an ex windmill dancer was a seasoned pro and worked on the routines with the girls. She was in her late fifties but still very agile and put the girls through their paces. Fat Albert had the use of the top floor of Cloughs, a disused cotton mill that he used for auditions. They had the dimensions of the stages on the vessel marked out on the warehouse floor in chalk, so they could work out the dance routines within these confines. All very slick, Florence was the ultimate pro, leaving nothing to chance. Further rehearsals would be done on board ship, but at least they would have pretty much the polished routines by then.

Sally Proctor, an experienced fashion designer and seamstress was tasked with designing and making all the different costumes for the girls; this was a huge task, it kept her and her assistants working around the clock. A vocalist, called Tony Sheridan was recruited, he styled himself on Frank Sinatra but he was a cocky individual. Most of the girls were swooning over this tuneless chap who thought he was God's gift. I wasn't a fan and would gladly have given him a kick in the nuts.

I had to create new material, cut the bad language, and make my act more family friendly. Not easy when my training and experience had been gained touring the northern clubs where the 'f' word and similar strong language, are the norm.

The cruise was to start in Barcelona, and then sail around the Greek islands stopping off at some of them, before returning to Spain, the trip would last fourteen days. Several more were planned for the summer, so if I enjoyed the experience, I could sign on for further trips.

It was the day of the final of the comedy spectacular from the heats at the Blue Garter, lots of new talent had been discovered, rumour had it Fat Albert had signed a very sharp and witty girl called Avril Jones from Wales. All the finalist had gathered for a quick a rehearsal at the TV station earlier in the day, not so much a rehearsal, more a lesson in where to stand, and don't pick your nose in front of the cameras.

After the rehearsal we were given instructions as to how the show was to run and what to expect. The vote was open to the general public; to be honest I was bricking it.

The compere was Bobby Brownlow, a smart-arsed southerner who gave the impression he resented having to travel north. The sheer mention of 'Bury Black Pudding' sent him into shaking convulsions. There was a panel of four new judges, or should I say old has-beens who were finding work hard to come by and would take any gig for the money.

One of them, Phyllis Todd, was an aging ballroom dancer, what she knew about comedy God only knows. She looked like her face would crack if she smiled with all the makeup that had been trowelled on in an effort to fill all the cracks and creases.

Brett Drumm, an aging DJ on one of the local radio stations was the youngest at sixty. The only thing this guy had in relation to comedy was his voice, he sounded like he had a bucket jammed on his head and spoke in a high-pitched Dorset accent.

Terrance Colby, a veteran comedian but long since retired was another judge, 'Laugh a minute Terry' he was know as, they must have been easily pleased in those days.

Lastly, Veronica Bull, who had started life as a holiday rep, before moving up the ladder and eventually buying the same company, she was classed as an entrepreneur. She was the last person on stage and was carried out and seated at the judge's table. As her fat arse hit the chair she let out a muffled fart and gave Terrance Colby an indignant look as if he was the culprit. The others had all managed to make it under their own steam, albeit with the help of a couple of Zimmer frames, this was going to be a fun evening. They would pass their cryptic comments on each act condemning them to comedy purgatory before it was put to the public vote at the end of the night. I had no doubt the general public would disregard whatever adverse comments this aging group of so called celebs would make. Comedy, don't make me laugh.

Brownlow, the compere, did a quick synopsis of the heats that had taken place at the Blue Garter, and after many acts this had been whittled down to these final six.

Avril Jones was the first one up; she was very slick and had the studio audience cracking up. She was tall and slim with auburn coloured hair down to her waist. However, I was seething when I realised she had used a couple of my gags, probably seen me in action somewhere. Not that I never got inspiration from other comics, but at least I change them to make them my own but she had copied my stories exactly. I like to think I created these, bang goes five minutes of my act; I'll need to find new material to replace it.

Then it was the time for the judges to pass their comments. She had impressed them all and got a favourable reaction from them. Ginger Nuts was up next, she was the bookies favourite but I don't know if it was nerves or what, but she was pure shite. Her timing was way off plus she looked as if she'd forgotten her routine. I had heard from Fat Albert during the auditions she was good and he may be interested in signing in her up, I doubted after this he would be going that route. She was savaged by the judges and left the stage in tears; at least they got that one right. Then the MC introduced me, "Ladies and gentlemen, please give a nice round of applause for Carter Dean."

This was my first time on television as I nervously walked out onto the stage and stood on the cross-marked on the floor, ready for my execution. What the hell was I doing there? Panic didn't come close to what I was feeling at that moment, after several seconds I was hoping someone would put a bullet in my head and put an end to my misery. My mind was a total blank, it was like my brain had been removed and replaced with a large void, not that I have a large brain but you know what I mean.

this impasse, he invited Brett Drumm to judge my act.

"I like you, I think you are very funny, your work is original you have a great collection of voices and accents, you are different I would say very refreshing I think you will go far."

That's what I wanted to hear, however it would be up to the general public to cast their votes at the end of the acts. I just had to listen to what Veronica Bull had to say, that's if they could wake her up from the comatose state she had lapsed into.

Brownlow asked her for her comments but she didn't answer, I could see the shows director pacing up and down off camera waving her hands in the air. The joys of live television. Then she woke up when Brett Drumm shook her shoulder, at which point she let out a rasping fart and almost fell off her chair with the fright. Jesus Christ, is this the best they can get, an aging entrepreneur who doubles as an expert in the art of flatulence? She gathered her composure looking very embarrassed, took a sip out of her water and after several seconds she uttered.

"I thought your act was refreshing, you are very funny, I think you have a great career in comedy. All your stories were original and your ability to mimic accents helped the delivery of your jokes, I think you will go far."

High praise indeed, but I figured she had slept through most of my act and she was winging it. I could see the show's director's career rapidly going down hill after this fiasco. The judge's panel were an absolute joke, although collectively they were a comedy act themselves.

As I left the stage I walked past the director who caught me by the arm, then prodded her finger into my chest, "I said no interaction with the audience, you deliberately disobeyed my instruction."

"Guess it's the firing squad for me then?"

Her lip was quivering her eyes narrowed to tiny slits, "This is serious, I said no interaction with the audience for a good reason, plus you overran your time by two minutes."

"Is that all? Think yourself lucky it could have been worse I could have stayed up there for a lot longer, I find it hard to stop once I get in full flow."

"Well it took you bloody long enough to start, it was like watching paint dry."

I guess that was to be expected, "Bitchy, but you've got to admit I was good once I got going."

She just glared at me, at this point, I thought I'd better leave her as she was waving a clipboard in a threatening manner; a strike against my jugular was imminent. I quickly went back stage and sat with the other comics, I let Avril Jones know I wasn't impressed with her stealing my material. Two of my best gags that took a long time to perfect she just stole and repeated verbatim. She didn't offer any kind of apology for doing so. I told her if ever she did this again I would sue her for plagiarism.

After the last act had performed, Brownlow, thanked all the contestants for a wonderful show he advised the voting was now open to the general public in a phone in. Meanwhile, a couple of gymnasts performed an amazing routine whilst the telephone voting took place. Eventually, the voting was over and all six acts were called out on stage to be given the verdict.

We all stood in line whilst Brownlow paced up and down the stage as he was given the result over his earpiece; nervously we eagerly waited for him to announce the results. With microphone in hand he turned to face the camera.

"Ladies and gentlemen, the phone lines are now closed, so please don't phone in as your vote will not be counted but you may be charged. In reverse order, here are the results of the viewers vote. In third place is," a long pause to build up the tension, "Steve Donovan, well done Steve."

He walked over to Donovan and handed him a cheque for £1,000 then shook him warmly by the hand.

"In second place," again there was a long pause, "is Carter Dean, congratulations Carter."

He shook my hand and gave me a cheque for £5,000. Better than the pot dog from Butlins.

"The winner by the smallest of margins is," there was a long unbearable pause as he tried to build up the suspense, Avril had a smug look on her face, she was convinced it was going to be her, "Kenny Taylor. I have to tell you there was only a difference of thirty votes in his favour."

That's a bummer; beaten by the smallest of margins I could demand a recount. Yes, that's what I want, a recount. The liberal MP in Bury demanded recount in the last election when she was beaten by fifty votes. What's wrong with me, this isn't a general election only a bloody talent show? But, I got some satisfaction that Avril Jones didn't figure in the top three. In fact by now she was in tears. Brownlow shook his hand, reiterated once again he was the winner and awarded him the first prize of £10,000

We all offered our congratulations to Kenny Taylor who I have to say was my favourite, I had seen him perform a good few times, his wit was sharp he could make an ordinary gag very funny. Fat Albert was in the audience he offered his commiserations to Avril and myself.

Whilst it was a disappointment to have come second, as a result of my participation I started to get more and more bookings, and my fees went up. As the booking for the cruise from Barcelona, approached I still had lots of material to finish off. At least twenty-eight shows to the same audience meant I needed lots of new material, no way could I repeat my act. This in itself was a huge task to come up with all the stories I would need, but eventually I managed it. Then one day I got a phone call from Cleo, she apologised for not getting in touch earlier, but she had been in Japan and China on business and had only arrived back in the UK that day. She asked me where I would be performing over the next few weeks, as she was thinking of meeting up again. I also told her about the booking for the cruise ship and if she was due a holiday, she should consider it. We chatted for over half an hour and agreed to keep in touch.

Chapter Four

It was almost time for my maritime excursion, although I had a few bookings to complete before then. One of them was at the Prestwich and District Dog Breeders Associations annual dinner. Incidentally, it was to be held at the Blue Garter were the heats for the comedy show were hosted.

I arrived at the venue about fifty minutes before I was due to go on stage, just as the last of the four hundred guests were finishing their meal. Anticipation and excitement was high, as 'Whizzo' and the 'Great Zedel' were about to entertain the audience to a spectacular display of what, can go wrong without really trying. They say, never appear with animals or children, after watching chaos unfold it was certainly true in this case. Whoever decided to book a dog act for the local dog breeders association, didn't have much imagination. I've no doubt they were now regretting it, after witnessing what can only be described as total mayhem.

Whizzo, he was the dog, a cross between a Jack Russell terrier and a greyhound, not sure how its parents managed to consummate that relationship, but I suppose, where there's a will there's a way. It was priceless, and at the same time shocking to see how this act unfolded. Zedel was in his mid sixties, slim build almost two metres tall. He had grey wavy hair, and a waxed handlebar moustache. His attire was a black tuxedo, with regulation satin stripes down the outside of his trouser legs, he wore a maroon bow tie and black patent leather shoes. He initially came on stage with six dogs of various breeds, who all sat obediently waiting their call to duty.

Whizzo was the first one called up, he had a

miniature red fez perched on his head, secured in position with rubber chin strap, like a tiny Tommy Cooper, standing upright on his back legs. The dog was obviously having a bad day, because he immediately walked up to the Great Zedel, dropped back on all fours cocked his leg 'Just like that' and pissed all over his patent leather shoes, much to the amusement of all the audience. Zedel gave a wry smile, he tried to give the impression it was part of the act, at the same time waiving his finger at Whizzo to reprimand him.

He shouldn't have done that, because as quick as a flash the dog jumped up and latched onto his finger. Zedel raced around the stage trying to get it to loosen its grip, all the time smiling at the audience. However, when blood started to drip profusely from his hand, it was apparent to everyone this little bugger meant business. What was he to do in front of an audience of dog lovers? He could hardly hit the dog, but he had to do something.

After doing about sixteen laps around the stage, like something out of a Benny Hill sketch, this rabid dog was still attached to his hand. The animal had no intention of releasing its grip, so he wound his arm around his head repeatedly, like an Olympic hammer thrower, and then launched the dog as hard as he could against a curtain. Zedel winced with the pain as the dog reluctantly let go of its grip, but not before tearing the skin out from between his fingers. Unfortunately, the curtain was covering a solid stonewall, as soon as Whizzo hit it, he let out a high-pitched yelp and dropped to the stage unconscious. There was a huge gasp from the audience; shouts of 'shame on you' to 'dog killer' were directed at the Great Zedel.

He wasn't sure what to do next, attend to the unconscious dog and bring an end to his act or, carry on with the remainder of his routine. He didn't need to worry; the decision was made for him. The rest of the dogs who had been patiently waiting their turn, raced to their comrade's assistance. Within seconds, Zedel had two dogs latched onto the cheeks of his arse; two others were shredding his trousers as they sank their teeth into his legs. It got more serious when the last remaining dog, a tiny Jack Russell launched itself onto his back and sank its teeth into his neck, at the same time taking an enormous dump onto his back. Zedel was screaming hysterically with the pain as he fell to the ground. Just then, a member of the audience climbed up onto the stage, with a few well aimed kicks and shouted commands, restored some semblance of order. She walked over to Zedel to remove the steaming pile from his back, and like a good detective she bagged the evidence.

The five dogs assumed their original positions; they sat there as if butter wouldn't melt in their mouths, whilst Whizzo was still spark out on the floor.

An assistant picked up the unconscious animal no doubt to give it a new leash of life, then, she led the other dogs off the stage. The Great Zedel wasn't so great; in fact he had serious injuries and was taken back stage to await the arrival of an ambulance.

The person who had restored some order to the proceedings, offered her comments as to why this had happened, in her view was the result of ill treatment. This lady was average height, quit stout, no, in fact she was obese, the last time I saw legs like hers was on a Queen Ann table at my grandmas. She was of advancing years with an abundance of nasal hair and a face like a bulldog. They do say if you live with your animals long enough you start to look like them. Her badge indicated she was president of the British Bulldog Breeders Association. She was wearing a tartan outfit and strutted around the stage like General Patton as she addressed the audience.

"It is not normal or natural for a dog to perform

tricks, I know there are dog trainers, some of them are my very good friends who can achieve great results with love and care of their animals, although I am against this kind of exploitation, but that's just my personal view. However, what we have witnessed here tonight, I think is retaliation for ill treatment, I can only assume these dogs have been beaten repeatedly to break their will power."

With that she stepped down off the stage to a rapturous applause, whilst the MC for the evening said there would be a short interval to let things calm down. Jesus, so these dogs were just getting their own back on the guy for ill treatment. If that was true it serves the bastard right.

After about fifteen minutes I was introduced on stage and started my stint, I wondered if I should tell some doggy jokes to break the ice although, I wasn't sure how they would react, what the hell this lot looked like they needed a laugh.

"Good evening it's nice to be here, wasn't that some spectacle? The last time I saw anything as entertaining as that, was when my mother in-law, just before she fell off her perch, crossbred a Doberman with a Hyena. It would bite the arse out of you then fall around laughing."

There was nothing, just a stunned silence.

"I'm a cat man myself, I think they're much brighter and far more independent."

This got an immediate reaction, there were boos and shouts of rubbish from several areas in the theatre.

"Obviously, some of you don't agree, but my cat Felix is really clever, he lets you know when he needs to go to the toilet. He stands at the door and meows, when I let him out he goes down the garden digs a hole then does his business, when he's finished he fills the hole in then comes back."

There was a call from the audience. "What's so

Get a Proper Job

bloody clever about this, all cats do that?"
"Oh really," I replied, "with a shovel?"
Laughter from the audience.
"Why do blind people skydive on their own? Because it frightens the hell out of their dogs."

Maybe not, there wasn't a hint of a laugh probably a bit too close to the bone, looking around, a lot of them still seemed to be traumatised by the previous act, revert to plan B. Eventually, they warmed up I managed to get a giggle or two but I had to work damned hard for my money.

After the canine debacle, I had two more gigs before I departed for a life on the ocean waves. I was booked to perform at the 'Comedy Club' in Blackburn and 'Mr. Beans Laugh a Minute' in Barnoldswick, talk about stardom, I was really moving up in the world. Cleo had been in touch as she had some leave due to her and wanted to make a booking on the cruise from Barcelona. This was great news so I gave her the name of the vessel, dates of the sailings and where to make the reservations. I was looking forward to the trip even more now.

I was on stage at the Comedy Club, when I spotted a face in the audience that looked slightly familiar but try as I may I couldn't put a name to it.

After I finished my routine, I went backstage to my dressing room, not so much a dressing room, more a narrow corridor where empty beer kegs were stored adjacent to a boiler house, no expense spared here. Couldn't see Frank Sinatra putting up with this crap. Not that I needed much space, just a spot to keep my flask of coffee and the sandwiches my mother had made for me. Of course, I risked getting a bollocking from the club for bringing in my own refreshments, rather than buying theirs, but seagull in a basket is an acquired taste.

"Really enjoyed your performance Mr. Dean, very original."

I turned to see the face from the audience, then it came back to me, he was the police inspector who made an early morning call to my parents home. What the hell was all this about?

"Remember me, I'm DCI Porter, this is my colleague DS Staunton?"

"How could I ever forget?" I said sarcastically.

"Could we have a quick word?"

"It'll have to be quick, I'm on stage at another club in Barnoldswick in fifty minutes and I'm cutting it fine as it is."

"This won't take long, we are just following up on the murder of Marcus Stone the singer near Shipley. When we interviewed you previously, you stated that night you were performing at The Pickled Parrot, is that correct?"

"Yes that's right, nothing has changed, why would you think it had?" I didn't like the way he said this, it was almost like he didn't believe me. Porter stared intently at me as he asked.

"Did you by any chance see two very tall men of heavy build, they looked like wrestlers or rugby players in the club that night? They would be in their mid thirties. One of them was bald probably shaven, the other was blond with a tattoo of a dragon on the side of his neck."

"Jesus, that's ages ago, I can't be sure if I would recognise anybody from tonight's audience let alone way back then. Are they responsible for the murders?"

"We're not sure, but it would appear they were seen at another venue where a murder took place, but it's too early to speculate, we are just following up various leads. We may want to speak with you again."

"Well if you do, can you arrange to do it elsewhere, it's not good for my image, plus people talk in this game? These murders are having a serious effect on the entertainment industry. If I'm linked in any way to this

Get a Proper Job

it could affect me, so if you have anymore questions I would appreciate it if you came to my parents' home. By the way, I will be out of the country for two weeks in May as I'm performing on a cruise ship, so don't be sending out the cavalry I'm not doing a runner."

"Very well Mr. Dean, we'll let you get to your next appointment."

With that they left, what the hell was that all about? It was almost like they thought I had something to do with these murders. They must have gone out of their way to track me down to this place, it was a hardly a chance encounter it had me worried, after all, this was the second time I had been interviewed.

As soon as I could I rang Fat Albert and I told him about the police tracking me down. He told me not to worry about it that it was probably just routine, but I wasn't so sure. The fact they had obviously gone to a lot of trouble to seek me out for a second time gave me a bad feeling.

The following day, I called into Cloughs textile warehouse to see the last of the rehearsals in preparation for the cruise. The dancers had some fantastic routines perfected under the guidance of Florence Patterson.

Fat Albert had recruited two vocalists for the cruise; the number of dancers had increased to 18. He said there were 3 theatres on board the vessel; they had to work out a schedule of how best to rotate the various acts to each of them. An added complication was that he had to work with an entertainments manager on board the ship who had already recruited a number of acts herself, from fire-eaters to sword swallowers. However, much to my disgust he had signed up Avril Jones as a backup comic. This was not I wanted to hear, when she told me she was on the trip I wanted to back out. Fat Albert said he was under pressure from the cruise ship company he had to cover for all eventualities, plus I couldn't back out as I had already signed the contract for the cruise. With this in mind, I told Avril in no uncertain terms, if she pinched anymore of my gags she would be going overboard.

Cleo confirmed she was booked on the cruise and would see me on board; she had secured a luxury stateroom with a sea view and was really looking forward to the trip.

The day of the cruise, we assembled at Manchester airport for the flight to Barcelona, although some of the entertainers who lived in the south flew out of Heathrow. Fat Albert was travelling with us along with Florence Patterson; rumour had it there was something going on with these two. It was the biggest booking Bonetti Entertainment had ever received, if it was successful could mean several more large paydays for him. Although, I was quite surprised that Fat Albert had managed to secure such a prestigious contract, I suppose it was down to his contacts in the entertainment industry.

When we arrived at Barcelona airport, a bus was waiting to take us to the *'Norseman Conquest of the Seas'* that was going to be our home for the next two weeks. There is a very narrow window of opportunity from when the vessel docked, the passengers disembarked, to the cleaning and restocking of supplies to cater for thousands of people, before taking on new passengers for the next sailing.

Once on board, we were shown to our cabins and I was in for a shock. I discovered I had to double up with the vocalist Tony Sheridan. Neither of us had been made aware we would have to share accommodation; we immediately made our objections to Fat Albert. He said he wasn't responsible for allocating the cabins, that was up to the cruise ship management. In fact, he told us some of the female dancers had to share three to a cabin. I told him if that were the case I would preferably share with the female dancers. That was up to us who we could get to swop, all he was concerned about was putting on a good show.

I wasn't a fan of Sheridan and I know I wasn't on his Christmas card list. I approached the management to see if they could help but I was told it wasn't possible. Obviously, they wanted as many cabins available for paying customers, although if I'd have had to pay for this shit hole called accommodation, I would have been bitterly disappointed.

We were in the bowels of the ship; the noise from the generators was like a constant throbbing, this would only increase once we were underway. On top of this, the cabin was very cramped it gave a claustrophobic feeling, coupled with extremely high temperatures as a result of poor ventilation. In short, it was damned uncomfortable but this was going to be home for the next two weeks so better get used to it.

We were given a schedule of the theatres and times we would be performing; my first gig was at 9:00pm that night in the *'Elhambra Theatre'* on C deck. I was running through my notes selecting stories for my opening show, whilst Sheridan was practising his vocals or should I say crucifying 'My Way' one of the crooner's best-known classics. Oh how I do wish he would bugger off and practise somewhere else. I was always a fan of Frank Sinatra but this guy was taking the piss, he sounded more like Frank Spencer.

My first gig went very well, I spotted Cleo in the audience, we met up after I'd finished my slot, although, we had been told fraternising with the passengers was out of the question. We tried to keep it low key I explained about my cabin arrangements not that I expected her to do anything about it, I was just voicing my disappointment that the management weren't prepared to do anything to help. Without any hesitation she offered to share her cabin with me. However, I thought it wouldn't be the right thing to do, especially as we didn't really know one another. I politely thanked her for her offer, but reserved the right to change my mind.

Chapter Five

DCI Porter, who was in charge of investigating the murders of 4 vocalists in the north of England, had called a meeting of his team. He was under pressure from his superiors about the lack of progress in apprehending whoever was responsible. His prime suspect, Carter Dean, was out of the country sailing around the Mediterranean. He had interviewed him twice; he thought he was too slick and his gut feeling was he had something to hide. His colleague, DS Staunton was bending his ear, he was convinced Dean fitted the bill because he'd been performing at, or near the clubs where these poor unfortunates met their tragic end.

"Good afternoon gentleman, I don't need to tell you the press are having a field day regarding these murders. I've been getting daily flack from a lot of people, today I got some disturbing news that another vocalist seems to have been murdered, or at the very least, has disappeared from onboard a cruise ship. The very same vessel, that our number one suspect, Carter Dean, is on. I'm not aware of the full facts yet, all I know is this chap was seen at midnight the night before last but seems to have disappeared between then and six am the following morning, despite the crew searching extensively for him. He was due on stage for a lunchtime show but couldn't be found.

"I'm flying out to Athens to meet up with the vessel when it docks there on Wednesday. It's on the return journey back to Barcelona; I need to speak with the passengers before they disembark. We have to be careful as this is a grey area, could be outside of our jurisdiction, but there are a troop of UK entertainers on board this British registered vessel. Their head office in London contacted Scotland Yard for assistance as soon as they were made aware this chap had gone missing in suspicious circumstances. It could be just a case of someone accidentally falling overboard, although they say this chap was sharing a cabin with Dean and neither of them were happy about this arrangement."

There were cries of, "Can we come with you, sir?"

"Sorry, my budget won't stretch for anymore to travel with me, this is not a 'Jolly Boys Weekend' despite what you might think. Even DS Staunton will be staying behind to follow up other information that has come in."

A lot of sniggering and out of earshot comments followed this, it was evident from some of the remarks he wasn't held in high esteem. He continued to outline what direction he wanted his officers to move in with emphasis on contacts of Dean.

DCI Porter arrived in Athens, on a British Airways flight from Manchester. He was met by a representative of the cruise company and then taken straight to their local office to await the arrival of the vessel. He was given a briefing by a senior member of the staff on what they knew so far about the disappearance of the singer. Every cabin and room on board the ship had been searched, but there was no sign of Sheridan. All they were aware of was that Dean and Sheridan did not get on, there had been a number of violent arguments. They had requested alternative accommodation but this had been denied. They were now regretting they hadn't done more to facilitate them. Hindsight is a great thing.

After being briefed on the situation, Porter was convinced more than ever that Dean was the culprit, however, there was a long way to go to get the necessary evidence that would convict him. The cruise company had a dilemma, as this kind of publicity can be bad for business. The situation had to be investigated

Get a Proper Job

thoroughly, but at the same time, they were conscious it had to be done in a way so as not to alarm passengers. Porter had been briefed on the need for diplomacy.

We were about eight days into the cruise; relations with Sheridan had gone from bad to worse. I found him totally objectionable, on top of this he couldn't sing, and I found it hard to listen to this talentless prick practicing his vocals. What amazed me was that Fat Albert had been taken in by this guy, who didn't have a note in his head, lots of bum ones but none in the right key. It all came to a climax, now there's a pun, when I came back to our cabin just after midnight and found him on my bed having sex with a passenger who was at the very most sixteen years old.

"Excuse me, what's wrong with using your own bed?"

"You know what you can do if you don't like it."

"All very funny, but I don't want you leaving crabs where I have to sleep, still trying to get rid of the last lot, despite the intervention of 'Rentokil'. By the way, that woman you slept with on Tuesday was here earlier, she's been to see the ship's doctor, he confirms she has contracted gonorrhoea, she's not pleased, says she got it from you."

The look on his face was bloody priceless, as his entertainment for the night was getting ready to make a quick exit, serves the little shit right. By now the young woman was in tears, getting dressed as quickly as she could. No doubt planning a trip to the ship's doctor at the earliest, I was enjoying this.

"Do your parents know where you are young lady, this prat is old enough to be your father?"

She didn't answer, just picked up her shoes, and shot out of the cabin like a scalded cat.

"If I ever find you having sex again on my bunk, I'll rearrange your vocal chords, who knows, it might improve your singing although, although I think that's a forlorn hope."

I was so enraged I left the cabin and decided to go and see Cleo, I couldn't put up with this pillock anymore, although it was going up for 1:00am and I wasn't sure how she would react. Luckily, she was still awake and invited me in. I explained what had happened, she told me not to give it a second thought but to move my things in with her. I didn't hesitate and immediately went back to my cabin to collect my belongings. Of course, Sheridan, was delighted I was moving out.

Her stateroom was the last word in luxury, a million miles away from what I had endured. There was a large double bed with an ornate carved wooden headboard. Honduras mahogany panelling was throughout, beautiful pictures adorned the walls. There were two comfortable couches also a small writing desk. The bathroom was equally over the top, with Italian marble on the walls and worktops. Gold plated taps, a Jacuzzi bath, as well as a shower completed the facilities. I couldn't believe the luxury; I was looking forward to enjoying some comfort. One thing that struck me was how quiet it was, plus there was no vibration that I had experienced in the bowels of the ship. Over the coming days we got to know one another, I had never felt so happy in a long time. My performances were going well the audiences were great plus I hadn't repeated one single gag.

Eventually, the news was leaked that Sheridan was missing; an extensive search of the vessel was launched. Naturally, as he was my roommate I came in for rigorous questioning, this placed me in a difficult position. How could I explain I had been sleeping in the quarters of one of the guests, knowing full well we had been told no fraternising with the passengers? Fat Albert was called I gave him the facts about finding Sheridan having sex with a young female passenger in my bed. This was just one of many objectionable things I had put up with but this was the final straw. I had made representations to the management regarding having to share accommodation but they refused to help. As a result, after his last despicable act I had moved in with Cleo. He fully understood how I felt and my reasoning for moving out, however, he told me to play that one down, in the interim, I should return to my original cabin. Reluctantly, I agreed, as I didn't want to complicate the issue, besides I wouldn't have to put up with his antics, and crap singing anymore plus, we were on the homeward stretch.

I explained to Cleo it was best if I moved back to my original cabin, and under the circumstances she fully understood my situation and reason for moving out.

There was still no sign of Sheridan, despite extensive searches of the vessel. Rumour had it, that a couple of irate husbands and fathers had visited this lecherous son of a bitch to warn him about his behaviour. In fact, for a couple of days he was sporting a thick lip, no Botox needed here, his injury was so bad he was singing with a lisp. These people had been interviewed but couldn't offer any indication as to where the missing vocalist was. It was a good thing Fat Albert had the foresight to have a backup singer, although I'm sure it never entered his head why he would need one.

Just after 10:00am one morning after we docked in Athens, I was summoned to the chief purser's office. What the hell's the matter now I wondered, as I made my way up top? As I was directed into his office, I was confronted by the smirking image of DCI Porter. Oh sweet Jesus, here we go again.

"Morning, Mr. Dean, I hope we didn't disturb your beauty sleep?"

Smart-arse comment. "For your information, I've been up since six-thirty, I like to get a few dozen laps around the deck before the passengers surface. Anyway, what did you want?"

"Just a few more questions if you don't mind."

"I thought you were looking for two rugby players, or was that just bullshit?"

"No it wasn't, but we have traced them and they've been eliminated from our enquiries."

"So you are back to try and pin it on me?"

"Murder seems to follow you wherever you go, Mr. Dean, it seems to be getting monotonous, and a pattern is developing. You appear on the bill then someone gets killed."

"I hope you are not accusing me of anything, think carefully before you answer that."

"What was your relationship with your room-mate Tony Sheridan?"

"No point in lying, we didn't have a good relationship, in fact, I couldn't stand the prick, although, you probably already know that. Neither of us was happy about having to share a room, but the management refused to help. But if you are suggesting I killed him so I could have the room all to myself, you're deranged. Anyway, how do you know he's dead, could have jumped ship anywhere, we've pulled into a number of the Greek islands, when we tied up in Lesvos he was the first one ashore."

"You seem to know an awful lot about his movements?"

"Not really, it's just he raced off as if he was on starting blocks, almost knocked one of the dancers off the gangway into the water. They say he has a girlfriend there. In fact, rumour has it he lived in Greece a while back and he's got women in a number of Greek islands, so he could be shacked up anywhere."

"His body was fished out of the Med yesterday morning by a local fishing boat, too early to say, but he has severe bruises to his throat, it looks like he was strangled before being thrown overboard."

Jesus, I know he was an objectionable prat, but I

Get a Proper Job

wouldn't have wished this on him. "Well it wasn't me, suggest you interview some of the irate husbands on board, he was sleeping with a different person every night."

"How do you know this?"

"Because I came back to the cabin one night and he was in my bed with a sixteen year old girl. Just one of many instances of his philandering ways. Another time he was thumped by one of the husbands after he found him with his wife naked on the upper deck. The guy was oversexed, couldn't keep it in his trousers, on top of that he was a shit singer, maybe someone couldn't stand the sound of his voice."

"There's no need to be flippant, Mr. Dean, someone has died, and it's my duty to find whoever is responsible."

"Well, it wasn't me, I get the feeling from our previous meetings you think I'm responsible for all these murders. I can account for my whereabouts when these people were killed, so I suggest you go back to the drawing board and find someone else to pin it on, because I'm not guilty."

"Where were you last Monday, between midnight and six am?"

"Can't remember, I finished my last appearance on stage about twelve thirty then met up with a friend for a drink."

"Was Mr. Sheridan in the cabin when you retired for the night?"

This was getting awkward, I didn't want to draw Cleo into the equation, but it was probably going to happen.

"I'm waiting Mr. Dean, anytime soon will do."

This guy was really starting to piss me off. If he was the calibre of expertise that the police were turning out I was dead and buried.

"Didn't return to the cabin, in fact I had moved out several days earlier because of his antics."

"That's interesting, can you tell me where you were?"

"I could, but I'm not going to do."

"Oh but I think you are."

"So, what's next, thumbscrews, the rack, or my balls in a vice?"

"You seem to think this is some kind of joke, it's a serious issue and you've got questions to answer, we can either do it here or I will have you arrested when we arrive in Barcelona and taken to the UK."

"I think we both know that's not going to happen, you can't just remove someone from a sovereign country, not without applying for extradition through the normal channels. We all know the Spanish authorities have never been helpful in that regard."

"I could have you taken off here in Athens, what do you say to that?"

"Not sure if you've noticed, but we left port about thirty minutes ago so, unless you can walk on water, and my gut feeling is you think you can, I'd forget it."

As soon as I said this, Porter had a startled look on his face; he jumped up from the table and raced to the porthole. At this point, he realised we had pulled away from the dock and left the harbour some time ago.

"You seem to have an answer to everything, except the questions I ask you."

"Look, you are concentrating on the wrong person, I left Sheridan to his devices and I moved in with a passenger and no, I will not reveal their name. I have no intention of ruining someone's holiday because of an over zealous Inspector Clouseau, who thinks he has someone banged to rights without a shred of evidence. Now, I've taken up enough of your time, so I suggest you spend the rest of it until we arrive in Barcelona making enquiries elsewhere. Good morning."

He stood there with a look of dismay on his face as I got up and left the office. I had to play it this way to show him that I wouldn't be pushed around. I was

Get a Proper Job

innocent but whatever I said this chap was convinced I was guilty. What could he do, he could hardly throw me in the brig, could he? However, my main concern was I didn't want Cleo dragged into this, we had started a relationship that had the potential to go the full course, anything that threatened this had to be avoided at all costs.

If I'd have given him her name, he would have gone in with his size twelve's interrogating her until she cracked, spilling the beans that gave him the impression I was the mad 'Vocal Strangler' that would have been the end of our relationship.

Not long afterwards, 1 got a visit from Fat Albert, "Carter, you've really pissed that copper off, he's been in to see me threatening all kinds of action. He said because this is a British registered ship he was going to instruct the captain to sail directly to Southampton. However, he didn't have much luck, they told him in a polite way to get stuffed. The vessel started its voyage in Barcelona, the passengers arrived there by air from all over the world, they have return tickets from there back to their home countries. Can you imagine the headache this would cause, repatriating in the region of two thousand passengers from the UK, it would be a logistics nightmare, not too mention the cost involved? The guy obviously isn't playing with a full deck, he seems totally incompetent and strikes me he couldn't wipe his own arse without a road map, but you can see he's under pressure to find the culprit."

"He's certainly gunning for me why, I'm not sure, I have an alibi for all the times these people were killed. Although, I hate that word alibi, it kind of gives the impression I have something to hide. But I don't, I'm quite prepared to sit down with another officer and answer any questions they put to me but not that prick. As far as he's concerned I'm guilty if he gets his way I'll be under lock and key at the earliest."

"Under the circumstances, I think you were wise to move back into your old cabin."

"Yes, I think you are right."

I decided to tell Cleo that there was a British police inspector on board, investigating the disappearance and death of Tony Sheridan. As his roommate I had been questioned in this regard. My main concern was that if DCI Porter saw us together he would undoubtedly put two and two together and want to interview her. This was the last thing I wanted, so I told her about the rule of no fraternising with the passengers that it was best we weren't seen together in public at least, until we got home. Much to my surprise she accepted this. Over the coming days, I saw Porter talking to various passengers; he would give me an intense look as I walked past.

"Can I have a word, Mr. Dean?"

"No, is the short answer to that, I'm done talking to you, now bugger off and annoy someone else."

"I intend to have you arrested when you arrive in the UK."

"Good luck with that, anyway, who said I was returning to the UK, I join another vessel after we dock in Spain for another four week cruise?"

I wasn't, but he didn't know that, just thought I would wind him up. He rushed off, no doubt to find my manager to see if it was true.

Once the vessel docked in Barcelona, I said goodbye to Cleo and agreed to call her just as soon as I was back home. Fat Albert caught the first available flight back to Manchester because of business commitments; the rest of us had to overnight in a cheap hotel then catch an early flight the next day.

Chapter Six

It was a miserable grey day as I stepped off the flight at Manchester airport. As I got onto the jet way, I was immediately approached by two burly men who identified themselves as colleagues of DS Staunton, I was told I was being arrested and taken for questioning to police headquarters in Rochdale. To be handcuffed in front of disembarking passengers was excruciating, not an experience I would recommend. As I was led away, Phoebe, one of the dancers and a good friend of mine shouted she would tell Fat Albert and inform my parents.

After a thirty-minute ride we arrived at the police station, I was then placed into an interview room. It was straight from Colditz, windowless designed to intimidate. The room was dark; illumination such as it was, provided by a single light suspended low over a bare wooden table, with two chairs on either side. Shortly afterwards the bald-headed figure of DS Staunton, and another officer entered.

"Lovely to see you again, Mr. Dean, this is my colleague DS Philips, he will be assisting me. I hope you are feeling refreshed and willing to answer some questions after your nice holiday?"

"I wasn't on holiday I was working as I previously told you I would be."

"My colleague, DCI Porter, tells me you were very uncooperative when he tried to interview you on the vessel, said you just walked away. I'm afraid that's not going to happen today, you will be kept here until you answer all my questions, is that understood?"

"I'm not saying anything until Alistair Bracken my lawyer gets here, you have no right to keep persecuting me like you are. It was unnecessary to arrest me at the airport in front of all the passengers, do you have any idea what that felt like?"

"No, but I'm sure you're going to tell me."

"To apprehend me like a common criminal, wasn't justified, I've had nothing to do with these murders, you are so far away from the truth pure incompetence springs to mind. How many times do I have to tell you, or is it a case you think you can stitch me up just to satisfy your arrest targets?"

"Not at all, we are duty bound to follow up all leads regarding these murders. Mr. Sheridan's body arrived back in the UK two days ago, forensics have established he was strangled before he was thrown overboard. The reason we need to talk to you is, because you were present at or near to the spots these people were killed."

"That's rubbish and you know it, the only one that had any connection to me was at the Pickled Parrot in Bradford where the singer was on stage prior to my act."

"On the contrary, you appeared at clubs that were only five minutes apart, giving you plenty of time to commit these terrible crimes and be on your way. The night you appeared at the Blue Garter, another victim was appearing at the 'Cotton Club' less than three miles away."

Shit, I wasn't aware of that, but if it's true it's purely a coincidence, however, this guy was like a dog with a bone, he was sure I was the culprit not prepared to accept my innocence, "I'm telling you the truth, what have I to do to convince you?"

"The truth is what we want, Mr. Dean, the truth."

"Ok, this is pathetic, we're just going around in dammed circles, let's play it this way, you seem reluctant to accept anything I say as the truth so, what's the point in me trying to convince you otherwise? From now on every question you put to me I will answer no

comment. You have no evidence of my involvement so I am reluctant to make any additional statement in case it is misconstrued."
"How was your relationship with Tony Sheridan?"
"No comment."
"So this is how it's going to be is it?"
"No comment."
"We do have enough evidence to charge you with these murders, my advice is to cut the bravado, start being cooperative and answer our questions."
"No comment."
This went on for at least an hour, Staunton was spitting feathers, and I was enjoying watching him slowly come to the boil. The veins in his forehead were standing out like the roots of a tree; his lips had turned blue he was trembling with rage. This was not a good sign, he might have a problem with his heart, needs to get that checked out. What's, wrong with me, am I getting concerned for his welfare? He's trying to give me the third degree and I'm hoping he doesn't have a heart problem. That's just my good nature showing through in the face of adversity.

He was twitching nervously, I knew he couldn't take much more, then suddenly, he slammed his fist onto the table in utter frustration, a glass of water was launched into the air the contents landing in his lap. Nice one Carter, a few more 'No comments' this guy will totally lose it, he'll be so wound up, and he'll start wrecking the furniture such as it was. Staunton sat there seething, clenching his fists gnashing his teeth, his face had now turned bright red and looked like one of those red arsed monkeys, he was not used to this kind of un-cooperation. Not long afterwards, the door opened and a constable entered the interview room, bending down he whispered in DS Staunton's ear. It obviously wasn't good news, because the expression on his face changed, something had wiped his arse. Shortly afterwards the cavalry appeared.

"Gentlemen, my name is Alistair Bracken, I'm here to represent my client, Carter Dean. I am aware he has endeavoured to give truthful replies to your questions in previous interviews but you will not accept that he is telling the truth. You have no hard evidence that my client was in anyway connected to these murders, so I suggest you put an end to this circus and release him immediately."

Was I glad to see Alistair? He was ex-marine well built and intimidating I was grateful he was on my side. Taking a seat beside me, he was his usual very confident, and matter of fact demeanour.

"On the contrary, because of his reluctance to answer any of our questions, we are thinking of applying to the courts for an extension to the length of time we can interview him."

"My advice to you is to think hard on this, as I will strongly object to this course of action. This is harassment pure and simple, it's a vendetta against my client without any hard evidence, you could be leaving yourselves wide open to a lawsuit."

Staunton was unmoved, he sat there with a look of superiority on his face but that all changed when Alistair said.

"You might also be interested to know the breaking news on Sky, minutes before I walked in here. They announced that another vocalist has been found murdered in Blackburn, the body was found on a waste ground early this morning. My client would have been on his way back from Barcelona when this murder was committed so, unless he has some magical power of transportation, he is not the culprit."

This shook them, Staunton left the room immediately, obviously to check if this was true. Alistair gave me a wry smile, he knew he had them and they would have to release me. Five minutes later Staunton returned.

"This interview is suspended, you are free to go, but we reserve the right to question you again should the need arise, don't leave the country."
"No comment," I had to have the last word.
My lawyer and I left the building; he was confidant the harassment would end here. "I don't think you will have anymore problems with them Carter, but if you do, contact me immediately."
"I'm grateful you appeared when you did, that bastard was getting ready with the thumbscrews."
"Your manager Albert called me, he gave me the background to what's been happening, you've been unfortunate, in the wrong place at the wrong time compounded by officers under pressure, also it would appear inept and grossly out of their depth. Why the hell didn't you let me know what's been going on?"
"I didn't want to bother you, I thought it would just blow over, it was only when Porter appeared on the cruise ship I realised I was in deep shit."
"I have to go Carter, I'm due in court just after lunch I'm a representing a client in a high profile assault charge, I can't be late for that, but remember, let me know if you get anymore agro from them."
"I will Alistair, thanks again."
I was grateful for his timely intervention after booking a taxi I made my way home. I doubted if that was the end of it, after all, they had interviewed me on four separate occasions. They obviously thought I had something to do with these murders, I couldn't see them changing their tack as far as I was concerned, but time would tell.

"Just when I thought we had him," said DCI Porter, "another bloody body turns up. Like his lawyer said, there was no way he could be in two places at once."
"It could be a copycat killer," said DS Staunton.
"Our colleagues in Blackburn say It's definitely the

same MO, death by strangulation with the sign of a snake indentation in the flesh, so it's the same killer alright. But there is a difference with this one, it's a female singer, goes by the name of Dame Nellie Ratchet, I assume that's just her stage name."

"Sounds like rat shit."

"Be serious Staunton, I'm getting flack from all quarters, I have a meeting in ten minutes with the Chief Constable no doubt for another ear bashing. I want you to get over to Blackburn, establish what they've found out so far."

"OK sir, I'm on it."

Staunton met up with the investigating officers in Blackburn; he discovered the body had already been removed from the crime scene to the city morgue, so they all headed down there.

The body of this beautiful woman was laid out on the slab, her head was resting on a block, in places her long blond hair was hanging off the table, her enormous breasts standing proud and firm as the pathologist got ready to perform the autopsy. All the officers watched intently from the viewing mezzanine as the pathologist, a scrawny little man with a miserable face, approached the table. He was clad almost from head to foot in a white rubber apron and wellingtons; he looked like a large condom. Using scissors, he started to remove her clothing. As he cut down the length of her dress and peeled it back, it revealed her perfectly formed breasts and slim figure, not an ounce of fat anywhere, the audience were impressed.

Then he placed the scissors at the top of her undergarments and proceeded to cut them away, as he did so, there were gasps from the viewing officers. Some of them even started to vomit, as the biggest pair of balls that wouldn't have been out of place on an elephant hit the table with a dull thud. What the hell was going on? It was at this point they realised, Dame Nellie Ratchet, was in fact a drag act. Staunton couldn't wait to tell his superior. DCI Porter had just finished his meeting with the Chief Constable when his sergeant brought him up to date on the investigation.

"You're not going to believe this sir, but Dame Nellie Ratchet, is in fact a bloke with the biggest pair of balls I've ever seen, not too mention tits like mount Vesuvius. Some of the guys here started to throw up when they realised what they were looking at, it was such a shock a major disappointment that this vision of beauty was indeed a bloke. Of course, a bit more investigation at the crime scene earlier would have discovered this, but apparently with all the recent rain the murder site was starting to flood, so they decided to remove body rather than risk contamination.

"This chaps real name is, Trevor Peters, he's from Brighton in Sussex, apparently he was a wonderful singer. Why the hell he had to dress as a woman I don't know, but he was very convincing with such an amazing body? Some of the guys here were raving about how beautiful she was, but after the unveiling of the biggest pair of nuts imaginable, they are probably never going to look at women in the same light."

"Jesus, what next, so far the killer has only picked on regular male vocalists, maybe he didn't realise it was a bloke he was just concentrating on a vocalist? Did the body have the distinguishing mark on the neck?"

"Yes sir, very evident in the pale flesh, probably the clearest image yet."

"What makes this guy select his victims, we know they are all vocalists, but there has to be a common denominator in all of this apart from them all being male of course, whatever the link is we need to find it?"

"I don't know what the link is sir, but man or woman the press are going to have a bloody field day when the news leaks out."

"Thank you, Staunton, I'm well aware of that, just had a testy meeting with the Chief Constable about our lack of progress. Get copies of their investigation details then get back here ASAP."

Each of the victims had the same distinguishing mark in their neck wounds. Probably because the killer was wearing a ring on their middle finger that had a snakelike shape on the outside of it that left an indentation in the skin. The police had never released this information to the general public purposely; they didn't want a copycat killer confusing the issue.

When I arrived home I had a lot of explaining to my parents as to what had happened, I told them it was just routine because my cabin mate had fallen overboard. Not sure if they believed me but I didn't want to tell them why because my mother was a born worrier. Then it occurred to me, my parents were with me the night I appeared at the Blue Garter, they were my alibi. However, if Alistair was correct I shouldn't be bothered by the police again so no need for them to become involved, at least for the time being.

Later that day, I rang Fat Albert and thanked him for contacting my lawyer. The next person on my to call list was Cleo, we arranged to meet up later in the week as I was appearing at 'Mr. Smiths' an up market club in Cleo's hometown of Preston.

It was show time and I was looking forward to putting my abduction and incarceration at the hands of PC Dickhead and his idiot friends behind me. I arrived in Preston early and met up with Cleo outside of the club. She had secured a front row seat, although she probably knew my act off by heart, having seen nearly all my performances over the last few weeks, although, I had prepared a few new gags.

It was a five-hundred seat club, however, I much

Get a Proper Job

prefer the smaller more intimate venues, where the smell of sweat and old spice gets into the nostrils, and that's just from the women.

"Good evening ladies and gentlemen, it's lovely to be back in Preston, may I say a warm hello to Cleo Sage who is somewhere in here." I knew exactly where she was, on the front row going a dark shade of pink looking extremely embarrassed. I was looking up into balcony as the audience were straining their necks to see the unfortunate person who had been singled out for a mention.

"This lady has just returned from a mission on board a ship, where she rescued a man in distress and cared for him until the vessel got back to port. She deserves a huge thank you for her dedication and caring in this unselfish act of kindness." The audience responded with a massive round of applause as they continued to look for the recipient of this praise. Meanwhile, Cleo's colour had climbed steadily up the chart until it had gone off the scale, I had the feeling I would pay later for my action.

"I was explaining to my wife last night, that when you die you get reincarnated, but you must come back as a different creature. She said she would come back as a cow. I said, "You obviously haven't been listening.

"She suggested I get one of those penis enlargers, so I did. She's 25 her name is Kathy.

"Did you hear about the new shade of paint made by Dulux, called blond? It's not very bright but it spreads easily.

"The misses went missing last week, the police said to prepare for the worst, so, I had to go down to the Oxfam shop and get all her clothes back."

I like to get a few short jokes and one-liners in; it helps me gauge the mood of the audience.

"A friend of mine joined a nudist colony. On his first day there he took off all his clothes and started to

65

wander around the complex. Anyway, a gorgeous petite blonde walked past and he immediately got an erection. She notices his erection, comes over to him, and says, "Did you call for me?"

"He replies, "No; what do you mean?"

"You must be new here, let me explain, it's a rule here that if you get an erection it implies you called for me." Smiling, she leads him away to the side of the swimming pool, lies down on a towel, eagerly pulls him to her, and happily lets him have his way with her.

"He continues to explore the facilities then enters the sauna, as he sits down he farts. Within seconds a huge hairy man lumbers out of the steam room.

"Did you call for me?" says the hairy man.

"No, what do you mean?" says my friend.

"You must be new," says the hairy man, "it's a rule that if you fart it implies that you called for me." The huge hairy man spins him around, bends him over a bench, and has his wicked way with him.

My friend staggers back to the office, where he is greeted by the smiling, naked, receptionist.

"May I help?" she asks.

He yells, "Here's my membership card, and my key, you can keep the £500 membership fee I'm leaving."

"But Sir," she replies, "you've only been here for a few hours you haven't had chance to see all our facilities."

He replies, "Listen lady, I'm sixty-eight years old, if I'm lucky, I get one erection a month but I fart twenty times a day! I'm outta here."

They loved that one; I could see Cleo breaking her heart laughing. After about an hour I thanked them for being a great audience, I got a huge round of applause as I left the stage.

That night I stayed with Cleo, as it would be some time before I saw her again. She was due to leave for the US the following day as she was leading a sales team to promote their products, they were starting on the west coast in Silicon Valley then moving east until they finished in New York. It would be at least four weeks before I saw her again.

Chapter Seven

I was putting a serious number of kilometres on my car; Fat Albert was relentless in promoting my appearances, to the point where I was getting exhausted and somewhat disillusioned with our relationship. I tried in a polite way on a number of occasions to get my point across, but he wasn't interested in listening. Some nights I had up to three gigs to do, a lot of them were 20-30 kilometres apart. I had only had one night off in the past two months and I needed to speak with him.

Whilst I was now making serious money, so was Fat Albert seeing as he took twenty-five percent of each booking. In my naivety I had signed a contract with him that I regretted, now I wanted out of this arrangement but I knew this wouldn't be easy. A lot of the entertainment managers were booking me direct, although I had to confirm with him to ensure there were no double bookings. It was easy money for him; I know I was the main attraction in his portfolio of performers.

One morning, whilst travelling home on the M6 motorway after completing a long corporate gig in Birmingham, I was utterly exhausted. Unfortunately, I fell asleep at the wheel. I hit the barrier on the central reservation before I woke up, but by the time I did, I'd lost control of my vehicle. I shot across the road and hit the barrier on the hard shoulder. It was fortunate that there were so few vehicles on the road at that time in the morning. I was shaken but not seriously injured, apart from a few bruises and a chipped tooth; the same couldn't be said for my car, it was extensively damaged at the front. It was towed away and put into a Mercedes garage for repairs.

After this near death experience, I decided to employ

Get a Proper Job

a driver; a chap named Bob Fletcher who lived nearby he came with glowing references. At least now he could shoulder some of the effort needed to get to and from venues, but something had to be done about the sheer number of bookings I was expected to do in one evening.

It was now even more imperative the situation was rectified, so, I phoned Fat Albert and told him we needed to talk. I wasn't looking forward to confronting him as I made my way up the steps into his office.

"Morning Albert, I've been wanting to talk to you for sometime about our contract."

"Really, what's the matter with it?"

"I want out of it, for the past year I've been feeling exploited with the program of bookings. I can't do the number of shows you expect, I've only had one evening off in the past two months. I can't keep going at this pace, I need to slow down and take some time to write new material."

"You ungrateful little bastard, I took you on when you were a snot nosed kid, I moulded you into the comedian that you are. I spent a lot of time and money promoting you, now you think you can just walk away? Think again sunshine, we have a contract I expect you to honour it."

By this stage he was on his feet, squeezing his knuckles as if he was getting ready to punch me, his eyes had venom in them as he stared me out. I was now seeing a different side to the man I knew. However, I wasn't going to be intimidated by him and decided to stand my ground.

"It's unreasonable to expect me to do two and three shows a night, I'm not doing it."

"You'll do whatever I tell you, I'm your manager, you go where I tell you when I tell you, it's not up for discussion."

"I had hoped that we could settle this amicably obviously that's not going to happen. If this went to arbitration I'm convinced they would term your employment tactics as exploitation.

"The level of commission you are taking is grossly over the top. Speaking with other performers they tell me I'm being ripped off. I feel I'm being prostituted. I wouldn't have signed your contract if I'd have known."

"Listen, you little shit, you wouldn't have had a career but for me, now you want to stab me in the back after all the money I've spent on you?"

"Oh, I think you've been more than adequately compensated with all the commission you've taken over the past number of years, it has to be in the region of several hundred thousand pounds. For what, sat on your bony arse making sure the golden goose never takes a breather. Rest assured, I'm going to have this contract rescinded I'll take care of my own career."

"Do you honestly think you can go it alone? With my contacts in the entertainment industry I can make it that you never work again."

"I didn't expect this kind of reaction, I thought maybe we could work things out, I would even have been prepared to buy my contract out, not anymore. I will continue with any existing bookings for the next month, purely because I don't want to let my fans down, but after this, you can go and get stuffed."

I turned and walked out of his office as he continued to yell obscenities at me. That went well. I wasn't sure what I would do but, the situation couldn't carry on as it was, he was exploiting me plain and simple. No entertainers were paying the kind of commission that I was; he'd taken advantage of a young inexperienced performer with this contract.

With a death toll at six and no one apprehended, DCI Porter was getting a severe daily ear bashing from his superiors. He had increased the number of officers on the investigation; they worked around the clock to find the culprit.

One particular addition to the team was a young detective called Danny Withers who had gained a reputation for tracking down and arresting villains. He talked with DCI Porter and suggested a different approach so it was agreed to do a television appeal.

About two weeks after my run in with Fat Albert, I got the keys to my new apartment. It still had to be furnished but with the pressure of work I hadn't been able to do it. Cleo had offered to help me but I would have to wait until she got back from the US. Meanwhile, I was still living with my parents, trying to convince my mother that I wouldn't starve to death once I moved out. One lunchtime, there was a TV appeal for information from the public to help catch the serial killer who had wreaked havoc in the entertainment sector.

We watched with interest, as a DS Withers made his appeal, my old sparring partners DCI Porter and DS Staunton were seated at the table.

"Good afternoon ladies and gentlemen of the press, this is also directed to viewers at home, my name is Detective Sergeant Danny Withers. As you know, there have been six brutal murders of members connected to the entertainment industry over the past few years. We are very sure these killings, have all been committed by the same person. Despite our lengthy enquiries, we have so far been unable to apprehend the culprit.

"However, today I am going to release details that have not previously been made public. It appears the perpetrator of these crimes wears a ring on their middle finger that has the image of a snake in it. An impression of this snake appeared in the necks of the victims, I'm appealing to anyone if they know of a person who wears a ring of this description to come forward.

"If you cast your eyes to this screen you will see an enlarged image of what this looks like. If you recognise this you can either contact us directly on this number or go to your local police station if you feel you can help. Any information you have will be treated in the strictest confidence. Thank you."

At this point a member of the press spoke up.

"Why is this information only being released now, surely if it was that important it should have been disclosed long before now?"

"This information purposely wasn't released so as to avoid any possible copycat killings, by withholding this detail it would exclude any person who committed a murder claiming to be the serial killer. However, we feel that it's now time to make this vital detail known. That's all, no further questions."

As soon as he said this, it was like being hit with a bolt of lightning, I couldn't believe it; Fat Albert sometimes wore a ring like this. He loved jewellery, had a variety of rings but, one in particular was gold with a serpent coiled around the outside with two ruby stones for eyes. Jesus, my mind was working overtime, surely he couldn't be the culprit.

Then I started to go back through my bookings to see if he had been there when these people had been murdered. He was definitely at the Pickled Parrot in Bradford when there was a murder in nearby Shipley. He was also at the Blue Garter the night there was a killing at the nearby Cotton Club. Of course he was on the cruise ship from Barcelona. It couldn't be him, surely not? These were people he was associated with, even employed one of them. It just didn't bear thinking about, yet, try as I may I couldn't get it out of my head. He had a nasty streak in him, I found that out to my cost, but could he strangle someone, indeed, would he have the strength? He was as thin as a rake although you don't probably need much strength to strangle someone.

I decided to Google him, what I found was quite surprising at the same time disturbing. Whilst he was classed as an impresario, representing a large number of performers, in his younger days he'd been a circus strongman, travelling throughout Europe with a number of different circuses. Could this be possible, that this man whilst looking like he'd just escaped from a prisoner of war camp, devoid of muscle had the strength of Samson? Then the thought occurred to me, had he been interviewed by the police? If not, should he have been? Of course I would never know. We were not close enough for him to divulge if they had spoken to him. If he was the culprit, it's kind of ironic, that at one point I was the number one suspect, yet this person had the opportunity to murder these poor unfortunates, but seemed to have slipped the net.

The following day, Cleo, returned from the US so I decided to ask her advice. She couldn't believe what I told her, but thought when taking everything into account, there could be something in my suspicion. However, seeing as I had decided to fulfil my bookings before I broke our agreement, I decided to put off making any decision until then. Meanwhile, I had an apartment to furnish. We set about picking furniture to complete my move and new-found independence.

The police had been inundated with calls regarding people who wore a snakelike ring. In fact, they got so many calls; DCI Porter was regretting the TV appeal. Numerous people had been interviewed and eliminated from their enquiries. Valuable time had been spent following this line of enquiry that so far had been proven fruitless; also his budget was under pressure because of the sheer volume of work.

I had to approach Fat Albert before I broke our agreement; he owed me several thousand pounds in booking fees. After our meeting at the beginning of the month, I had tried to avoid him, keeping contact to a bare minimum. But I wanted what he owed me for past performances.

I approached his office with a degree of trepidation, not knowing how he would react but there was no way I was going to part company without being paid what I was due.

"Albert, as I told you at the start of the month, I will be going on my own from now on, but, before I do, I want my fees for the past two months that by my reckoning is thirty four grand. I would appreciate payment now if you don't mind."

He looked up from his desk, his face was pure rage, "The door is open, so I suggest you go through it before I throw you through it."

"You don't frighten me, if you think I'm leaving here without what you owe me, think again."

He got up from his seat and raced across to confront me. He grabbed my lapels and pulled me towards him, his face was inches away from mine, I could smell has disgusting breath. I wasn't going to put up with this so I shoved him away and raised my fist. He backed off, surprised that I would defend myself.

"You're not going anywhere, you are still under contract to me, if you think you can just walk away, breaking a legally binding contract you are mistaken. I will bring so much legal shit down on your head you won't know what's hit you. As for what you are owed, Nancy in accounts has a cheque for twenty grand I signed it this morning. The balance I haven't received yet, in fact the corporate gig you did in Birmingham didn't go down too well, they are disputing the invoice, as is the Buccaneer club in Derby, they didn't feel you were value for money."

This was bullshit, he was just trying to justify not to paying me. I got a fantastic reception in Birmingham, in fact so much so, I got a booking for their Christmas party, so I knew what he was telling me was pure lies. At the same time, rubbing salt into the wound seeing as I had a near death experience on my way home from this particular gig.

"I remind you that you have two performances tonight, at the Adelphi in Leeds and the Bucket of Laughs in Bolton."

"I think you need to switch your hearing aid on, you and I are history, if you don't pay me the other fourteen grand, I will take it that is a severance payment. As for legal shit, I've already taken advice; we will be taking action against you to formally wrap this association up. Regarding tonight, I suggest you contact these clubs and advise them I will not be performing."

With that I went straight down to the general office to collect my cheque.

Shouts of, "You'll be sorry you little bastard" followed me down the steps. I was shaking with fright, this guy was vicious, and not to be crossed, I couldn't wait to get out of the place.

For the next two weeks I fulfilled my own bookings, I was enjoying being out from under the yoke of Fat Albert. My lawyer had been in touch with the other side in an effort to legally wind this relationship up but he hadn't received any response from them. It would be difficult to break this agreement because it was a pretty watertight contract, but he thought the level of commission was unreasonable. His approach would be that I had been taken advantage of; the level of remuneration was way above the norm it was excessive. Combined with the level of bookings, the travel involved was above what could be expected as acceptable. Efforts to seek back damages by way of arbitration could well sway him to end the contract amicably.

However, after three weeks I got a shock, when I was served with an injunction effectively stopping me from performing on my own. It was very detailed, even stated that any fees earned since my departure would be subject to a deduction for Twat Albert. The bastard had taken it to a new level. My lawyer was on it immediately and regrettably advised me to comply with the injunction.

Being on 'Garden Duty' gave me lots of time to think, especially about Fat Albert and his violent reaction to me. Could he be the killer? Highly likely, he had the character and temperament as I had seen first hand. Although, it was hard to get my head around the fact he was in the entertainment industry, why would he want to murder vocalists? Was he a failed singer, jealous of people who made it in this competitive field?

It just didn't seem possible that he could be the culprit that was responsible for the killings, not to mention spreading fear and trepidation amongst vocalists.

Several weeks went by, I was still watching paint dry literally, I was putting the finishing touches to my gleaming new kitchen. Cleo was a frequent visitor and I was quite enjoying my newfound freedom. My lawyer was trying to get the injunction lifted, as I was not being allowed to practice my craft and earn a living.

Going back to my previous situation was out of the question for the reasons already stated.

One morning, I got a visit from DS Withers; could I spare him a few minutes for a chat. He was in his mid thirties; tall with sandy coloured hair dressed casually in jeans and a black leather jacket.

"I know you have previously been interviewed by my colleagues and eliminated from their enquiries."

"It took them long enough, I was up in front of the firing squad more than once, I don't think your gaffer is playing with a full deck, couldn't organise a prayer meeting in the Vatican. They only came to that conclusion when they realised I couldn't be in two places at the same time."

"Let me say at the outset, you are not a suspect and

the reason I'm here is to try and pick your brains to see if you could throw any light on who you think it could be.

"We have interviewed and eliminated, literally hundreds and hundreds of people, we are no nearer to finding the culprit now, than we were six months ago. You are an entertainer you have been on the tour of the clubs; does anyone come to mind that could fit the bill, anyone at all? Obviously, any information you can give us would be treated in the strictest confidence."

"Up until a few weeks ago I wouldn't have had a bull's notion, but as soon as you mentioned about the snake ring during the TV appeal, it triggered something that I've thought about constantly. There is someone that I think could be responsible."

That got his attention; his notebook came out quicker than a hooker dropping her knickers.

"Who might that be?"

"My old manager, goes by the name of Albert Bonetti or Fat Albert to those that know him. His office is in the precinct, Bonetti Entertainment. He sometimes wears a thick gold ring on his middle finger; it has a serpent around the circumference with two ruby stones for its eyes. He doesn't always wear it, but he definitely has one. I'm not saying it's him, and it would take a giant leap of faith on my part to accuse him outright, but I know from my own experience he has a very short fuse. It could be that you've already interviewed him, but if you haven't he deserves a visit."

"The name does not ring a bell but I will check with DCI Porter to see if we have already talked to him, thanks."

Chapter Eight

The breaking news on television was that a man believed to be a northern impresario had been taken in for questioning regarding the murder of the six entertainers.

No name was divulged, but I was sure it had to be Fat Albert. Jesus, if it was him, it didn't take them long to act, seeing as I only spoke with Sergeant Withers earlier in the day. Could it be him only time would tell? But whoever was responsible, it was about time the police made some progress, because the perpetrators had wreaked havoc amongst the entertainment community. Nobody felt good about performing, especially vocalists, it's hard to sing whilst keeping one eye over your shoulder.

Myself, I was still not able to perform; I've never been so frustrated. It was ridiculous to prevent me from earning a living. However, my lawyer was confident he could get the injunction lifted; it was a form of restrictive practice, and as so, was against European law.

The following day, it was announced the suspect taken in for questioning was released without charge, we had no idea who it was, but it wouldn't take long to find out.

Cleo had prepared dinner and we had just sat down to eat, when the door of my new apartment was almost kicked off its hinges as whoever it was attempted to gain access, fortunately, the toughened metal door held firm. Security had been a major selling point on the apartment with CCTV cameras covering every aspect of the complex, a concierge was on duty twenty four seven, as well as steel doors activated with an electronic key card.

They had somehow gotten past the guard and attempted to smash their way through the toughened steel door. With a degree of trepidation, I engaged the security chain and opened the door. It was Fat Albert, and boy was he pissed off, I could see the flames shooting from his nostrils. He normally had the appearance of an albino with very pale skin and white hair. However, today his face was bright red like a slapped arse, the veins in his forehead stood out, pulsing as if ready to burst.

He thrust his bony arm through the gap, I tried to slam the door shut, but he'd placed his foot inside. He reached in and managed to grab hold of my throat and pulled me towards him.

I tried to break free but he held me in a vice like grip, I couldn't free myself and could barely breathe as he attempted to squeeze the life out of me. I started to go faint as I sank to the floor, fortunately, Cleo raced to my assistance, she raised her arm up high then slammed a carving knife deep into his shoulder, he let out sharp cry and released his grip.

He staggered back with the knife still embedded in his flesh, blood starting to pour out of the wound as he continued to make threats. I slammed the door shut and realised that without the intervention of Cleo, he may well have killed me.

How did I find out where I was living, I sure as hell didn't tell him? Cleo immediately called the police. This could get ugly; I could hear him screaming at the other side of the door, accusing me of naming him as a murder suspect. After a couple of minutes, I opened the door again but with the chain engaged and standing well back, I attempted to diffuse the situation. From what he was shouting, it was all too evident the police had told him that I gave them the information that he was the culprit, so much so for anonymity.

"Who the hell do you think you are, attempting to break into my apartment, and attacking me? You're not going to get away with this, you bloody nutcase, I suggest you sling your hook, because the police have already been called."

It didn't make any difference, he continued to shout insults and make threats of what he was going to do to me. Fortunately, I had switched on the camera on my phone in video mode, so I was filming, and recording everything he said. By now, other people in the apartment block came out to see what all the screaming and shouting was about.

Thirty minutes later the police arrived, after a discussion it was evident to them he had caused damage to my property, as well as assaulting the concierge who had attempted to prevent him from entering the complex. An ambulance had been called and the concierge was taken to hospital suffering from facial injuries.

He denied threatening and assaulting me, but Cleo was able to confirm he had tried to strangle me. Footage from the CCTV showed him entering the building, then attacking the concierge. The camera on my floor showed him attempting to break in. This coupled with the video from my iPhone convinced the police of his guilt as it showed his aggressive and threatening behaviour. After this they didn't hesitate, he was cuffed, cautioned, arrested, and escorted away.

"Thank you Cleo, he was intent on putting my lights out but you came to my rescue, that's the last bloody thing I expected, I gave the police that information on the understanding it was in the strictest confidence, so much for anonymity, that's the last time I help them."

"That was so scary, Carter, he's a real thug trying to break in and attack you like that, God knows what he would have done to you if he'd got in, he was like a man possessed."

"He may well have played into my hands, with this recording of every bit of bile that came out of his mouth it shows his violent nature towards me, probably towards six vocalists who sadly are no longer with us. Not sure if it could be used in court, but it may help in getting my injunction lifted."

The first thing I did once I'd changed my underwear was to contact, Alistair Bracken, my lawyer, and inform him what had just taken place. Irrespective of what had happened and I had recorded; he was confident the injunction would be lifted at a court hearing later in the week. We could also apply to the courts for a restraining order to keep him away from my home. How do you like them apples Albert?

I always felt comfortable with Alistair, he was an ex-Marine who had gained the rank of sergeant; he worked as a private eye after he left the service. He had studied law during this time, eventually graduated as a lawyer. After this incident, I thought that a phone call to DS Withers was in order, seeing as the information I gave him in confidence was somehow passed onto Fat Albert.

"I am very sorry, Mr. Dean, it did not come from me I am afraid it was DCI Porter, not sure if it was intentional or it just slipped out in error. In any event, we had to release him; there was no evidence despite getting a warrant having his office and home searched thoroughly. We found a number of rings and items of jewellery, but none like you described, are you sure you weren't mistaken?"

"Absolutely positive, he wore it most days, you can bet your life he got rid of it the minute it was reported in the media. Up to that point, it probably never occurred to him the ring was the thing that linked the murders together that this could identity the perpetrator. In any event, that's the last time I help the police, he came around to my apartment, tried to break the door down, and he also assaulted the concierge on his way in. He tried to strangle me; we had to call your lot to remove him. He's an evil bastard, I can't get over the fact I've been associated with him for over seven years I had no idea he could be so violent and nasty. Suggest you keep your eye on him, because the fact you couldn't find the ring means he got rid of it, so that has to tell you something, I wouldn't rule him out of the equation just yet."

"It's regrettable we put you through that, I can understand how you feel, all I can do is apologise for what happened, I am sure it was not intentional."

"Not so sure about that, Porter was after me from day one, he was pissed off when I had the nerve to stand up to him. I don't rate him as a policeman, he's not too bright, in fact, I'd go as far as to suggest his pilot light has gone out."

Withers laughed, apologised once again, and then hung up. Cleo and I sat down to try and come to terms to what had just happened. It had been a frightening incident I was hoping it didn't put Cleo off from staying with me. "Thanks for doing what you did Cleo, there's no way he would have released his grip without your intervention."

"Just sorry I had to resort to doing that, I've never done anything like it before, but I wasn't prepared to let him do that to you."

"It did the trick, serves the bastard right, notice he didn't mention that to the police."

Not long afterwards, the maintenance team arrived to carry out repairs to my doorframe. Whilst the door had held firm the surrounding plasterwork needed some attention.

Later that week, Alistair Bracken contacted me with some good news; he had been successful in getting the injunction lifted. There was still the point regarding commission plus other elements in our contract that had to be resolved by both parties sitting down and

Get a Proper Job

discussing it. That should be interesting, but in the meantime, I could go back to work on my own and practice my craft. Whatever money I earned, I was determined that bastard wouldn't get any of it.

My time in exile had allowed me to write some new material, I immediately started to notify my contacts that I was available once more. Word soon got around that Fat Albert had been taken in for questioning, it must have been having a serious affect on his bank balance regarding the other acts in his stable because of the number of cancellations he was getting.

The incident at my apartment hadn't done my reputation any good either, some of the residents refused to acknowledge me, the concierge was quite standoffish once he'd recovered from his injuries and returned to work. Fat Albert's visit had more of an impact than I had anticipated. My main concern was whether or not the police would follow up their investigation of Fat Albert. I was even more sure after attacking me the way he did, he was the culprit, the fact they didn't find the ring that he wore most days was even more telling. However, life goes on, I had to put recent events regarding that head-case to the back of my mind.

My return to the stage was to be at the Apollo Gentlemen's Club in Leeds, I was looking forward to getting back in the saddle.

From now on my program would be done at a pace that I was comfortable with, not multiple gigs spread halfway around the country. However, I would need some help, so I decided to see if my driver, Bob, would be willing to do more for me. He was very smart and at one point in his career had been an accountant, before the company he worked for closed the branch down.

I approached him to see apart from being my driver, would he be interested in taking on more responsibility, managing my affairs, looking after some of the bookings, and arranging my schedules. He was delighted to be offered this new position, we worked out suitable remuneration for him, however, I would not be signing a contract, our arrangement would be based purely on a gentlemen's agreement.

   It would take several months to get him up to speed but he was willing and a joy to have as a travelling companion. Cleo was away in China for a couple of weeks I was concerned the incident at my apartment may have a lasting effect on our relationship. It shook her up because she was very quiet afterwards, not her usual bubbly self, but who could blame her.

   It was showtime, but the weather was particularly nasty as Bob and I headed off to Leeds. Heavy rain started to fall; by the time we got to the Apollo it was torrential. As a result, there was serious flooding on some of the roads. I just hoped it didn't affect the number of people attending the club. However, as I peered from the wings there seemed to be a good crowd but I was slightly nervous as I waited for the master of ceremonies to introduce me.

   "Ladies and gentle put your hands together for a welcome return to Mr. Comedy himself Carter Dean."

   I walked out to a loud applause, I realised at that point how much I'd missed not been able to perform.

   "Why does Mexico have no Olympic team? Because everyone who can run, jump and swim is already in the US.

   "Why did God invent alcohol? So ugly people can get laid.

   "What do you call a prostitute with a runny rose? Full.

   "What's the difference between a bitch and a whore? A whore sleeps with everyone at a party, a bitch sleeps with everyone at a party except you."

   I hit them with several short more gags to get the measure of them and soon I had them eating out of my hand.

"A couple attending an art exhibition at the National Gallery were standing at a picture that had them completely confused. The painting depicted three black men, totally naked, sitting on a park bench. Two of the figures had black penises, but the one in the middle had a pink penis. The curator of the gallery realised they were having trouble interpreting the painting and offered his assessment. He went for nearly an hour explaining how it depicted the sexual emasculation of African-Americans in a predominantly white patriarchal society. "In fact," he pointed out, "some serious critics believe that the pink penis also reflects the cultural and sociological oppression of gay men in contemporary society."

After the curator left, a Scottish man approached the couple and said, "Would you like to know what the painting is really about and not that bullshit?"

"Now why would you claim to be more of an expert than the curator of the gallery?" asked the couple.

"Because, I'm the guy who painted it," he replied.

"In fact there's no African-Americans depicted at all, they're just three Scottish coal miners, it's just the guy in the middle had been home for lunch."

They loved that one, "A bus stops and two Italian men get on. They sit down and engage in an animated conversation like Latin men do. The lady sitting behind them ignores them at first, but her attention is galvanized when she hears one of the men say the following:

"Emma comes first. Den I come. Den two asses come together. I come once-amore. Two asses, they come together again. I come again and pee twice. Den I come one lasta time."

"You foul-mouthed sex obsessed swine," retorted the lady indignantly. "In this country, we don't speak aloud in public places about our sex lives."

"Hey, coola down lady," said the man, "who talkin about sexa? I'm just a telling my friend how to spell Mississippi." This got a good laugh

"The tax office decided to do an audit on a synagogue as they thought there might be something dodgy regarding their annual returns so they sent out an inspector. Hoping to catch him out, the inspector asked the Rabbi.

"What do you do with all the wax that runs down the side of the candlesticks?"

"Oh we scrape it all off then send it back to the candle maker, they reuse it and now and again they send us some free candles." said the Rabbi.

"What about all the matzo purchases, what do you do with the crumbs?"

"Oh we sweep them all up, send them back to the manufacturer and periodically they send us a free box of matzo balls."

Determined to catch the Rabbi out he asked him, "What do you do with all the leftover foreskin from the circumcisions you perform?"

"Here too, we do not waste," answered the Rabbi, "what we do is save up all the foreskins, send them all to the Tax Office, and about once a year they send us a complete prick."

Rapturous applause, that went down well, after another thirty minutes I bid them goodnight then Bob and I left for home. I was back in the saddle and thoroughly enjoying myself.

After about six weeks of bookings, things were going particularly well, Bob was getting up to speed and gaining in confidence as he started to take on more and more responsibility. Then I got news of the court date for the trial of Fat Albert; of course I had to attend. Thankfully, he pleaded guilty to assaulting the concierge and myself, so this avoided a prolonged trial at the crown court and was being dealt with in the local magistrates court.

He was also charged with assault, criminal damage of my property, trespassing and threatening behaviour.

The magistrate took into account Fat Albert's unblemished record, and he was reluctant to impose a custodial sentence, however, any similar actions in the future would not be tolerated and he would have no hesitation in sending him to prison. Pity. He was ordered to make restitution to the concierge for his injuries and loss of earnings, in the amount of two thousand pounds. He imposed a further fine of five hundred pounds for breach of the peace then was hit with a further five hundred pounds for property damage. He was bound over to keep the piece. A restraining order was issued meaning he couldn't come within a two hundred metres of my apartment.

He thanked the magistrate, apologised to the concierge for assaulting him, then assured the magistrate this would never happen again.

Myself, I would have added to his discomfort with several months' community service with him dressed in a loincloth. The most damaging aspect for him, would be all the negative publicity, word soon got around and rumour had it he'd already received a lot of cancellations for a number of his acts, no doubt he would be blaming me for that.

Alistair had been working on finding a permanent solution regarding my contract. Since the attack on me by Fat Albert, it was unlikely that we would ever be able to work together again, nor would I want to do. A face-to-face meeting wouldn't be ideal also it wasn't guaranteed to find a solution. Alistair was able to come up with an idea that if all parties agreed could once and for all settle the issue.

He managed to acquire the services of a mediator who was prepared to listen to both sides, he would rule on the issue. Fat Albert eventually agreed, the meeting was arranged in the offices of the mediator, Judge Patrick Swanson, who was a retired High Court Judge. He appeared quite frail with a sallow complexion and a very bad stoop. Of course, there was no guarantee that he would rule in our favour, but at least I would know one way or the other. He was in possession of our contract, along with all my gigs undertaken since the signing. They showed an ever-escalating figure of performances along with an ever-increasing number of kilometres incurred travelling to and from the various venues. He also looked at the commission he had taken. The judge was seated at the top of the table; I sat with my lawyer facing Fat Albert who was with his lawyer. The judge asked pertinent questions from both parties, taking notes all the time.

This went on for over an hour, at which point he spoke to deliver his verdict.

"Gentlemen, I have looked very carefully at this contract, there are a number of issues that I have a problem with that have influenced my ruling."

I didn't like the sound of this; I could see the look on Fat Albert's face change to concern. One of us was going to be unhappy.

"Whilst the contract is what you would call, water tight, I have to look at elements that I feel in light of recent events makes this unworkable. Firstly, I feel Mr. Dean should have had legal representation when he signed this contract, however, he didn't. You could argue that was his fault and he must pay the price, but he was naive and not worldly wise in legal matters. He was a young man desperate to launch his comedy career, to be perfectly honest I think he was taken advantage of. The degree of commission taken by you Mr. Bonetti, whilst legal as far as the contract goes is in my opinion excessive.

"I have looked at the program of bookings, the amount of travel involved, particularly in the last two

Get a Proper Job

years. This was in my mind excessive. I think it was unreal and unfair to expect Mr. Dean to carry out this level of activity. I understand he approached you about this work rate but you wouldn't listen to his problem. I would point out that slavery was abolished over a century ago."

"What are talking about, slavery, that's bullshit, there's no way you could call it slavery?"

"Mr. Bonetti, you agreed to this mediation, I'm in the process of giving my judgment, I suggest you listen."

What the hell was Fat Albert doing; that wouldn't have helped his cause?

"There is also the incident of assault on Mr. Dean and the current restraining order from preventing you from visiting his home. This situation, whilst you could say is not relevant to the contract, it does have a bearing, and in my opinion it would prevent a good working relationship. You have been more than adequately compensated during the lifetime of this contract. The number of bookings Mr. Dean was asked to undertake, was excessive, obviously influenced by your greed.

"There is also a health and safety issue for the amount of travel involved. My view is he was taken advantage of when he signed the contract and he is still being taken advantage of. Having taken all these elements into account, there is no doubt in my mind this contract is unfair, unjust, it is heavily biased against Mr. Dean, therefore, I rule in favour of Mr. Dean and declare this contract null and void.

"Furthermore, I understand there is an amount of fourteen thousand pounds belonging to Mr. Dean that is retained by you. I'm instructing you to pay this money to Mr. Dean immediately. I would hope that both parties would accept this ruling and move on, that is my decision thank you."

It took several seconds for what he said to sink in, then Fat Albert jumped to his feet, he raced up to the top of the table to confront the judge, who was a frail old man. But before he could do anything, my lawyer stepped in between to prevent him. Alistair was a huge man approaching two metres tall and built like a brick outhouse. He held Albert by his coat lapels whilst advising the judge to make a quick exit.

"Back off you clown, assaulting a high court judge, got a death wish have we?"

"This is a fucking joke, you're not going to get away with this Dean, and I'm going to appeal."

My lawyer looked at him, "You agreed to this mediation, the terms being that you would accept the verdict of the judge, there is no appeal process. This was all spelled out to you beforehand and you agreed, now it's gone against you you're complaining. I suggest you move on before you get in serious trouble, as the judge said you have been more than adequately compensated. This golden goose has stopped laying, at least for you."

"You're not going to get away with this, Dean, I'll see to that, if I were you I'd watch your back."

At which point he stormed out of the room, leaving his lawyer standing there speechless, looking more than embarrassed.

"Threats against my client will not help his cause, you were witness to his comments, perhaps you would convey to him the seriousness of what he has just said, as he is already under court orders to keep the peace."

His lawyer nodded and left the room, hopefully to try and knock some sense into this boneheaded prick. I was elated, we retired to the George & Dragon for a celebratory drink then, I phoned Cleo with the good news.

Chapter Nine

I was just out of the shower, when Percy the concierge said I had a visitor, it was that super sleuth, DCI Porter requesting an audience. Not this stupid prick again. Reluctantly, I told him to send him up.

"Inspector Porter, back again, you should change you're name to Herpes."

"I assume that's not meant as a term of endearment?"

"You got it one."

"Nice place you have here, must've been expensive."

I didn't respond, "I gather it's not a social call, what do you want?"

"Can you tell me where you were between twelve and two on Sunday morning?"

Here we go again, how many damned times do I have to tell this bonehead I'm not responsible for whatever it is he's investigating.

"Let me see, I murdered one bloke in Burnley, that would have been around twelve, then I hot footed it over to Bolton, strangled another chap around two, then I came home totally knackered after a good nights work."

Porter stuck his finger into my chest, "I get the feeling you think this is some kind of game?"

"That could be construed as assault, another charge to add to your continued harassment, plus God knows where you've had that finger."

"This is a serious matter Dean, I want your cooperation."

"It's just that you bring the worst out in me. You were responsible for Bonetti trying to break into my apartment and trying to kill me. I gave information to the police in the strictest of confidence, yet you chose to release this information to him, knowing full well it would piss him off and he'd take action against me."

"Where did you get that information from?"

"From your associate DS Withers."

Porter didn't like this, no doubt Withers would be in for a bollocking later on, "It may have slipped out in error, I can assure you I would not have done this maliciously."

"Really? That is exactly what you would do. You've had it in for me from day one, the way you have hounded me without any evidence it's sickening. Anyway, I'm trying to put all that behind me, I'm in the middle of something so why are you really here?"

"There was another murder on Saturday night, a vocalist called Max Stafford, found in the Rochdale canal. He'd been strangled and dumped in the water near Leeds. He appeared at Browns Club on the outskirts of the town earlier in the evening and was found early yesterday morning by a group of canoeists."

"Suggest you try Fat Albert, rather than harassing me."

"Unfortunately, we can rule him out as he's not in the country, he's on a cruise. We contacted his office; they confirmed he is currently sailing around the Greek islands has been for the last two weeks"

What the hell, "Is it the same M O ?"

"Unfortunately it is. The same snakelike image was found in the neck of the victim."

I was stunned, I was certain it was Fat Albert who was the murderer.

"Can you tell me where you were?"

This guy was really starting to piss me off; I'm the number one suspect again,

"I was on stage at the Apollo in Leeds, finished around one, then I came home, arrived back here around one forty."

"Leeds, that's interesting, Mr. Stafford was murdered

there."

"Well I wasn't responsible, I did my show then came straight home."

"Can anyone confirm this?"

"Yes, my driver Bob, also Percy the concierge would confirm what time I arrived back, because everyone coming and going is logged in a book. If that's not good enough for you, there will be CCTV footage showing time of my entry. Now I will say this only once, I'm not responsible, suggest you back off and look elsewhere. I still believe Fat Albert is the culprit."

"We didn't find the ring that you said he wore, despite obtaining a warrant and searching both his home and business premises extensively. The general feeling amongst my colleagues, is that you fabricated this story so as to deflect attention away from you. It's well known there is bad blood between the two of you."

"Is it any wonder, when you repeated to him details I gave you in the strictest of confidence."

"Like I said, it was an accident, it just slipped out." he said with a smirk on his face.

"That's bullshit and you know it."

"Afraid we'll have to disagree."

I was fuming with this idiot, he had had it in for me from the beginning, now he was back, trying to pin something on me, and he wouldn't be happy until he achieved that goal.

"Where can I find your driver?"

I wrote his name and number on a slip of paper that was as far as I was going to go. I showed him the door, and then rang Bob to advise him that inspector shit for brains would be contacting him. There had been no further murders for nine months, then this. I would have to be very careful and watch my step if the police thought I was the prime suspect again, or maybe it was just the opinion of Porter. I called my lawyer and advised him what had taken place. Alistair sounded concerned, he asked me to meet him at his offices at 10:30am.

"Morning Carter, grab a seat, so we have another murder?"
"Yes, unfortunately it doesn't look like its Bonetti, seeing as he's on a cruise around the Greek islands."
"Do they know this for sure?"
"I assume they do, or at least that's what they told me. They've been on to his office and were told he'd been away for two weeks."
"I think this needs clarification because I'm sure this guy is involved with the killings. Leave it with me, I'm going to make some enquiries we'll see if it's true."
I thanked Alistair, and then returned home to prepare for my gig at Foxes Club in Derby.

Alistair Bracken had a number of contacts in the travel trade. He found six direct routes from various Greek islands into Manchester.
Once he had this information, he made contact with the airlines to see if it was possible to obtain passenger details. Naturally, they were reluctant to release this information, because they would be in breach of the Data Protection Act. But, when he told them it was regarding a murder enquiry, he was able to get the material he wanted. Coincidently, he found that two passengers with the name Bonetti had travelled from Greek airports. One was from Lesvos, the other from Kos, ironically, both had the Christian name beginning with the initial A. One had travelled to Manchester two days before the murder on a one-way ticket, the other arriving the morning of the day of the murder from Lesvos. This passenger had returned to Athens the day after the murder. The next thing would be to get a positive ID. Carter was able to supply him with this from his iPhone coverage of the encounter at his apartment.

Get a Proper Job

This was presented to the immigration authorities at Manchester airport and at Lesvos. With the latest biometric passports, confirmation soon came through that Albert Bonetti had boarded a flight in Lesvos the morning of August sixth, flying into Manchester, and had returned to Athens on August eighth. Alistair was of the opinion Bonetti used Athens to link up with the cruise ship. Contact with the cruise company, confirmed that Bonetti had rejoined the cruise in Athens.

I was just about to go on stage at the Mr. Sloan's Club in Oldham, when I got a call from Alistair.

"Carter we have him, I've established he flew from Lesvos into Manchester the day of the murder, he returned to Athens two days later. We have a positive ID from both countries."

"Jesus, how the hell did you manage to find that out?"

"I've a number of contacts in the travel trade also a few friends in immigration, so it wasn't that difficult really, once I convinced them it was important."

"Have you told the police yet?"

"No, I thought I'd give you the good news first."

"It will be interesting to see if they do anything about it, seeing as they are convinced I'm the culprit."

"If they've any sense, they'll wait until he flies back into the country, then arrest him. If he gets wind of his impending arrest beforehand there's a good chance he won't come back," said Alistair.

"I'm afraid sense is something Porter is lacking. The other thing that strikes me is, he could well say his return home was business related, how can you prove otherwise?"

"Let's not get ahead of ourselves Carter, Porter said his office told them he was on a cruise and wouldn't be back in the UK for another week."

"He's a sneaky bastard, he could just say it was an

emergency and had to come back. Anyway, we'll see how it pans out. I must go Alistair, my audience awaits."

One week later, it was announced that a suspect in the murders of seven entertainers had been detained at Manchester airport. I was sure it had to be Fat Albert. Later that day, Alistair called me and confirmed it was definitely he.

Albert Bonetti, was arrested the minute he disembarked from a British Airways flight from Barcelona, he was then taken to Rochdale for interrogation. Protesting his innocence all the way there to the arresting officers, but his charm offensive failed; they didn't answer him. This wound him up even more, in fact, by the time they arrived at the police station he had become quite violent, so much so, that he was placed in handcuffs. He was put in the interview room to wait for the arrival of DS Porter.

"Hello again Mr. Bonetti, thank you for coming."
"As if I had any bloody choice."
"I'm sorry to inconvenience you. We are making enquiries into the murder of the entertainer Max Stafford. Can you tell me where you were on the evening of August sixth?"
"That's easy, I've been on a cruise around the Greek islands with some of my team for the past three weeks. We sailed from Barcelona on July thirtieth returned there last Tuesday."
"So, you've been away for three weeks?"
"Correct, after the vessel docked I got the first available flight home then I was met by your goons at the airport."
"Goons, that's hardly a term of endearment, did you return to the UK at any stage in the past three weeks?"
Fat Albert was stunned, he tried not to show it but it deeply worried him, his mind was working overtime.

Was he just fishing, or did they know he'd been back, had someone seen him? He thought about it for several seconds. If they did know, how the hell had they found out?

"Anytime soon will do."

"Actually, just remembered, I had to come back for a business meeting at noon on August sixth. I returned to Greece on August eighth and rejoined the cruise in Athens on August ninth."

Porter didn't believe him; first he's been away for three weeks, but when pressed says he forgot he returned home on August sixth. He was lying, the truth didn't figure in this chap's make-up.

"So now you are changing your story, suddenly you remember you had to come back to Manchester, what urgent business necessitated you returning home?"

"My business has been expanding recently, I've been in talks with a Russian entrepreneur about doing luxury cruises around the Black Sea. We would supply a number of acts for these sailings. He called me out of the blue to see could I meet him in Manchester, I didn't have much choice but to travel back."

"What's the name of this gentleman, and where can I find him?"

"His name is Alexi Petrov, I think he's based in Moscow I'm not too sure, but he was leaving the UK the day after I met him."

Porter looked at Bonetti, he didn't believe one single word this guy uttered, and this was some cock and bullshit story. "Do you have a number for him?"

"I don't, he contacted me. After our meeting he was going away to study what we could offer in the way of entertainment, then if he was interested he would get back to me, that's all I can tell you."

All very convenient, it was going to be very difficult to disprove what he was saying.

"If you don't mind me asking, how did you know I

returned to the UK?"

Porter thought about it for a while, then he decided to have some fun, "Your old mate Carter Dean passed the information on to us, one friend of his who's a private eye did some digging and he was able to establish you'd been back."

Fat Albert was seething with rage, he tried not to show it but after this knife in the back he was determined to seek retribution.

Porter was sure it was either Bonetti or Dean who was responsible for these murders, so he thought if he threw a hand grenade into the equation it might yield results. He thought the best thing was to let him stew for a while. He left the room and his colleague took over the interrogation.

"Morning Mr. Bonetti, I'm DS Withers, can I get you anything, tea, coffee, a truth pill?"

"What do you mean by that?"

"I don't believe your story, initially you said you were away for three weeks, then when pressed you forgot you'd returned for an urgent meeting. If it was that urgent, surely you would have remembered it?"

"What can I say, my memory isn't as good as it used to be."

"You mean selective, can you tell me where this meeting with yourself and Mr. Petrov took place?"

"Yes, at my office."

"Can someone confirm this, your secretary or anyone else?"

"She doesn't work on a Saturday, there was just me and Petrov."

Withers looked at him, this guy was some slippery customer. "I don't believe you, I don't believe there is a Petrov, I don't believe you came back specifically for a meeting, I think it was something a lot more sinister."

"Whether you believe me or not, I don't care, I'm telling you the truth."

Withers left the room to consult with his superior. "He's lying, Sir, I was watching him through the two-way glass, when you mentioned about him returning home, the look on his face was utter shock, he almost fell off his chair."

"That may be so, but I don't think we can hold him much beyond the end of today. We have nothing that links him to any of these murders, no DNA, or fingerprints, no witnesses, in fact, bugger all. Let the bastard stew for a few hours then let him go."

"Are you sure?"

"Unfortunately, I don't think we have any option, but put a tail on him, in fact on both of them."

"You mean Dean as well, really, I don't have enough men to spare for that, especially as Fat Albert and Dean travel all around the north? It would be a major task just to keep tabs on any one of their movements."

"OK, I understand what you're saying, but it would only be in the evening, see what you can do. The commander is on my back non-stop, he's talking about taking us off the case that wouldn't do either of our careers any good."

Life was interesting; it was great to be back on the road again doing what I loved most. Unfortunately, I hadn't seen much of Cleo due to both our work schedules, but we had arranged to meet up later in the week for dinner at my apartment as I had a night off.

Friday arrived, I was just putting finishing touches to our meal, Cleo's favourite, prawn cocktail, the main course of grilled fillet steak with hot chilli salsa, caramelised onions with my special peppered chips, followed by that old stalwart, hot apple pie and ice-cream. My cooking skills are limited, but steak was one thing I could do. She liked her meat medium rare so I would wait until she arrived before I put it on to cook.

The table was set; I had a nice Merlot ready to pop

the cork. Seven o'clock came and went, but there was no sign of her. By seven thirty I tried her mobile, but all I got was her voicemail, this was strange. I repeatedly called her number, but each time got the same result.

By ten thirty I was convinced something had happened to her, all manner of thoughts went through my mind. Had she had an accident on the way over, had she got a last minute travel request to see one of her overseas customers, but if she had, surely she would have called me?

I didn't sleep that night the first thing next morning I decided to drive over to her apartment in Preston. I parked in the visitors bay and walked across to the glass-fronted unit. The concierge acknowledged me as I entered the building, then I took the elevator up to the fourth floor. As I opened the door to her apartment, I could hear the sound of her radio playing. I called out her name but there was no reply, as I searched each room there didn't seem to be anything out of the ordinary, her bed was made she had neatly laid out clothes on it. Was this what she was going to wear last night but somehow had been disturbed? I didn't like it, I had a stomach churning feeling as I walked around the apartment and tried to make sense of the situation.

I left the apartment then took the elevator down to the underground car park. Her blue BMW wasn't in her parking space. I was now convinced more than ever, something had happened to her. I went up to the ground floor to see the concierge; maybe he could throw some light as to where Cleo was.

"Good morning Sir, can I help you?"
"I hope so, I'm Carter Dean."
"Yes sir I recognise you."
"Do you have any idea where Ms. Sage from apartment 4D is? She was supposed to meet me for dinner last night but never showed up."
"One moment sir, I'll check."

He scanned through CCTV footage until he spotted her car entering the underground car park.

"She arrived here at two minutes past five last night. Just one moment, let me check the cameras to see if she went out."

He fast-forwarded the cameras.

"Here we are sir, that's her following the blue Jaguar out at five thirty-three last night."

"Can you freeze that? Just go back a bit, there stop it now." I looked at the image but it wasn't very clear, if it was Cleo she was wearing a hat, something that I'd never seen her do. Where the hell was she going? I had no idea what to do next.

"Do any of the cameras cover the various floor levels or the elevator?"

"Afraid not sir, the cameras only cover the main pedestrian entrance into the building and the underground car park. The management team is of the opinion that's sufficient. Of course I keep a log of visitors coming and going so it's very secure."

He checked the cameras to see if she'd returned to the apartment but she never did. I thanked him then left the building, not sure what to do next.

Her mother was still alive and lived in Cornwall, had she gone there? I think she said she had a B&B in St. Ives. I contacted directory enquiries and found three numbers with the name Alice Sage. The first two numbers I called I drew a blank, and then the third number was the Alice Sage that I wanted. I had to be careful; I didn't want to alarm her. I explained who I was, Cleo had obviously told her about me. Unfortunately, she wasn't there, I tried to play it down so as not to upset her unduly, but I'm afraid that's exactly what my phone call did. She hadn't spoken with Cleo for over two weeks and had no idea where she could be.

I gave her my number and asked her to let me know

if Cleo made contact. The only other thing I could think of doing, would be to contact the company she worked for, however, with it being the weekend I would have to wait until Monday. Meanwhile, I had two bookings to fulfil one for that night in York and the following night in Horwich, at least it may help take my mind off things.

Chapter Ten

Just after nine on the Monday morning, I placed a call to the company that Cleo worked for. I explained who I was and the fact that she hadn't kept our appointment on the previous Friday evening. I was eventually put through to the Managing Director, Peter Barnes, when I explained what had taken place with her he was very concerned. She hadn't arrived for work that morning, something that she had never done before.

Normally she would be in her office at 8:30am. In fact, she was supposed to head a sales team to Bosnia later that day. He couldn't suggest anything, apart from going to the police to report her as a missing person. We exchanged numbers then I headed straight over to Preston to the police station that serviced her area. I gave them a photograph of Cleo, along with her address and details of the car she was driving. She was immediately classed as a missing person; her details were issued to various forces around the country.

Where the hell was she, I feared the worst? It was like she'd vanished into thin air. She was constantly on my mind I knew if she didn't turn up soon it would affect my work. I had a show to do in Derby, that night, to be honest my heart wasn't in it and I would have cancelled it if I could, but I knew this would have serious implications if I did. I cannot deny it was difficult to give my best, even Bob my driver commented I wasn't on song. This would only get worse unless she was found safe and well.

Two days later I was just out of the shower, when Percy the concierge buzzed me to say I had visitors, it was the police. I told him to send them up. I assumed it was the local police with news about Cleo. However, when I opened the door, it was DCI Porter and his colleague DS Withers.

"Morning Mr. Dean, may we come in?"

"If you must."

Porter walked inside and parked his bony arse on my sofa, "Do take a seat why don't you?"

"We gather your friend, Ms. Cleo Sage, has gone missing? What can you tell us about that?"

"How do you know about Cleo?"

"It comes natural to me, I'm a spiritualist."

"So I've heard, two bottles a day isn't it?"

"Funny, I forgot you're supposed to be a comedian, on a far more serious note, what can you tell us about the circumstances regarding her disappearance?"

"Not a lot, she was supposed to come for dinner last Friday night but she never showed up. Anyway, how come you've become involved, I reported her disappearance to the police in Preston?"

"Her disappearance was circulated to forces throughout the country and coupled with information we have received, it appears your relationship wasn't what you would call, harmonious."

He had a smug grin on his face, I was close to punching him, "That's utter bollocks, who told you that?"

"Afraid I can't tell you, it was anonymous but was quite detailed in the accusation, so much so, we are duty bound to follow the information up."

His associate DS Withers looked uncomfortable, almost like he didn't want to be there.

"I don't know what all this is about, all I know is that my girlfriend has gone missing and the two of you have the nerve to come around here because you have received anonymous information that throws a bad light on our relationship. Well, I can tell you, nothing could be further from the truth, we had even discussed the possibility of getting married. Anyway, I don't see why I should be discussing our personal relationship with you; it's of no business of yours. Maybe the person who gave this information has something to do with her disappearance, did you think about that?"

"As I said, the information was from an anonymous source so I can't really comment on that."

"No, but you are quite prepared to point your grubby little finger at me inferring that I'm behind her disappearance. You said the information was quite detailed, such as?"

"There have been incidents of the two of you rowing in the street when you assaulted her and she needed hospital treatment, also being asked to leave a club because you were fighting inside, want me to go on?"

"This is pure rubbish, nothing like that ever happened plus, you'd be hard pressed to find the hospital that attended to her. I'm not going to stand here and listen to this bullshit any longer. I'm calling my lawyer now, this is pure harassment, this discussion is over."

I opened the door, "Get out the pair of you, I'm sick and tired of your inept bubbling investigating. You tried to pin the other murders on me now you are here insinuating I had something to do with Cleo's disappearance, I didn't, now get lost."

The pair of them just stood there, obviously not being used to this kind of reaction. This could go two ways, either they would do as I suggested and bugger off, or they would arrest me. Thankfully, they walked to the door, Porter turned to face me.

"This isn't over, I've a feeling we'll be back."

"I've a feeling you are not going to be in your current job for much longer."

"Really, what makes you think that?"

"Information I've received."

"What information might that be?"

"I can't say, it was from an anonymous source."

Two can play at that game. I slammed the door shut behind them and immediately called Alistair.

"Do you know what Carter, it's possible that Albert Bonetti has something to do with Cleo's disappearance, it's his style? He has it in for you, this was pretty evident when he tried to break into your apartment and attack you. Also, remember the threats he made during the appraisal meeting? To be honest, I'm surprised he's not under lock and key. I think we need to look into this further."

"I don't know what to do, Cleo's disappearance is affecting me very badly, I'm finding it very difficult to go on stage and give it my best."

"Leave it with me Carter, try not to worry I'm gonna call on some muscle."

Alistair had been a private investigator before he qualified as full time lawyer. He was still in touch with a number of former colleagues from his time in the Marines, some he still used when needed. He arranged to meet with two of them later that day.

"Marvin, and Dexter, good to see you both again, thanks for coming."

They were former friends who had served with Alistair in Afghanistan and Iraq. They were trustworthy and dependable. Almost like twins in appearance, they were both approaching two metres in height, weight around 100 kilos of solid muscle. The only obvious difference was Marvin had dark brown hair; Dexter had lost most of his.

"I've got a little job I hope you can help me with. There's a chap I want you to keep an eye on, he's called Albert Bonetti or Fat Albert to those that know him. This is a photograph of him, as you can see he's very pale what I would term peroxide, almost looks like an albino, very tall weighs about sixty kilos. He's what they call an impresario, manages a number of acts from an office in the precinct in Bury. He's a violent son of a bitch, he's

Get a Proper Job

threatened one of my clients, also we think he might be linked to all the recent murders of entertainers, vocalists to be precise, as well as the disappearance of my client's fiancée, a lady called Cleo Sage.

"He's a slippery bastard, the police haven't been able to nail him, although that's hardly surprising seeing as the investigating officer is, Detective Chief Inspector Porter, who it appears couldn't organise an orgy in a brothel. So far, I've been able to establish he spends his daytime in his office, then travels with some of his acts to various venues around the north of England. I want you to tail him for a couple of weeks see what he gets up to, daily rates and expenses as usual, if that's OK?"

They both nodded their approval.

"Let me know as soon as you see anything out of the ordinary."

"What kind of vehicle does he drive?" asked Marvin.

"A black Citroen Picasso, a small people carrier, that's the registration.

"He normally parks his car in the underground garage next to his office."

Over the coming days, Marvin, and Dexter, took it in turns to follow Fat Albert. They were used to covert surveillance, making sure not to be noticed, taking the step of using a different vehicle each time they followed the Citroen.

There was no set pattern to his movements, but all involved visits to nightclubs around the north of England. After two weeks they called with an update, "Alistair, its Dexter here, got some interesting news re our friend. Firstly, we are not the only ones tailing him; I think the police also are keeping an eye on him. They are not very good though and have comprised our investigation, because he has now realised he's being followed. For over a week we tracked him without a problem, then these two muppets in a navy Ford Mondeo gave the game away. He came out of a club one night and caught them red handed examining his car, since then he's been over cautious. Each time he sets off, he's doubling back then doing all kind of things to lose them they haven't a clue how to keep up with him. Make no mistake he's a clever bugger, now he knows he's being followed he'll be even more elusive.

"However, what we've been able to establish is, Fat Albert, is supplying drugs, probably on a big scale. We saw him doing transactions on six separate occasions; we managed to get photographs of him in action. He handed over large packs, looked about a kilo of what we think was pure coke outside on the car parks, probably to other dealers."

"You're positive?"

"Absolutely, we've also established he has a lockup building near Oldham, we followed him there one night after he left his office. He was inside for about ten minutes, and then came out with a hold all over his shoulder. Marvin's gone over to see if he can get in but it's like Fort Knox.

"It will be difficult to get access without him noticing, but he's taken a friend who is a locksmith so, if anybody can pick the locks, this guy can, however, the place is probably alarmed. This visit is more of a recce to see if we can take a look inside without giving the game away."

"Jesus Christ, drugs are the last thing I expected you to find. Maybe that's what's behind all the recent murders."

"Don't know about that Alistair, but from what we've both observed he's definitely handing over large packs of Columbian marching powder, we think to other dealers who probably then break it down and sell it on."

"Thanks Dexter, tell Marvin to call me as soon as he gets back."

"Will do."

Bob and I were driving to the Apollo club in Leeds

when Alistair called me.

"Just had Dexter on the phone, you are not going to believe this Carter, but they've been following Fat Albert for the last two weeks. He's been seen handing over large bags of what they are sure is cocaine on six separate occasions."

I was stunned it didn't register immediately what he said, "Coke, Hells bells, are you sure?"

"As sure as I can be, let's put it this way, they are hardly handing over bags of sweeties."

"I wonder how long he's being doing that?"

"Don't know is the answer to that, but Marvin and Dexter are of the opinion he's a major player and he's been working with a lot of dealers. Each time he went to a club where one of his acts was performing, he was seen doing a transaction out on the car park. Obviously, it's great cover travelling around the country meeting up with various dealers."

I was finding it hard to take in what Alistair had just told me. In all the years I had worked with him, I had never seen him dealing in drugs. However, he didn't accompany me to every show, he would rotate with various acts, sometimes he wouldn't even travel at all, "I wonder if this is what's behind the murders, you know, coke heads who couldn't pay their bills?"

"Don't know Carter, it's a possibility, but, as well as that, they've discovered he's got a lockup in Oldham, Marvin is at the location now to see if he can get in."

As soon as he said this, I immediately thought of Cleo, could she be held in there against her will?

"What do we do now, tell DCI Porter about this, or maybe he already knows if his guys have been on his tail?"

"I wouldn't hold my breath on that one Carter, Dexter said they stuck out like a sore thumb, bumbling I think is the term he used. Let's wait until Marvin gets back with whatever he's managed to find out, then we'll decide what to do. I know it's imperative that we find Cleo but we might be better going it alone in view of past run ins with Porter."

I was in shock after what Alistair had told me, I found it difficult to concentrate on my presentation. An hour later, I was just off the stage in Leeds when Alistair called again, "Marvin just phoned me, the place is so secure they couldn't get in. There are no windows on the ground floor, and only one door in. There was originally what appeared to have been a wide roller shutter door over a loading bay, but this has now been recently bricked up. The one and only entrance is made of heavy gauge steel with three locks that they were unable to pick.

"On top of this they think it's alarmed, seeing as there is a large what looks like a siren on one side of the building with a bell box on the other. Why would you have a building so secure, unless you had something housed inside that's valuable?

"There are a few old warehouses in the complex, the whole area is a disused textile mill, pretty derelict probably has been for years. Yet, this building stands out because it's so secure. Marvin's thinks the only way in is with some C4 explosive, either that or weld a large steel hook to the door and try and pull it off with a tractor. These are both extreme methods but it's probably going to take something like that to get in."

"I've not heard from Cleo now for almost four weeks, the local police haven't had any information from the public, apart from a sighting in Wigan that turned out to be an off duty copper who looked like her. My gut feeling tells me she is dead, I just hope I'm wrong, but despite a public appeal she seems to have disappeared off the face of the earth. I think we should make every effort to get into that building, but, don't pass any of this info on to inspector Nob head."

"I think you're right Carter, I've got a couple of

contacts who are still in the Marines, one of them works in the quarter masters stores, so getting hold of some C4 and a detonator shouldn't be a problem, I think I can still remember how to set up a charge. But, if we manage to get into the building, it will have to be a straight in and out as quickly as possible. The noise is sure to attract some attention. The only thing that might help is, Dexter says there is a mosque less than a mile away. When they call the Muslims to prayer, the sound from the loudspeakers should hopefully mask some of the noise, but we won't know for sure until we actually set off the charge."

"When do you think you'd be in a position to do it?"

"I'll place a call straight away, I should be able to get hold of the goodies within the next day or so, leave it with me."

Chapter Eleven

Once Alistair was in receipt of the C4 plastic explosive, along with Dexter and Marvin they headed over to the warehouse in Oldham. It was just after 8:00pm when they drove into the disused complex. Making sure they were not observed, they wove their way around piles of rusting old textile machinery, parked their vehicle in one of the old buildings out of sight, then made their way to the nearby target. Alistair examined the door and the heavy metal frame.

"He was making certain that nobody would get in here without a great deal of effort, this bloody thing must weigh a thousand kilos if not more. I think we need to attack the frame rather than the door. If we can sever the frame from the concrete block-work, that should release the door.

"Several small charges down the sides and along the top linked together should do the trick. However, it's sure to activate that large siren above us and that bell box on the far side, it has a large blue light on that will be visible from a long way off. Let's hope the alarm isn't linked directly to a police station. Speed will be of the essence, we'll have minutes at the most to get in, search each of the five floors, and then get out. I don't have to remind you that what we are doing is highly illegal, however, in the scale of things I think the end justifies the means. If either of you have any misgivings or, are having second thoughts, now is the time to let me know."

"I think I speak for Marvin as well as myself, we are committed one hundred percent to get inside and see what this bugger has been up to, who knows, if we find the biggest stash of Columbian marching powder we might get a knighthood."

"Not sure that will be on the cards Dexter, plus I wouldn't trust Prince Charles with a sword near my jugular, anyway let's get on with it."

Alistair proceeded to break off small pieces of the putty like explosive then mould it into a long strip. He did this several times, pressing them against the metal frame and the concrete block work. He placed a small detonator into each one and linked them all together to a timer and set it for ten seconds.

"As soon as they start calling for prayer, I'll hit the timer then we need to take cover behind that wall. With a bit of luck it should remove the frame and door in one go. I estimate each floor is about five hundred square metres, but they may be divided into a number of rooms, we just won't know until we get in there."

Just after 9:00pm, the sound from the loudspeakers on top of the Minarets on the Mosque boomed out the Adhan echoing around the valley, calling Muslims to prayer. Alistair was glad he didn't live in the vicinity of a Mosque, the noise sounded off the scale. He hit the start button on the timer and they raced for cover, he hoped the blast wouldn't be heard.

    They only just made it, when there was a huge flash with an enormous bang, the door and frame shot out, landing about twenty-five metres away in a pile of dust and debris. They had more than achieved their goal as most of the wall over the door came crashing down as well, bringing with it the siren, which bounced several times as it hit the ground, surprisingly, it was still working.

    The noise was like an air raid warning sounded during the Second World War it would have woken the dead. Dexter quickly picked it up then dropped it into a large nearby tank that was full of rainwater, it continued working but slowly winding down until the sound was now more of a glug. However, the bell box located on the other side of the building was ringing, the flashing blue strobe light would be visible from a long way off.

"I haven't had this much fun since we blew up an al Qaeda armoury in Helmond Province, in Afghanistan, although, I think I used a bit too much C4. That old line of Michael Cane in the Italian Job 'You were only supposed to blow the bloody door off' springs to mind. Anyway, now is not the time to reminisce, let's get inside."

The three of them stumbled in through the gap they had created, although, visibility was poor the atmosphere was full of concrete dust with the acrid smell of cordite. As they scrambled over the debris, they shone their torches to find a light switch, flicking each one to illuminate the room then start their search.

 The first floor contained five rooms situated at one end of the warehouse, each one was empty, apart from benches on which sat some old sewing machines. In one corner of the room a sheet was draped over a car, when they removed it a blue BMW was revealed. This got Alistair's attention but they had to move on time was critical. There was an ancient hoist that went up to the various floors but they decided against using it, the last thing they needed was to get stuck in a lift.

 Having completed their search of that level, they raced up the stone stairs to the second floor; this room contained about twenty old weaving machines all past their sell by date. Alistair was getting worried, so far they had found nothing, what if they'd got it wrong and there wasn't anything to find?

 They raced up to the third floor and threw the light switches, as the fluorescent lights stuttered to life, what they found took their breath away. Shackled in one corner of the room was Cleo, she didn't respond to their presence she seemed barely alive. Alistair used his first aid training and quickly checked her condition; she had a faint pulse, but was unconscious. Whilst he attended to her he had a dilemma, call the emergency services and explain how they came to find her, or, treat her themselves. First he had to free her from the chains that secured her to a large steel ring anchored into the floor. On a nail high up on the wall was a bunch of keys, Alistair tried each one until he found the key that unlocked the shackles around her legs and wrists. As he removed the anklets, her legs were swollen and red raw from being restrained in this manner. It was the same with her wrists; both of them were raw and bleeding. Alistair was seething when he saw this, how could you do this to a harmless woman? Once she was free he had to act quickly, he picked her up and headed towards the stairwell.

Meanwhile, Dexter and Marvin raced upstairs to check the remaining floors, level four was empty apart from old textile machinery. As they rushed onto level five and threw the light switches they stopped dead in their tracks, bingo! Cocaine and lots of it, packed in one-kilo bags, a quick count estimated at least two hundred of them sat on a wooden pallet near to the elevator door. Marvin took out his pocketknife, punctured one of the packs, and tasted the contents.

"I'm no expert, but I'd say that's coke alright."

Once they had gathered their breath, the two of them raced down the stairs to tell Alistair what they had discovered.

"We found it, hundreds of bags of coke, didn't stop to do an accurate count but at least two hundred, I don't know what the price of coke is but I'd say on the street it's worth a bloody fortune." said Dexter.

"Good so we found what we came for, we need to get

Cleo out of here and get her treated, poor girl she's barely alive doesn't look like she's had much to eat or drink nor allowed toilet breaks going off the state of her clothing."

Alistair carried Cleo to the stairs and they headed down the old worn stone steps to the ground floor, he was expecting any minute to be met by the police on their way in to investigate the blast. So far so good, they exited the building, raced over to their car then placed her on the back seat. Marvin sat in with Cleo's head resting on his lap doing his best to make her comfortable.

They drove out of the complex slowly so as not to arouse suspicion, weaving in and out of piles of rusting machinery from a bygone era, it looked like the aftermath of a World War One battle. Once they were clear and on the main raid, Alistair put his foot down, they raced as fast as possible to Fairfield Hospital in Bury. On arrival, they quickly made their way into A&E calling out for help. Doctors and nurses raced over to give their assistance. Alistair explained who she was, that she had been abducted and held in appalling conditions. The staff wasn't interested in the politics, they could see she was in difficulty and barely alive, she appeared severely dehydrated, they immediately sprang into action to treat her. Alistair told Dexter and Marvin to beat it, the police would have to be called there was no point in involving them, although he asked Dexter to place an anonymous call from a pay phone to DCI Porter to advise him that a large haul of Cocaine belonging to Albert Bonetti could be found at a warehouse on the Dingle Industrial Estate in Oldham.

I was just on my way to perform at the Portland Club in Wigan, when I got a phone call from Alistair with the best news I could have hoped for. He had found Cleo.

"Thank you my friend, from the bottom of my heart,

how is she?"

"Alive, but only just, that bastard kept her chained up like an animal, she has the scars on her limbs to prove it. I don't think she would have lived another day. I'm here at Fairfield Hospital; they have just moved her to intensive care. I spoke with one of the doctors a short time ago he says she is very poorly he thinks there's only a fifty-fifty chance she will make it. They are getting as much fluid into her as quickly as possible, she is severely dehydrated, assuming they can get her stable they will run more tests on her to see if she has suffered any permanent damage to her organs.

"I've got to go now the police are here waiting to interview me, I'm going to come clean and tell them how I found her in a warehouse owned by Fat Albert. Incidentally, we found about two hundred kilos of coke, so he's going to have some explaining to do when they get hold of him. We also found her car, he parked it in there then bricked up the doorway so it wouldn't be found."

"What a bastard, thanks again Alistair, I'm going to head over to the hospital as soon as I've finished my slot."

Whilst it was great news she had been found, from what Alistair said it seemed it was touch and go whether she would make it. If she didn't, I vowed to go after that swine and inflict my kind of retribution on him. Meanwhile, I had a show to do and it was going to be difficult to muster the enthusiasm, but I kept telling myself Cleo was tough she would make it.

Alistair was asked to accompany the police to headquarters in Rochdale, and then placed in an interview room.

"Good evening Mr. Bracken, I'm DCI Porter as I'm sure you are aware, I understand you found Ms. Sage? May I ask how this came about?"

"An anonymous tipoff."

"Really, there seems to be an awful lot of that about these days, how did this tipoff manifest itself?"

"They told me where to find her, said she was held on the third floor of this old warehouse. Seeing as you lot hadn't got very far I thought it was worth investigating myself."

"That's what you do is it, investigate?"

"Yes, I used to do a lot of it before I became a lawyer, so I'm well capable of carrying out an investigation successfully, not like some people I'm aware of."

"I hope that comment isn't directed at me?"

"If the cap fits, wear it."

Porter was raging; who did this so-called lawyer think he was making smart-arsed comments like that?

"So you say you got a tipoff, by way of a phone call I assume, man or woman?"

Alistair thought about it for a while, then he thought he would wind him up, "It was a woman, spoke with a strong Jamaican accent, and the call was from a public call box."

"That narrows it down a bit," he said sarcastically, "did she say why she was giving you this information?"

"Afraid not, just told me where to find her, but when I got there the building seemed to have suffered quite a bit of damage. The only way in was through a large hole in the wall at ground level. I searched inside until I found her then, rather than wait for an ambulance and to save time, I drove her straight to the hospital myself."

"Whilst you were there, did you notice anything else out of the ordinary?"

"Such as?"

"Drugs, cocaine to be precise."

"I wasn't aware of drugs, I certainly didn't see any, I was just looking for Cleo, as soon as I found her I didn't look elsewhere, I drove her straight to the hospital."

"Would it interest you to know that the door into the

building was blown off by someone using plastic explosive? I understand you're an ex-marine, probably had training in the use of this material during your time in the service."

"Is that a question or a statement?"

"Mr. Bracken, we can go on all day sparring so let's cut to the chase, did you blast your way into that building?"

"Good heavens, no, is the short answer to that, when I got there it had already happened. You said there were drugs in the building, maybe, that was what they were after."

"I don't believe you, I think you planted C4 explosive to gain access into the building using your experience obtained in the service to achieve this."

"Not me, now if you don't mind I've had enough of this conversation, either charge me or release me."

"What time did you arrive at the building?"

Alistair thought about it before he answered, the timeline was critical.

"I got there at precisely nine thirty, noticed all the damage to the door but as there was no other way in I scrambled over the rubble to get inside."

"We have reports of the sound of a large explosion at nine o'clock, are you sure about the time you got there?"

"Absolutely, I remember looking at my watch."

"Why?"

"Why what?"

"Why did you need to look at your watch?"

"There's no point in wearing a watch if your not going to check the time."

"Local police arrived at the site at nine forty-five, I'm surprised you didn't bump into them."

"It took them long enough if as you say the blast was reported around nine, good job it wasn't an emergency."

Porter glared at him, this guy was responsible, but how could he prove it.

"Doesn't it strike you as odd, we get the report of an explosion at nine o'clock in the vicinity of Dingle Mill, coincidently you just happened to be visiting the exact same place at nine thirty. Can you see my difficulty in accepting what you are saying?"

"Maybe, because you've always had the problem in accepting what people tell you as the truth."

By now, Porter was ready to throw the book at him

"Would it interest you to know that we found on the top floor, two hundred and thirty kilos of pure cocaine? I think you went there to steal this but for whatever reason changed your mind when you found Ms Sage, you were probably intent on returning to claim your prize, once she was taken care of."

"Where do you get this kind of bullshit from, I put it down to the kind of comics you are reading? If I were you I'd stick to the Dandy and Beano, they're less stressful and far more educational. Now if that's all you've got I take it I'm free to go."

"We are going to swab your hands for explosives residue, what do you have to say to that?"

"If as you say, plastic explosive was used, residue would almost certainly be on my hands from climbing over the rubble, what do you have to say to that?"

Alistair had taken the precaution of wearing gloves to avoid any direct contact with the C4, so any residue would be minimal. His hands were swabbed but the swab had to go to Manchester, as this was the nearest station that would be able to analyse the sample.

It was midnight before the result came back; DS Withers went to break the news to his superior.

"Results are back sir, there's no explosives residue on the swab, not a trace."

"This guys too clever by far, I was sure we'd find something."

Get a Proper Job

"We may have to release him, we've nothing that connects him directly to the blast."

Porter was in no hurry to let him go anywhere until all his questions had been answered. For the time being the test results would be positive.

"Mr. Bracken, you may be interested to know the test for residue was positive."

"Like I said, it's hardly surprising, I had to climb over a pile of rubble to get into the building that's probably why. If that's all you've got its not enough to hold me any longer, I demand you let me go."

"You'll be kept here until I'm satisfied with your story."

Alistair was confident there was no residue on the sample; this was just Porter telling porkies that he would eventually be released. In the meantime he thought he would pursue his own line of questioning, "By the way, may I ask who owns that building?"

"I'm not at liberty to say who owns it, but there is currently a warrant out for their arrest."

"Are you not going to tell me DCI Porter, maybe I should hazard a guess, is it Albert Bonetti?"

"I'm not able to confirm or deny this to you."

"In view of past encounters with you that's hardly surprising. But if you have a warrant out for whoever is responsible for this drugs haul, there is no reason to detain me any longer, I'm a lawyer, not a drug dealer."

"Our enquiries are ongoing, you'll be kept here until I'm satisfied with your story."

Porter was enjoying this encounter, making life difficult for Alistair because of their past history. After six hours he decided to release him.

"Was that really necessary to detain me, purely because of our previous encounters? I will be making a formal complaint to your superiors."

"Feel free, but I suggest you leave before I change my mind and charge you."

"With what, let me see, wasting police time, now there's a laugh, nobody has been wasting more police time than yourself? We pointed you in the right direction, regarding Bonetti months ago, yet you chose to ignore our information. You were convinced my client Carter Dean was the culprit without any evidence whatsoever, now that shows how incompetent you are. I am trying to talk him out of suing you for harassment, but I'm not holding my breath, good evening."

Porter was furious, he wasn't used to being spoken to like that by a jumped up lawyer. He was sure he was more involved than just rescuing Ms. Sage, but he had nothing to connect him. However, the thing that was hurting him the most was the fact Bracken had been able to find the missing woman, when all his efforts and those of his associates had proven fruitless.

His only chance of redeeming himself in the eyes of his superiors would be to find the culprit responsible for the murders of the entertainers, stretching back almost two years. Bonetti had been suggested as the culprit, now that drugs had become involved it now seemed more plausible that this could be a motive and he was somehow connected to their deaths. Yet his own officers who had been tailing him hadn't noticed anything out of the ordinary. As a result he had taken them off the operation after two weeks because of their lack of progress.

There was now a degree of urgency as police armed with arrest warrants raided the home and offices of Albert Bonetti but he was not to be found. An appeal was then made on television with a photograph of the suspect. The public were advised not to approach him directly, but to notify the nearest police station.

Chapter Twelve

Within minutes of the discovery of drugs there was now an all police watch out for Bonetti, his picture was flashed across TV stations as police appealed for help in locating him. To me it was a bizarre situation, trying to come to terms with the man I had worked closely with for over eight years, being a murder suspect, as well as a major player in the drugs world. Of course, he was responsible for kidnapping my girlfriend and keeping her chained up in the most appalling conditions without sufficient food or water. He was pure evil of that there was no doubt, probably by now at his most dangerous.

As I pulled into the car park at Fairfield Hospital there were several outside broadcast vans parked up, a group of people were huddled together, probably from the press. Obviously, word had got out that Cleo had been found; I walked past quickly then headed to the information desk. I explained to the nurse who I was and that I wished to see Cleo Sage, she made a quick phone call then shortly afterwards, DCI Porter put in an appearance.

"Mr. Dean, I'm afraid it's not possible to see Ms. Sage at the moment, she is in the care of our protection unit. As she is the only person who may positively be able to identify who kidnapped her, she is under armed protection until we apprehend the suspect Albert Bonetti."

"I can understand that, but I would like to see her as I'm her good friend as you are aware."

Porter looked at me, he was enjoying this moment of power, seeing me beg, after all our past run-ins he was not going to forgive or forget.

"Maybe tomorrow, but at the moment we are in the

process of making sure every aspect of her safety is covered. Bonetti is dangerous as you know, we can't take the risk of him attempting to take the life of Ms. Sage."

"Finally you've realised what an evil son of a bitch he is, pity you didn't come to this decision earlier because if you had, we wouldn't be in this position now."

"Good policing is all about strong evidence and thorough investigating."

"Thorough investigating, there's a laugh, you couldn't investigate your way out of a paper bag. You've given me grief these past few years, I don't know what I ever did to piss you off, but rest assured I am now coming after you. My lawyer has been instructed to sue the police for wrongful arrest and harassment, I'm sure your superiors will enjoy that."

"Sorry you feel that way, l was just doing my job."

"My view is you are incapable of doing the job you are employed to do, even now you are trying to make things as difficult as ever for me."

"Like I said, we are in the process of making that floor safe so no unauthorized people get in. It's possible him or his criminal associates may well want to mount an attack on Ms. Sage, make no mistake we can't take any chances with her safety."

I could equate to that, reluctantly I found myself agreeing with this arsehole.

"Very well, I'll check back tomorrow."

I left him to enjoy his moment of victory then went to the nurse's station to enquire about Cleo's condition. I was told by one of the doctors she was now stable and conscious and making good progress although, seriously underweight, they were still doing tests to ensure there was no lasting damage to any of her vital organs. I thanked him and immediately called Cleo's mother to bring her up to date with recent events. She was grateful that she had been found alive, but appalled about the circumstances.

Fat Albert drove his Citroen Picasso down the off ramp of the car ferry in Zeebrugge, Belgium, once clear of formalities at the port, he made his way into the centre of Bruges. He needed to find sanctuary and gather his thoughts. He'd left home in a hurry, without even time to pack a toothbrush. When he visited his warehouse to replenish supplies, he found a heavy police presence outside. It was better to vacate the area; it was only a matter of time before PC plod came knocking.

For years he'd been anticipating this event, always thinking ahead, planning to keep one step in front of the posse. Now, he hadn't a clue what to do, he'd a huge problem, not least was the fact he had lost 230 kilos of high grade Columbian cocaine, the property of one, Eduardo Castellar, one of the top five drug lords in that country. He currently had a bounty of fifty million dollars on his head, dead or alive, placed there by the American Government.

He was not someone to be crossed. Fat Albert knew he was in serious trouble. It was only a matter of time before Castellar got the news. It now dawned on him how lax and complacent he'd become after years of dealing drugs successfully. On top of this, he'd abducted Cleo Sage who was probably dead by now, seeing as he hadn't been to the warehouse for the past week. If she were dead, it would be an added complication in what was becoming his worst nightmare. His decision to abduct her from her apartment building in a moment of madness was something he was now regretting. Although, at the time, this was the perfect way of exacting revenge on Dean.

It was easy to establish where she lived; when the door of the car park was activated he slipped in unnoticed and followed her inside. She parked in her bay as she opened the door he dragged her from the car and knocked her unconscious. After binding her arms and legs and placing duct tape over her mouth he threw her in the trunk of her car. He waited for a while then started the engine of her BMW he followed another car exiting the building, making sure he kept his face and head covered. An anonymous call to inspector Porter completed this vile act, however, since then things had not gone his way he needed to cover his tracks.

He would have to keep a low profile, Castellars's reach was long, and there were numerous incidents documented of him having eliminated people who crossed him. Not knowing how he would react when he got news of the drugs loss, he decided to alter his appearance. Being well aware of his distinctive look and how people compared him to an albino a cosmetic update was needed.

On his way into the city, he stopped off at a supermarket, purchased, hair dye, fake suntan, and spectacles. He booked a room in a cheap hotel with basic facilities, the kind where a room can be rented by the hour and they don't ask too many questions. Then he set about changing his appearance. The next day he emerged a new man, sporting a healthy suntan with dark brown hair, and wearing horn rimmed spectacles.

Eventually I was allowed to see Cleo although it was a moving encounter. She was taken out of intensive care and placed into a single ward. An armed officer was positioned at the end of the corridor, only hospital staff with full ID were allowed past, outside of her room another armed policeman stood in attendance. Seeing as I satisfied all the criteria I was allowed into her room.

As soon as she saw me she broke down in tears, "Nothing has changed then, I'm still having the same effect on women, although I would have been worried if you'd started laughing."

"Come here and give me a hug you big clown, I've

missed you so much, at times I thought I would never see you again."

"We never stopped looking for you but I have to say a big thank you to my lawyer and good friend Alistair, he discovered where you were being held. He had a couple of his contacts follow Fat Albert and discovered his warehouse. They had to blast their way in that's when they found you. Of course, DCI Porter doesn't know that he told him he'd had an anonymous tipoff where you were being held. He called me just as soon as he found you; I was so relieved I gave my best performance of the year. Can you remember what happened, was it Fat Albert?"

"I remember driving into my building and opening the car door, after this nothing, until I woke up with a splitting headache in a cold damp building with my hands and feet chained to the floor I also had a blindfold on. I can't say for sure if it was him, because I never saw him even after I managed to get the blindfold off, there was no light in the building plus he always approached me from behind. He never said anything other than 'food' and placed it next to my hand.

"Food was a loose term for what he left, sandwiches that tasted like the kind you would get in a motorway service station, bland butter-less and unappetising along with bottled water. I was never allowed to use the toilet and eventually peed my pants then had serious bouts of diarrhoea, but after a while soiling my clothes didn't seem important anymore, I was convinced I was going to die. The next thing I was aware of, was waking up in hospital in an intensive care unit. The police told me I had been rescued by a member of the public and brought to the hospital, I didn't realise it was Alistair."

"He's been brilliant, but for him you would have died in there, it's because of his exploring he uncovered Fat Albert's drug operation. Hopefully, they will get him and convict him for the murders as well."

"Thanks for keeping my mum up to date, I really appreciate it, she wants me to go and stay with her for a while."

"Not a problem, I've been so worried about you I haven't slept for weeks according to Bob my driver, not giving my best."

"I need to get out of here, I've been kept locked up now for weeks, I feel I've just swopped one prison for the hell-hole that fucking nutcase kept me in."

"They are just looking after your interests, they think Fat Albert or some of his cohorts might attempt to take your life. When they do release you, I think it's a good idea to go and stay with your mum until they get this lunatic. I'll drive you down there, I've never seen that part of the world."

"It's a nice idea, but I can't really take anymore time off, my career is important to me, although Mr. Barnes rang me yesterday he told me to take as long as I needed."

"There you are then, problem solved."

I said my goodbye and left to prepare for that nights show in Burnley. I was looking forward to it; I had a new zest for life now Cleo had been found alive, although she was battle scarred.

We arrived at Darcy's, an up market club I had played at a couple of times before. After a warm introduction from the MC I walked out to loud applause.

"Thanks very much for that great welcome, are you all enjoying yourselves?"

There was a huge chorus of 'Yes'.

"It's nice to be back here in downtown Burnley, but I only just made it, got held up on the way here. I was stopped in traffic for ages, and then I saw this guy who was walking along, going from car to car. I wound the window down and asked,

"What's going on?"

"Terrorists have kidnapped Theresa May, Jeremy

Corbin, and Vince Cable. They're demanding a ransom of ten million Sterling, otherwise they're going to douse them with petrol and set them on fire. We're going from car to car, taking up a collection."

"I asked him, "How much is everyone giving on average?"

"About a gallon."

That went down well.

"One day a farmer was sitting on his porch when a young man drives in and comes to his door.

"Sir, I was driving by and noticed you had a lot of milkweed in your pasture. Would you mind if I went out and got some milk?"

"You don't get milk from milkweed!" the farmer replied.

"I have a degree in agriculture from Cambridge University, I know all about it."

"Well then, help yourself."

Shortly afterwards, he saw the man coming back to his car with two buckets full of milk. The next day the farmer was sitting on his porch when the young man drove up again.

"Sir, yesterday when I was here I spotted some honeysuckle growing along the hedgerow and wondered if I may collect some honey?"

"You don't get honey from honeysuckle!" said the farmer. Again the young man explained about his degree from Cambridge, so the farmer agreed to let him collect some honey. Not long afterwards, he saw the young man going back to his car with two buckets of honey. The next day the young man drove up to see the farmer.

"Sir, when I was here yesterday, I noticed some pussy willow down by the river."

The farmer said, "Hold on, let me get my shoes."

Lots of laughter and applause

"An Amish lady was driving her buggy to town when a police officer pulled her over.

"I'm going to cite you," said the officer. "I just wanted to warn you that the reflector on the back of your buggy is broken and it could be dangerous."

"Thank thee," replied the Amish lady, "I shall have my husband repair it as soon as I return home."

"Also," said the officer, "I noticed one of your reins to your horse was wrapped around his testicles. Some people might consider this cruelty to animals so you should have your husband check that too."

"Again I thank thee, I shall have my husband check both when I get home."

True to her word, when the Amish lady got home she told her husband about the broken reflector, and he said he would put a new one on immediately.

"Also, said the Amish woman, "the policeman said there was something wrong with the emergency brake."

I was on a roll, I had them eating out of my hand. I was enjoying myself so much I didn't want to finish but I had to do, from the corner of my eye I could see the next act waiting patiently in the wings, so after I'd been on stage about an hour, I told my last story and finished to a standing ovation. I could get used to this.

After ten days, Cleo was released from hospital, she did as I advised and decided to spend some time with her mother. Initially the police were reluctant to let her leave their jurisdiction, however, when she pointed out her mother lived in a secure place in St. Ives, Cornwall and no one would know she was there, they agreed to let her go. I drove her down to this beautiful county; I was impressed by the scenery and the small boutique style hotel, that her mother owned.

I stayed overnight and would have loved to have spent more time with her but had to leave early the next day because of a previous booking. Once I was sure Cleo was settled in OK, I returned to the north of England. Afterwards, I called her several times a day as she continued her road to full recovery.

The Chief Constable requested Detective Chief Inspector Porter's presence. He didn't like the sound of this but wasn't prepared for what happened next.

"Morning, Porter, take a seat I'll cut to the chase, I've got some bad news, I'm taking you off the Bonetti case. It has come to my notice; information that he was responsible for the murders of seven entertainers was given to you, yet you chose to ignore this and instead went after one Carter Dean, without any hard evidence. In fact it has been described as a vendetta, in view of your past actions this force may well be sued for harassment. In an effort to prevent this, I feel a direct apology to Mr. Dean is the only thing that will help. Bonetti is still at large despite in the past you having him in custody before releasing him."

"With all due respect sir, I didn't have enough evidence to charge him."

"I don't accept that, in my opinion you have been inept and incompetent in your investigation into these crimes, if you'd have been more thorough you would have uncovered the necessary evidence needed. Good lord man, if a member of the public can find out what this chap has been up to, it puts this department in a poor light, not to mention receiving a considerable amount adverse publicity. Questions have been asked in Parliament, I've been grilled in a committee about the lack of progress, each time I've defended my investigating team, but you have placed us in a position that we can no longer tolerate. Apologise to Carter Dean, do it now to fend off a possible harassment charge. Detective Chief Inspector Brian Lawson, is being transferred here from Liverpool, he is taking over this investigation. That's all, get out."

Porter was stunned, after all his years coming up through the ranks being spoken too like some raw recruit from Hendon Police College. To apologise to Dean was something he was not prepared to do. Sure he had got it wrong, but how many police before him have got things wrong, did they apologise to people taken in for questioning? He was sure they didn't and he wasn't going to do either. This would be a major setback in his career it would also affect his team but not to the same extent. For days afterwards he couldn't think of anything else and was considering resigning but if he did he would loose certain elements of his pension.

Just after 2:30am, a fire broke out in the underground car park next to the Movenpik Hotel, Bruges, Belgium. Fire-fighters were hampered because their appliances were so tall they couldn't gain access to the car park. By the time they had transported hoses and other equipment down to fight the fire, it had spread to two levels and fourteen cars were now on fire. The heat was so intense, some of the vehicles literally melted. It took a full twenty-four hours with firemen wearing breathing apparatus to extinguish the blaze.

Forensics established the fire had started in an electrical substation in the basement level, before spreading to the upper floors. There was one fatality, probably that of a male found in a Citroen Picasso, but the remains were so badly damaged it would not be possible to extract accurate DNA. However, they did manage to find the chassis number of the vehicle and enquiries lead them to establish it was registered in England to an Albert Bonetti, of Bury, Lancashire. A roll call was carried out at the adjacent Movenpik Hotel, but they didn't cater for long-term residents, with the exception of the client in room 21B who owed several days rent but couldn't be accounted for. When police gained access into his room they found the passport and other documents in the name of Albert Bonetti. They gathered this and other items, a hairbrush and drinking glass to extract DNA from, this was processed and eventually passed on to Interpol.

DCI Porter was getting ready to hand over the investigation to DCI Brian Lawson who was due to arrive later that day, when DS Withers entered his office.

"Morning sir, got some important news, Interpol have just forwarded us details take a look at this."

Porter took the document and studied the contents; the report confirmed the demise of one Albert Bonetti, burned to death in a car park in Belgium. Found in his car burned beyond recognition. He had been staying in the nearby Movenpik hotel, when they checked his room after the fire; they found his passport and driving license. DNA taken from articles in the room confirms it was he. Also the chassis number of the vehicle he was found in corresponded with what was registered with the UK vehicle registration authorities. The general consensus was that Bonetti had been overcome by fumes and lost consciousness whilst in his car.

"Well, beat my buttocks with a Bury Black Pudding, what's DCI Lawson going to be doing now? If Bonetti was responsible for all those deaths it's going to be damn near impossible to prove it. Anyway, as of today, it's no longer my problem in fact, I'm thinking of handing in my resignation. I've given everything to this job, sacrificed my marriage because of the unsociable hours, and regretted not having time for kids, for what? Only to be called inept and incompetent by the Chief Constable. If anyone's incompetent its him, he only got the job because of his fathers contacts. It's all down hill for me after this so I'm going before I get pushed."

"Are you sure about this sir?"

"Yes, Withers, given it a lot of thought, it's time I moved on."

"Well, I'll be sorry to see you go, I know I've not been

here too long but I've enjoyed working with you."

"Thank you Sergeant, likewise."

With that, Porter went down to the evidence room to check the paperwork he had on Bonetti. In a secure caged area all the drugs recovered from various criminals was held prior to destruction.

On a pallet in one corner, was the huge haul of pure cocaine found at the warehouse in Oldham. Once this was cut on the open market it would be worth many millions, equivalent to some countries national debt.

Chapter Thirteen

The media was full of the demise of what was now being termed, 'The Northern Strangler.' It was reported in great detail as to how he perished in a cheap hotel in Belgium, whilst on the run from the police for murder and drug dealing. I thought they were jumping the gun seeing as Fat Albert had never been publicly linked to the killings before, nor had he been charged with drug offences, he cleared off before they had chance to arrest him. Although, we all thought there was more than enough circumstantial evidence to link him to the murders. It was still difficult for me to come to terms with recent events. I had been associated with him for eight years, most of which I had enjoyed with the exception of the last couple. The fact that he was dead caused major problems for his employees, bookings had dried up, and contractually they weren't sure where they stood.

Word had got around that I had broken ranks with Fat Albert and gone on my own, four people approached me to see would I be interested in looking after their affairs. Bob was gaining in experience day by day, when I put it too him about taking on more responsibility, he was more than happy to do so. The fact that Fat Albert was dead meant that their contracts had effectively become null and void. Even though they were with Bonetti Entertainment, there was no one else in the company to take up the reins; it meant they had become unemployed.

He had never married or had any living relatives; he was a one-man band. Several phone calls to the secretary confirmed it was a ship without a rudder. After giving it some thought I decided to take on these four entertainers, two singers, the comedienne Avril Jones and a ventriloquist.

We decided to form a new agency; we called it 'Phoenix Entertainment Management'. I rented a small office on Bolton road in Bury, then took on a smart young girl called Denya to answer the phones also do general office duties.

I started to advise clients about the change of management, almost immediately we secured bookings from them. Within a matter of a few weeks, virtually every person who had been employed or, was under contract to Bonetti Entertainment, approached me to take on their contracts. A few old pros decided to go it alone, but I now had thirty people on my books, life as an impresario was getting interesting, plus I would be earning nice commission for looking after their needs.

Drugs were being moved out of the evidence room for disposal. The fact that there would now be no individual prosecuted as a result of the drug seizure, and no court case with the number one suspect being found dead, the decision was made to destroy the drugs. As a result they were being transported to a furnace at a special unit in Bury. All the cocaine and paperwork was loaded into a police van and driven off.

Once it arrived at its destination, an official checked the pallet and counted the number of packs against the paperwork. Satisfied everything was in order, he signed the delivery docket then proceeded to strip the pallet and throw the contents into the incinerator, one by one. He had disposed of about eighty packs, when he noticed something wasn't quite right. Some of the packs he examined looked like they had been opened, because powder was falling out. Closer examination and tests with a chemical kit, revealed the contents were not cocaine, but what appeared to be chalk. Someone had switched the contents, but who? He tested the remainder of the packages and ninety-five kilos had been replaced with chalk. The officer immediately notified the station in Rochdale about the discrepancy.

Ex DCI Porter, was enjoying his retirement, after he had resigned from the force. He moved to Marbella in Spain, where he purchased a small apartment close to the beach. He could often be seen frequenting bars, always with a young attractive female in tow.

Life was good, my new business was thriving, Cleo and I had become very close it appeared she was at that point in her life when she wanted children. The more she bent my ear, the more I realised how important it was for her to satisfy her maternal instincts. And when I'd retrieved my arm from up my back, we decided to get married so we set the date for November fourth. Since then, she'd been actively planning the big day. I asked Alistair if he would be my best man and I was delighted when he agreed. The agency was growing weekly, I found myself auditioning young hopefuls wanting a taste of the bright lights. I had signed up a new singer called Dale Byrnes, who, within a very short time became very popular with clubs on the northern circuit. I predicted big things for this talented chap.

Denya proved very capable in running the office, one day she received a call asking if we did private shows. Mr. Oliver Rem from Doncaster, was enquiring about entertainment for his wife's upcoming fortieth birthday, she was a big fan of Carter Dean. I had never done a private show before, apart from large corporate events held in hotels, so I told her to get full details of where I would be performing and to add ten percent to my normal fee. If he was in agreement to organise a contract and payment terms, so I left it in her capable hands.

DS Withers and the sergeant in charge of the evidence

room had been summoned to the chief Constables office.

"Gentlemen, I assume you know why you are here?"

"Not really sir, we just got a message late yesterday to come here to meet you." said DS Withers.

"Well, let me enlighten you, at least ninety-five kilos of pure cocaine from the evidence room has been switched by someone for what appears to be chalk, French Chalk to be precise. The amount may be a lot more, because some eighty kilos of the two hundred and thirty packages had already been destroyed before the switch became evident. We estimate its value was at the very least, two million sterling, a sizeable amount. This was pure so, by the time it was cut and hit the streets, probably treble that.

"Sergeant Baron, you spent most of your time looking after the evidence room, do you have any idea how this could have occurred, because its evident the switch was made at the Rochdale station?"

Baron looked decidedly uncomfortable, he had prided himself on running the evidence room with meticulous efficiency. No one was allowed in without his or a higher authority. He was six months away from retirement; this was a serious blot on his unblemished career. Drugs had gone missing in the past from the evidence room, long before his time, as a result he had been diligent in his mission to make sure it didn't happen under his control.

"I'm sorry sir, no one is allowed into that room without prior permission from a senior member of staff. In fact, the area where drugs and other contraband are stored is in another even more secure area. I've no idea how this could have been breached, it certainly didn't happen on my watch."

"Detective Sergeant Withers, have you any comment to make?"

"No sir, I've only been here at this station for six months, I was in the evidence room on one occasion

Get a Proper Job

only, that was in the presence of DCI Porter."

"Where is ex DCI Porter now, any idea?"

"I understand that after he took early retirement he went to live in Spain, I've had no contact with him since he left the force." said DS Withers.

"His departure was a bit sudden wasn't it?"

"He'd been talking about it for quite some time, after his marriage broke up he said he had no ties in this country and often talked about emigrating to warmer climbs. He suffered quite badly with arthritis in his hands, he thought somewhere like Spain would help his condition," said Sergeant Baron.

"Well it strikes me as odd he left at this time, however, this is a serious matter, and can't be left as it is, I will be convening a meeting of all officers from this station within the next forty-eight hours. Sergeant Baron, I want you to convey to all members of staff, whether they are on duty or not, to meet in the staff canteen at ten-thirty on this coming Thursday. I also want the CCTV coverage from the evidence room."

"The recordings only go back about twelve weeks sir, then it's starts to wipe the drive and record over it," said Sergeant Baron.

"We just have to hope the recordings for this period throw some light onto how this switch took place, that's all."

Sergeant Baron was furious, in all the years he had been involved with the security of the evidence room, no one had ever questioned his integrity. Now the Chief Constable was pointing his finger at him, inferring this incident occurred on his watch. He had never stolen anything from the secure area, stealing was not his style, nor had he seen anyone take anything without signing for it. In most cases it was just documents but they all had to be signed for.

The first thing he did when he got back to the control room was to retrieve the data from the CCTV cameras covering the evidence room. One camera was focused on the entrance and counter, another covered the secure cage where drugs and stolen items recovered from police raids were kept. He played the recordings back for the previous twelve weeks but found nothing out of the ordinary. DCI Porter visited the area on eight separate occasions to retrieve documents, just before he retired then again to return them; on each occasion he signed the register.

It took him until late into the evening, fast forwarding until someone entered the room then he logged the details. He made a note of the time and day and who the officer was. In total, eight individual officers visited the area thirty two times to retrieve data, then again to return it. At no time did any officer gain access to the secure caged area, until the day the drugs were being transported for destruction. This meant the switch had to have taken place on route; it was down to the two officers that had transported the consignment. This gave him a degree of comfort and it was two fingers to the Chief Constable.

Phoenix Management was going from strength to strength, and it soon became apparent that our office was far from ideal, we needed more space as well as taking on extra staff. The building in the precinct in Bury where Bonetti Entertainment had been located was now vacant and had been for a number of weeks. It had been repossessed after non-payment of rent. It would seem that he never paid on time and was always in arrears. The bailiffs had visited him on a number of occasions to collect unpaid money.

At the time of his disappearance he was in arrears for six months, after his death was reported, the property owners wasted no time in applying to the courts for repossession. As a result, I was able to secure a discounted rate with what I considered was a good deal with rent reviews only every ten years.

Once the contract was signed, the building was given a fresh coat of paint over the two floors both inside and out, after we had removed all reference to Fat Albert, we moved in. As our new venture continued to grow, I found myself spending more time managing my acts so I decided to cut down on my own appearances. There are only so many hours in the day so I decided to restrict myself to doing three shows a week.

The Chief Constable had all his officers assembled in the staff canteen. Some of them looked extremely nervous, as he read the riot act to them. Sergeant Baron, with the assistance of his superior had compiled a shortened video of all entrants into the evidence room; the Chief Constable questioned each one as to why they were there. Nothing was apparent from the video; no one was seen entering the secure caged area. Then he turned to the two officers who had transported the cocaine to be destroyed

"Officers, Holmes and Wilson, you signed for the consignment, your mission was to deliver this to the incinerator in Bury for destruction, have you anything to add?"

The two officers looked decidedly uncomfortable, every person in that room had their eyes fixed on these two men. They were the number one suspects. Officer Holmes spoke up. "We signed for the goods in good condition, we didn't examine each pack because it was on a pallet covered in shrink wrap that's how it was when we delivered it to the depot in Bury, that's how it was signed for. We are not responsible for any shortfall, whatever you or anyone else thinks."

As soon as he said this you could cut the atmosphere in the room with a knife, the Chief Constable glared at him, furious he had the nerve to respond the way he had. His face was a picture of rage as his eyes scanned around the room, all he had achieved was to give the impression they were all suspects and could not be trusted.

"What about you PC Wilson, did you notice anything out of the ordinary?" Wilson glared back at him, who was this arsehole inferring they were somehow responsible for the theft.

"No, like PC Holmes said, it was all sealed in pallet wrap, were we expected to cut it open and examine every pack, I don't think so? We delivered exactly as it was we didn't open any of it." They stood their ground,

The Chief Constable's stare was still fixed firmly on them.

"We don't seem to be getting very far, but I can assure you this investigation isn't over. This is not the first time drugs have gone missing from this station, I'm determined to get to the bottom of this incident and find out whoever is behind it, take note, someone will be found accountable for this theft."

"What about DCI Porter, he left about the time this went missing, has he been interviewed?" said PC Wilson, determined to deflect attention away from him and his colleague.

The Chief Constable glared at Wilson for having the nerve to question him.

"We have requested him to make contact with us, we have only just established where in Spain he now lives. However, as you saw in the video he didn't enter the security cage, but we'll see what he has to say for himself. Let me say this, the investigation will continue until we get to the bottom of it and we establish who's responsible for this theft."

I was just putting some new material together, when my mobile rang, I could see it was Alistair, "Hi Carter, just thought you might be interested in this. Apparently, some of the cocaine we found has gone missing from the police station. They moved it from Rochdale to Bury for incineration at least ninety-five kilos was discovered to have been stolen it was substituted with French chalk."

"What the hell's French Chalk?"

"I think it's the base for talcum powder, anyway, the Chief Constable, a chap called McClintock is doing his nut, it's not common knowledge yet so keep this under your hat. I've a good friend called Alison in the accounts department, she brought me up to speed, seeing as she knows indirectly we were responsible for finding the drugs. Apparently, all the staff were brought in and given the third degree. They all suspected it was possibly DCI Porter, because he resigned after a row then buggered off to Spain. Anyway, video footage showed he never went near to the evidence area where everything is kept. The end result is they are all under suspicion, everyone is pointing the finger at one another so it's going to be interesting to see how it all pans out."

"My money's on Porter, all a bit suss don't you think, he sods off to Spain then they discover some of the drugs are missing? Too much of a bloody coincidence if you ask me."

"I know he's given you a hard time Carter and I agree it looks like he's the culprit, but I'm not convinced it's him."

"Anyone in mind?"

"Could be a connection of Bonetti, I know he's no longer in the land of the living, but it's too much to think some of his cohorts don't want to get their hands on the stuff."

"You mean you think the police and Fat Albert go hand in glove?"

"I wouldn't go as far as to say that, but it's a possibility that they somehow got at the drugs, either in the evidence room or, on route to be disposed of. Apparently fifty kilos of heroine disappeared from this same station ten years ago, they never did find out who was responsible."

"You have me worried now Alistair, seeing as we were responsible for them discovering the stuff. Fat Albert would certainly want revenge if he'd been alive, who's to say his associates won't be thinking the same."

"I wouldn't worry about it Carter, I didn't mean to alarm you."

"That's exactly what you've done Alistair, I thought after Fat Albert got incinerated that would be the end of this bloody nightmare, now I'm not so sure."

I put the phone down, somewhat disturbed after what he'd said, however, there was no time to dwell on the subject it was the day of the private birthday party in Doncaster, I needed to put this to the back of my mind. Cleo decided she wanted to come with me so it would be a good opportunity for her to judge my new material.

Later that day, our driver Bob collected us from the apartment and we headed for Doncaster. Thirty minutes later, we turned off the A1 then headed for a small place called Carcroft, shortly afterwards, the voice of Victor Meldrew on my sat-nav directed us up a long narrow gravel road to "The Willows' a large period residence. As we approached the house we could see the outline of an imposing tall building against the night sky. It was in total darkness, there didn't seem to be much evidence that anyone was at home.

"I hope we've got the right place?"

"According to the sat-nav we have, but they've been wrong before," said Bob.

Just after we parked the car, a gentleman carrying a torch appeared from the side of the building.

"Mr. Dean I assume, my name's Rob Glenister, I'm the MC for this evening."

Glenister was short and fat; in the gloom I could just make out he was bald with a moustache.

"The party is being held in the Orangery at the rear."

Get a Proper Job

"What the hells that?"

"It's a conservatory to you and me and it's a big one, although there is no one here yet, we are the first."

We walked around the side of the house; Glenister shone the torch picking out the narrow pathway, the gravel crunched under foot. Then we came to a large beautiful Victorian domed shaped building made of glass. Several large ornate chandeliers suspended on chains anchored to cast iron beams provided the lighting.

"At last, signs of life."

Glenister directed us inside, "There is a small stage at the far end and a couple of dressing rooms and toilets just behind. There are seats laid out for two hundred people although, I'm not sure what time they've been told the event kicks off."

"I understand the birthday party is for the wife of Oliver Rem, any idea what's she called?"

"I think it's Vanessa, not one hundred percent sure, my agency took the booking. I was a late substitute the other guy is sick, I'm usually an after dinner speaker, golf clubs, rugby clubs that kind of thing. I was told it was a surprise fortieth party for his wife, for the entertainment there was a comedian, a singer and a dance troupe."

"I think the surprise might be on us, seeing as there's no one here yet." I was getting a bad feeling about this booking, wishing I'd got more information from Denya, although my fee had been paid in advance. It was a bizarre situation, a bit like the Mary Celeste. We all sat down to pass the time and wait for developments. Cleo and Bob my driver started to play patience, mine on the other hand was being tested. After an hour there was no sign of anyone showing up so Glenister and myself decided to investigate further. We walked out to the front of the house but it was securely locked there was no sign of anyone home. Dust on the rusty door handle indicated it hadn't been opened in a while. Every window we tried was firmly secured; it looked like it had been that way for some time. Enough was enough, it was time to sod off, after all, what had I to lose my fee had already been paid?

As we made our way back to the rear of the property we heard a loud bang.

"What the hell was that?" asked Glenister.

"Sounded like a gunshot, to me."

We raced back to the Orangery, as we got inside we discovered Bob laying on the floor. At first glance it appeared he'd been shot in the stomach, he was writhing in pain and bleeding profusely. As I looked around the room there was no sign of Cleo. I immediately called the emergency services. Glenister tried to make Bob comfortable but he wasn't in great shape, he was very pale and his breathing was laboured. I grabbed the torch and raced outside through the rear of the building, all the time calling out for Cleo but got no response, it appeared she'd simply vanished.

Chapter Fourteen

Just after 8:30pm the emergency services arrived, first it was the ambulance, and the crew immediately started to work on Bob, but he'd lost consciousness. We needed to speak to him to find out exactly what had taken place, but until he came around, this wouldn't be possible. There was a serious amount of blood leading into the washroom at the rear, it was smeared along the wall and was on the door.

My heart sank when I saw this, it would seem that Cleo had been badly injured. I went outside but in the dark it was nigh impossible to see anything in great detail, the light from the torch wasn't very good I could just about see my feet. I called for Cleo constantly but there was no reply. I phoned Alistair and told him what had occurred and had just finished, when through the avenue of trees I could see the blue flashing lights as a convoy of police cars skidded to a halt, scattering gravel in all directions.

"Are you Dean?"

"That's correct."

"I'm DS Lofthouse, can you tell me what's gone on, I've a report of a shooting?"

Lofthouse was in his mid thirties, tall and lean, square jawed and was almost bald, he had an intense stare, his piercing blue eyes cut right through me like a laser.

"Not very sure, other than my driver Bob has been shot, and it would appear my fiancée has been abducted."

"Really, attempted murder and abduction in one night, can't remember when that happened last." he said with a smirk on his face. It was almost like he didn't believe me; we had to convince him this was exactly what had occurred.

"Let me explain."

"I wish you would."

"My name is Carter Dean I'm a comedian, I was supposed to perform here for a fortieth birthday party, this gentleman here is Rob Glenister he's the MC for the event. Our agencies took the booking for the party for this evening but there is no one here."

"Are you sure you got the right house?"

"This is the Willows isn't it?"

"That's correct, but no one lives here anymore."

"Are you sure?"

"Believe me, I'm sure, now why are you really here?"

His stare intensified, he obviously didn't believe our story.

"My agency got a booking from a chap called Oliver Rem from the 'Willows' a good few weeks ago, it was for his wife's fortieth birthday, it was supposed to be a surprise party. It would appear the surprise is on us. We've been here since seven-o'clock, when no one showed, we went to the front of the house to see if we could find any sign of life but, we couldn't raise anyone. On the way back we heard what sounded like a gunshot, when we got back to the building we discovered that my driver had been shot in the stomach. There was no sign of Cleo my fiancée and there is a serious amount of blood all the way out through the rear door."

Then Glenister spoke, "He's telling the truth. We are both here from different agencies. My agency wouldn't have got involved unless a contract had been signed and either payment in full or a substantial deposit had been paid. It seems like someone's idea of a sick joke but with deadly consequences."

"Well, I can tell you, this house hasn't been lived in for the past two years. It was owned by the Battersby family, but since Godwin the last family member died it's been empty. Nobody comes here anymore, apart from one chap who has a key and keeps an eye on the property; it's been unoccupied since then. Although, my chaps were here about a month ago because something had tripped the burglar alarm, but they didn't find any sign of a break-in, it seemed it was just a fault."

What the hell was going on, why would someone go to the trouble to make a fake booking, I couldn't believe what had taken place and judging by the remarks of DS Lofthouse, neither could he. My mind was racing, who would do such a thing? Of course Fat Albert was at the fore but since it was reported he'd died in a fire in Belgium, we could rule him out. Then I started to think about what Alistair had said, maybe an associate of his wanting revenge. But, why would someone want to do this, after all, we didn't have the drugs? This was just one of many thoughts going through my mind as I tried to make sense what had taken place, it didn't seem credible it could be drug related, so eventually, I dismissed the idea.

"I'll need a full description of your fiancée and what she was wearing, also I'll need a statement from both of you. It would appear our hopes rest on your friend to tell us exactly what occurred."

"That's not going to be easy, he fell unconscious not long after he was shot."

"Did he say anything, about what had happened?"

"Afraid not, we found him on the floor writhing in pain, I asked him what had happened but he didn't speak, I could see he was in acute discomfort. Eventually he just rolled his eyes then flaked out. We just tried to make him as comfortable as possible until the ambulance got here. We kept talking to him but got no response."

"What makes you think your fiancée has been abducted, could she have shot your colleague and then left the scene?"

What the hell was this idiot saying, I could feel my temperature rising and my fist clenching I would gladly have punched his lights out? Before I did anything stupid, Glenister barked.

"That's bloody ridiculous, think about what you are saying, call yourself a detective, someone else is responsible. Mr. Dean's driver has been shot by an intruder who it appears then abducted his fiancée."

"I only have your word for what's taken place."

"Well that's as good as your going to get, meanwhile, while you are trying to discredit our version of what has occurred, this maniac is on the loose and will probably be long gone."

Lofthouse studied the two of them, maybe he was misjudging the situation, and they were telling the truth.

"My girlfriend was kidnapped by a drug dealer called Albert Bonetti recently and held captive in an old warehouse in Oldham. I'm sure you've heard of him he was on Interpol's most wanted list until they found his body in a burned out car in Belgium. She was found chained up and barely alive and was only just getting used to her freedom, and now this."

"Sounds like she's been unlucky, and yes I did here about this chap before, but seeing as it happened at another patch I'm not that familiar with the details."

"While we are trying to convince you what has taken place, she could be in all kinds of trouble."

"They won't get far, we'll mount a search of the surrounding area. I've already called for more backup to assist."

"The sooner that starts the better, who knows how badly injured she is," I couldn't grasp what had just taken place it was a mind blowing situation, surreal didn't come close to describing how it felt. Shortly afterwards, a police bus arrived with several dozen reinforcements, they were immediately given instructions then dispatched throughout the grounds to

Get a Proper Job

widen the search.

Forensics arrived shortly afterwards, once Bob had been removed to hospital, the area was secured as a crime scene. Glenister and myself filled the sergeant in on what we knew; neither of us could fathom what the hell was going on. Whilst the search continued, DS Lofthouse said he wasn't one hundred percent happy with our version of the night's events and asked us to accompany him to the station to make a full statement. I couldn't blame him; I was finding it hard to come to terms with what had taken place.

It was just after 4:00am when we finished giving our version of events, after signed our statements we were allowed to leave.

There was still no sign of Cleo; the latest report regarding Bob's condition wasn't encouraging. Glenister left to retrieve his vehicle from the Willows; I hailed a taxi then made my way to Doncaster Royal Infirmary, the hospital where Bob had been taken. I arrived just as Alistair was parking his car.

"Any news about Cleo or Bob?"

"Hi, Alistair, thanks for coming only just arrived myself, there's nothing further about Cleo, I was just about to go into A&E and see what they can tell us about Bob."

We made our way inside but he was still in the emergency room receiving treatment. As we waited for news, I took the opportunity to update Alistair on what had taken place. Like me he was finding it hard to take in what had happened. About an hour later, we were told Bob was out of surgery and was in the recovery room. He was conscious but not yet ready to accept visitors. He was eventually moved into a private ward, shortly afterwards, DS Lofthouse arrived and was taken straight through to see him. Thirty minutes later, he came out to speak to us.

"It would appear that your driver was shot by

someone who was trying to abduct your fiancée."

Finally, it would appear he was prepared to accept our version of events.

"Apparently, she put up a spirited fight, striking her assailant over the head with a chair. It would appear all the blood was probably from his head wound so we are doing DNA tests to see if we can find a match. Do you have anything we can get a DNA sample from to eliminate your fiancée, like a brush or a comb?"

"There's an empty water bottle in the rear of my car that she was drinking from, would this be ok?"

"That will do fine, I'll get forensics to bag it. Your driver told me he intervened, after this chap got up from the floor and attempted to grab hold of Ms Sage. Apparently, this fellow came in through the rear doors, grabbed hold of your fiancée from behind, but she jerked her head back and butted him full in the face, breaking his glasses, as well as spreading his nose across his face. Then she picked up one of the metal chairs and struck him on the head.

"As she ran out through the doors at the back, this chap got up off the floor and attempted to follow her. He was obviously badly dazed because he was stumbling about and crashing into the wall. It was at this point your driver tried to restrain him but the assailant pulled a pistol out and at close range shot him in the stomach. He's been very lucky, even though his spleen has been removed, but it could have been a lot worse, the doctor says he should make a good recovery."

"Did he give you a description of this guy?"

"Yes, he was over one and a half metres tall, of extremely thin build with long dark matted hair and he was initially wearing spectacles. The guy didn't utter one word during the attack, it all happened so quick but it would appear Ms. Sage got in a couple of telling blows, judging by the amount of blood in the place he's suffered a serious injury. His blood stained broken glasses were found on the floor. We've told the A&E staff to be on their guard if anyone seeks treatment for a head or face wound, also we are alerting hospitals nearby to keep a close eye out for this guy."

"Is there any sign of Cleo?"

"Not so far, we've brought in extra tracker dogs and have set up additional road blocks outside the immediate area. There's also a police helicopter with thermal imaging coordinating the search. Some of the surrounding ground cover is very dense, she could just be hiding until she feels it's safe to come out. I wouldn't be worried about her, it seems like this lady can handle herself."

"Yes, so it would seem, after we were both physically attacked by some nut-job at my apartment, I decided it would be a good idea for the two of us to get some lessons in basic self defence, it would appear in her case, it was time and money well spent."

Just then his cell phone rang, after taking the call he walked towards us,

"Excuse me for a minute, I've got to contact the mobile incident room."

"Can we see him?"

"That's up to the nursing staff, I would have liked to have spent more time interviewing him myself, but he wasn't up to it."

I didn't know what to do but had to do something to help, just to hang around waiting for developments didn't seem like the correct option.

After clearing it with DS Lofthouse, Alistair took me back out to the Willows to retrieve my car and show him the scene of the incident. There were police everywhere, dog handlers coming and going, the constant chatter of police radios, periodically dwarfed out by the deafening noise of the chopper overhead as it made another pass in its continued search. Trees and shrubs did a wild dance under the intense down draft from the helicopter;

loose debris from the ground was whipped up, battering us like stinging shrapnel. A mobile command centre was now in position, there was no doubt it was being treated as a major incident.

The orangery was a secure crime scene, but in the daylight it was easy to point out to Alistair through the glass walls where the incident took place. Two forensic staff clad in white sterile suits were still inside gathering evidence, one police photographer was taking stills of the crime scene another officer was videoing every inch of the area.

Outside, the search was being carried out in a measured methodical grid pattern but so far without any success. We stayed at the scene for about an hour then, before we left, checked with an officer in the command unit if any progress had been made.

"Despite searching over 200 hectares, so far we've drawn a blank. But, I've just received a report from one of our mobile units that a male who appeared to have been injured flagged down a lady about four kilometres from here. When she stopped, he produced a gun then dragged her from her Range Rover, before he hijacked it and it sped off towards Doncaster. It appears he was on his own and he was covered in blood. Thankfully, apart from being badly shaken by the incident the lady wasn't harmed. I've just directed the chopper to engage in the pursuit. The latest report we have is that the car was heading in the direction of a multi-storey car park in the city centre. We've a number of units in hot pursuit. He won't get far. Meanwhile, we will continue to carry on searching here until we find your fiancée or, we are one hundred percent sure she's not in the area."

If this statement was meant to console me, it did exactly the opposite, I feared for her safety more than ever. If she had have been in hiding, surely with all the police activity she would have shown herself, the fact she hadn't meant she was either dead, God forbid, or

Get a Proper Job

had somehow gotten outside of the search area. Alistair and I decided to leave and await contact from DS Lofthouse.

By the time I got home, press and TV reporters were camped outside my apartment but I was in no humour to be interrogated by these people. How do they find out? I know they were only doing their job, but after everything that had occurred in the previous twenty-four hours, this was the last thing I needed. Under the circumstances, I decided to spend the night at Cleo's apartment just in case she made her way home. As I entered the underground car park, I could see her parking slot was unoccupied. I parked in the visitors bay, then made my way up to her apartment. I poured myself a stiff whiskey then settled down to what was going to be a long night.

Periodically, I checked the news channels but there was nothing further to what I already knew. I was constantly thinking that I had brought her nothing but trouble since we'd met. Her near death experience at the hands of Fat Albert, now this, I couldn't help feel I was responsible. Eventually, I succumbed to the effects of several large glasses of Famous Grouse whiskey. I was awoken just after seven the next morning by my mobile phone belting out that wonderful tune, 'Galway Girl'.

"Hello, Carter Dean."

"Mr. Dean, it's DS Lofthouse, sorry to call you so early but it's important, I'm afraid I've got some bad news."

My heart sank; it would appear my worst fears were about to come true.

"We have found the body of a dark haired female, aged in her thirties. She was wearing a navy jacket over a pale blue blouse and dark grey slacks. There was no identification on the body so we need you to identify if it's your fiancée or not. She had been shot in the side and it appears she bled to death, one of our search teams found her on the banks of a stream about five kilometres from our initial search area. We are treating this as murder. I'm sorry to have to break this to you, there is a possibility it's someone else, although I don't really think so, she matches the description you gave me."

Even though I had been expecting bad news I was stunned by what he said, from the description of her clothing I was in no doubt it was Cleo. I immediately started to throw up and couldn't stop. Lofthouse obviously heard my distress.

"Are you OK Mr. Dean?"

I reached down and retrieved my phone from pools of vomit, "Sorry about that, where is she?"

"She's been sent for a full autopsy, obviously we would like a positive ID beforehand, we'd be very grateful for your assistance in this regard, if you like I can send a car for you."

"Normally, I would say no that's not necessary, but I'm afraid I've got too much whiskey in my system I would not be fit to drive."

I gave him the address then immediately called Alistair to give him the bad news.

"Jesus, Carter, that's shocking, what can I do to help?"

"Not sure, I've to go over to Doncaster to identify her before they start the post mortem, although it appears she was shot and just left to die."

"OK, I want to come with you, I'll head over to Cleo's apartment, if I leave now I should be with you in half an hour."

This gave me time to shower and freshen up. The driver took us both straight to the city's mortuary where DC Lofthouse was waiting. We were taken inside where a body was laid out on a stainless steel table it was covered in a white sheet. I hesitated as I looked at the veiled figure on the table.

"Let me know when you're ready Mr. Dean." said Lofthouse.

Get a Proper Job

I nodded and an attendant the pulled the sheet back, there was no doubt it was Cleo. Her face and hair bore traces of dried mud I couldn't speak, other than to say, "Yes, that's Cleo."

Alistair placed his arm around my shoulder and led me outside where we took a seat. I've never lost anyone close before; it's a dreadful gut wrenching feeling.

"What ever I can do to help Carter, you only have to ask, I can't imagine how desperate you are feeling, it's too shocking for words."

"Thanks, Alistair, it doesn't seem real to see her lying there so cold and lifeless, all our plans for our future gone. She'd been busy for weeks arranging our wedding, talking about having kids and what we would call them, it doesn't seem real. Now I've got the awful task of informing her mother."

"Would you like me to do that?"

"Thanks Alistair, but I think I'd better do it, God knows how she's going to take it."

"I'm not sure if you've heard Mr. Dean, but her assailant who we chased into the multi-storey car park, somehow managed to evade capture. They found the stolen Range Rover abandoned on the second level, a search of the complex revealed nothing.

"It then became apparent, he'd shot a delivery man then got through our cordon in a 'Mr. Crusty' bread van. He was waived through wearing a white coat and hat, like a uniform, the kind that people delivering food normally wear. The officer was under the impression he was a genuine driver who'd been delivering bread to one of the supermarkets based in the complex. He checked inside the back of the van then satisfied he was genuine, he waived him through.

"I don't need to tell you this idiot has been placed on leave whilst we consider disciplinary action. It was only later during a search of the car park; they discovered the body of the real driver in a waste skip. He'd been shot in the head. The van was recovered early this morning burned out on the outskirts of Stockport."

    I couldn't believe what he'd just said, her killer managed to escape despite the involvement of dozens of police throwing a so-called impenetrable cordon around the building. Cleo deserved better than this. We were driven back to Cleo's apartment, once there I phoned her mother to give her the awful news. As you can imagine she was heartbroken, her one and only daughter taken in such a cruel and barbaric way. Now, instead of planning our wedding, we had to concentrate on organising her funeral, but first we would have to wait until the pathologist had conducted the post mortem and released her body. This would take a few days.

    Alistair stayed with me for the rest of the day whilst I made a number of phone calls. I rang her employer and spoke with Mr. Barnes who broke down when I told him what had occurred. Then I called a number of clubs where I had bookings for over the next few weeks. Under the circumstances I would not be appearing, but rather than let them down I agreed to supply Glyn Thomas a talented young comedian recently signed up by my agency. I was finding it hard to function properly. As I ticked off things I had to do, there was no doubt in my mind that my life as a comedian was over.

Chapter Fifteen

I have always found funerals difficult, I'm not particularly religious, even being inside a church makes me feel uncomfortable. Cleo's funeral took place at St. Walberg's Catholic Church in Preston, where she attended at least a couple of times a month when she wasn't travelling. This was followed by cremation at Longridge Road Crematorium, her mother's choice, not mine. There was a huge turnout of people, all her friends and relatives including all the staff from the company she worked for, as well as clients from overseas. I found it amazing that people from China, Japan, Malaysia, and the US had travelled so far to pay their respects. This was an indication that she was held in such high esteem. Unbelievably, some of my old school friends put in an appearance; I hadn't seen them for almost twelve years. John Stevenson who had been following my career, contacted most of my old classmates by social media when he heard about the atrocity. Under different circumstances it would have been great to see them all again, but all I could do was to thank them for coming. For most of the day I was in a complete daze, functioning on autopilot. It was the most difficult day I've ever known, I was thankful that I had Alistair by my side. My life would never be the same; I was in a very dark place. It didn't help matters when her killer had never been found to date there was no indication to their identity.

Bob was released from hospital after ten days. He said he was comfortable to work from home and would look after the bookings for the agency. I was grateful to him for the offer, my life wasn't in it anymore. Alistair was in touch constantly, checking to make sure I was

OK, he knew the depths of my despair for me it really was living one day at a time.

Reports were coming through on Sky, about a serious shooting incident on the Costa del Sol, Spain, regarding a British subject. Initially, it was thought to be a terrorist related incident, but soon afterwards clarified as a drugs operation. An ex-patriot had been injured as he returned to his apartment in Marbella.

Spanish police had mounted dawn raids on properties in Marbella, Puerto Banus, San Pedro, and Estepona. The raids all took place simultaneously, mounted by the drugs division of the local police in an effort to stem the flow of class A drugs that were flooding the area. It was later revealed that ex-Detective Chief Inspector David Porter had been challenged by police as he entered his apartment building. He refused to comply when instructed to lie down on the ground; instead, he pulled out a pistol and fired several shots before racing into the building. Armed police chased after him into the unit and a gun battle ensued that lasted almost an hour.

Eventually, after breaking a hole in the door into his apartment they fired in teargas to flush him out. When the police considered he was no longer a threat, they broke down what was left of the door and raced inside to find him lying unconscious on the floor. He'd suffered several gunshot wounds and was taken away for treatment. After searching his apartment, police found ten kilos of pure cocaine along with €65,000 Euro in cash. Another unit had raided a villa in San Pedro to apprehend Eduardo Castellar. They encountered stiff resistance and a serious gun battle developed in which two policemen were killed and three others seriously injured. Castellar evaded capture, stealing a police car then headed in the direction of Gibraltar. The car was later found burnt out in a wooded area near Punta Mala, there was no sign of him. Raids in Estepona and Puerto Banus resulted in four other people being detained and several hundred kilos of cocaine being seized, along with €500,000 Euro in cash.

I had just finished a phone call from Bob, who'd been bringing me up to date with the state of play at the agency, when the concierge buzzed to say Alistair was downstairs, so I told him to send him up.

"Morning Carter, have you heard the news?"

"Only just got out of bed, haven't seen any news, finding it difficult to motivate myself these days."

"You need to get back in the saddle, Carter, I'm sure if you got back on stage your love for the game would come back."

"That's easy for you to say, Alistair, everyone's giving me advice on what I should do, but you don't know what's it like. I can't sleep at night without dosing myself with Valium, and they make you feel like shit the next day."

"Stop taking those bloody things, they can become addictive."

"What else can I do, if I don't take anything I just lay awake all night staring at the ceiling?"

"Look, Carter, I'm not going to say it will get easier with the passing of time, because I know how badly you've been affected. But you've got to snap out of this, only you can do that. I honestly believe if you could force yourself to do one show, I'm sure it will help, at least think about it because I'm getting concerned about you. You're a guy with an amazing sense of humour who has to ability to make people laugh, it's a gift you have, don't throw it all away."

It was genuine concern from Alistair, I know he was only thinking about my wellbeing, but at that point in my life I couldn't see myself doing it.

"Anyway, what news did you mean?"

"Your old buddy, Porter, shot and seriously injured by police in Spain investigating drugs. They tried to arrest him but he resisted, produced a gun, and shot at them. Barricaded himself in his flat until they flushed him out with teargas. Apparently, they found loads of coke and cash in his apartment. It was the first thing on Sky this morning and is ongoing; they've been rounding em up in dawn raids. In another raid, one nutcase, a Columbian called, Castellar, shot dead two cops, and seriously injured three others. He stole a police car then took off towards Gibraltar but seems to have disappeared. Apparently, he's got a huge bounty on his head, evaded capture on a number of occasions in several South American countries, not a pleasant sort.

"From what has been reported, it looks like Porter was involved with drugs all along, probably responsible for the theft from the station in Rochdale, it wouldn't surprise me if his sidekick Staunton was in cahoots as well."

I couldn't believe what he'd just told me, Porter, a pillar of the community turns out to be a pillar of shite, "That's unbelievable, what a scumbag, when I think how difficult he made things for me, hounding me at every opportunity, never missing a chance to make my life a misery, what an evil bastard. You don't suppose he was connected to Fat Albert's drug business do you?"

"Who knows, Carter, on the surface you'd have to say no, especially after his reaction when drugs were discovered in the lockup in Oldham. He interrogated me for hours. Bonetti certainly didn't seem to be flavour of the month. But, maybe it was just an elaborate ruse, and they were connected. Or could be it was just too much of a temptation for Porter, seeing the pension fund going begging in the station lockup. He bided his time, scheming how best to steal it."

"You could be right, Alistair, when I think about it there was no love lost between them, he had Fat Albert arrested at the airport on his return from Greece, on another occasion he was taken in and interviewed about the ring, before he came to my apartment and attacked the two of us. It's hard to be imagine doing all that if they were in cahoots dealing in drugs."

"My gut feeling is it was just too much for Porter to resist, pension fund staring him in the face. But, at this stage, Carter, I wouldn't rule anything out, bizarre and unlikely as it seems."

The whole situation seemed unreal; at least if nothing else, the morning's encounter with Alistair took my mind off thinking about Cleo. That is, until Alistair said, "There's still no sign of the murderer who killed Cleo, I've been in touch constantly with DS Lofthouse, but they've not been able to trace them and have no idea as to who it was."

"What about the tests for DNA, surely they have the results back by now?"

"No match for anyone in the national database."

"That's disappointing, I was sure that would yield something."

"Same here, it would appear they have absolutely nothing to go on. The specs they recovered from the crime scene were not by prescription, just plain glass, imported into Europe from China in there millions plus there were no prints on them."

The nightmare continued, whatever I thought about these people peddling their misery in drugs, my main concern was no one had been caught for the murder of Cleo and I wouldn't rest until they were.

The following day, just after 10:00am, a newsflash on Sky gave the breaking news of a developing situation on the Rock of Gibraltar. A hostage situation had occurred when police raided an apartment to apprehend a Columbian wanted in connection with an incident earlier in the day in San Pedro, Spain. Again, he evaded capture by racing along rooftops before dropping down onto the top of a delivery van, but as police closed in on him he took refuge in a small cafe. The report was live and showed Gibraltar's senior police officer negotiating through a loud hailer in an effort to reach a peaceful solution. A young girl and twelve customers had been taken hostage, their abductor confirmed as Eduardo Castellar threatened to kill them if any rescue attempt was made. Three hours passed as police tried to negotiate with this lunatic. He was demanding safe passage off the rock with a plane fully fuelled to take him to Libya. Armed police had their weapons trained on the small cafe where Castellar had barricaded the windows with tables. This situation was being beamed live around the world and a tense standoff ensued.

I was just out of the shower when Alistair called me.
"Have you been watching TV?"
"No, only just got up, why?"
"Switch onto Sky, one of Fat Albert's cohorts has taken hostages in Gibraltar, he's threatening to kill them if they attempt a rescue. It's going out live, bloody unbelievable, just goes to show you what a sick bunch he was mixed up with."

As my TV sprang to life, gunfire could be heard followed by two or three large bangs from stun grenades according to the to presenter. It became evident that the attacker had agreed to release one hostage, only to shoot them in the back as they exited the cafe. The chief of police obviously concerned this would turn into a public execution, gave the command for the UK Special Forces unit to intervene. They were on a training mission in the Mediterranean and just happened to be in Gibraltar for twenty-four hours R and R, and had been on standby to mount a rescue mission. It was all over in less than thirty seconds, Castellar was dead, unfortunately, so were two of the café customers,

Get a Proper Job

but in the scheme of things and what could have been, probably an acceptable level of collateral damage.

"Jesus, Alistair, what next?"

"I know, from what was reported earlier he was a major player in the drugs world with huge bounty on his head. No doubt the source of all the crap that Fat Albert was peddling. However, it would have been better if they'd got him alive, there are still a lot of unanswered questions and blanks in the story that he could have filled."

"Yes, he may well have known who was behind the murder of Cleo."

"That's possible, they've established he had a direct link to Fat Albert."

"How do you know that?"

"My friend Alison in the accounts department at the station, throws me odd bits of information, she says they've uncovered direct communications between the two of them so putting two and two together he would not have been best pleased when all the cocaine was confiscated."

"Did it not occur for you to tell me this before?"

"Look Carter, you've been in the throws of deep depression for the past few months, I didn't think it would do your state of mind any good."

"Sorry Alistair, you've been the best mate anybody could have, it's just like a gaping wound in me, not knowing who was behind her murder."

"Me also, but hopefully something will turn up."

Over the next day's, more information was released that did indeed show a direct link with Fat Albert and Eduardo Castellar, but the authorities were confident that this particular group responsible for the massive volume of narcotics flooding European countries was now out of business. Only time would tell.

I had been very fortunate that Bob had picked up the baton taking care of running our fledgling business.

It had been six months since Cleo had been murdered yet nobody had been apprehended for this heinous crime. I made it a mission to keep chasing DS Lofthouse; I would call him at least once a week demanding an update, although I never got any satisfactory information. He assured me a team of detectives were working tirelessly to find the killer of Cleo and the delivery driver, who had been shot and dumped unceremoniously in a waste skip.

As time went by, I got the feeling that more and more of my calls were being met by 'I'm sorry he's not available' but I was determined her death wouldn't be put on the back burner.

Eventually, I slowly started to come out of my depression. I found that going for a run each morning helped me face the rigours of the day. Just a few kilometres to start with, eventually building up to ten. I began to get more involved in the running of our business and like people say, time does heal. We had some exciting talent on our books as I got increasingly more involved, I began to realise how much I missed performing on stage, seeing first hand the responses we were getting about some of our acts, so I decided to come out of retirement.

Bob and I were on our way home after doing my comeback show at the Falstaff Club in Derby. My return to the bright lights had gone very well, I realized then that Alistair had been right all along. Suddenly, a large truck with headlights on full beam loomed large in the rear window on a remote stretch of the A6 road as we travelled through the Peak District. Bob thought it would be prudent to go this route rather than on the motorway when traffic reports indicated huge tailbacks after a serious incident. The truck seemed to be trying to overtake on this narrow moorland road, weaving from side to side before it suddenly slammed into the rear corner of my Mercedes, in what the police would call a pit manoeuvre. Bob did his best to control the car, but the impact was so great we spun around about three times before we shot off the road and dropped several metres into a field. We landed nose first, the impact was so great we somersaulted twice before landing back on four wheels. The front and side airbags inflated creating a cocoon that cushioned us from the impact. When we extricated ourselves from the car, we could see the truck hadn't stopped but sped away.

"Are you OK, Bob?"

"What the fuck was all that about?"

"Don't know, but that was no accident."

"You're right, Carter I could see in my rear-view mirror his headlights on full beam, the way he was lining up behind me weaving from side to side, he was intimidating. We'd better call the police."

"Also the AA, although I have my doubts if they will be able to pull us out."

The police and the AA arrived after twenty-five minutes, just as a breakdown service screeched to a halt and volunteered to pull us out for a fee.

"How the hell do these people get here so quick, the bloody police haven't arrived yet?"

"I'm told they tune in to police radio frequencies, programmed to listen for RTA's I think they call them ambulance chasers." We declined their offer.

The near rear side of my car was badly damaged, although, there was only minor damage to the front, which was surprising seeing as we had nosedived off the road. But, apart from sitting in about half a metre of boggy moorland the car seemed otherwise intact. There were traces of dark blue paint streaked along the side of the rear also; part of mudguard probably belonging to the truck was lying in the road. The name of a company Dillard was embossed onto it, but this would be the name of the coachbuilder however, it may help narrow the search for the truck.

Whilst Bob and I spoke with the police, the AA mechanic hitched a steel cable to a tow hook on the front of the Mercedes then began to winch it back onto the road.

We were unable to give the police a registration or description for the truck, other than it was a dark coloured box body. However, they took the mudguard with them in an effort to trace the company. Police up ahead were notified in an effort to intercept the truck but this was only going through the motions, he'd be long gone and without a positive ID unlikely to be found. After the mechanic checked the car he determined it was drivable after he had prised the rear panel away from the wheel, although the rear lights were not in great shape. He did his best to cobble together something that worked that would enable us to limp home, once he was happy with his temporary fix we departed, shaken and most definitely stirred.

There's no doubt in my mind that Bob's expert driving saved us from a potentially life threatening situation, narrowly avoiding a dry-stone wall placing the car through a narrow gap between it and a large dead tree. It has been a frightening experience, the more I thought about the more it seemed it was a deliberate attempt to kill us. We later learned from the police, they had traced the company that owned the vehicle. It had been stolen from a motorway service station; the driver had been beaten senseless with an iron bar he was in a critical condition in hospital. This was a serious incident that had been the reason for tailbacks on the motorway because the truck had hit a number of cars as it raced for the nearest exit. Despite exhaustive checks the truck hadn't been found.

Chapter Sixteen

Two weeks after we were run off the road, I was just about to retire to bed for the night, when the police called me with an update that left me absolutely stunned. The stolen truck had been located, hidden inside a disused warehouse on the Dingle Industrial Estate in Oldham; it had been taken away for forensic tests. The officer was hopeful that they would be able to retrieve some fingerprints or DNA to identify the person who had stolen the van and left a trail of destruction in their wake. The driver who was beaten senseless with an iron bar had since died, so this was now a murder enquiry, as well as trying to kill us and causing mayhem on the motorway resulting in several vehicles being totally destroyed and their occupants badly injured. I immediately called Alistair; we agreed to meet the following day.

I spent a restless night in bed; I couldn't sleep thinking about the significance of where the truck had been discovered, and what it could mean.

The next day, somewhat bleary eyed the two of us were enjoying the sunshine having lunch outside in the garden of Toni's Bistro on Bolton road, discussing the implication of where the hijacked truck had been found.

"There's no doubt in my mind it's connected to the drugs operation, it's too much of a bloody coincidence not to be."

"I think your right, Carter, could well be one of that lot wanting to inflict some kind of revenge for the loss of their merchandise, it certainly fits with your previous experiences."

"I agree, it would appear we've stirred up a real hornets nest. God knows how many of them there are."

"We need to cover our backs, it's common knowledge where you live and it wouldn't be difficult to locate where I operate from."

"I'm sorry Alistair, I never thought it would escalate to this, you've been a good friend I'd hate to think they have you in their crosshairs."

"Don't worry, it's nothing compared to my time in Afghanistan or Iraq, all the same we need to be on guard."

I felt bad for drawing Alistair into this bizarre situation, I'd become too dependent on him, not realising I was drawing him ever more into my apocalyptic ordeal. Just then my mobile rang, the number I recognised belonging to the police in Derby.

"Mr. Dean, it's DI Wilson, after exhaustive tests, we've been able to identify the person that is responsible for the murder and theft of the vehicle, not too mention your incident and the numerous cars destroyed on the motorway."

"Don't keep me in suspense, who was it?"

"There's an outstanding warrant out for his arrest, it's probably someone you are familiar with, we were able to get a match to him on the police national database, his name is Albert Bonetti."

I froze when he said this, it can't be, after catching my breath, "That's bloody impossible, he's dead, burnt to a crisp in Belgium."'

"Well if he is, he did a very good interpretation of someone being alive. We were able to get matching DNA and fingerprints off two items. The steering wheel door handles had been wiped clean but we found a partial print on the rear view mirror, a water bottle provided a match for his DNA. Guess he just wasn't as smart as he thought he was. He obviously went to some length to avoid leaving anything behind that could identify him. Probably just forgot about the water bottle but it's pretty conclusive I'm afraid, he's the culprit."

Get a Proper Job

I couldn't believe what he'd just told me, for months I was under the impression he was dead, confirmed by the police after he was found burnt to a crisp in Belgium, I switched my phone to speaker mode so that Alastair could hear.

"Are you absolutely sure?"

"Yes Sir, we've double checked, from his file it appears he was a suspect in the murders of entertainers in the north, he was taken in and interviewed but was released without charge. Later, it was discovered he was involved in kidnapping and the dealing of drugs but evaded capture and fled to Belgium. His file goes on to show he was found dead in a car park in Bruges. DNA taken at the time from his possessions at a nearby hotel confirmed the body found in a burned out car was his. Somehow they got that wrong, don't ask me how this came about. But it would seem it was a deliberate attempt to fake his own death, however at this stage we don't know why, could be drugs related or something else entirely. It seems it was an elaborate ploy to give the impression he perished in the fire. Working with other forces, we have now established there is direct evidence that links him to the other murders as well as the truck driver. I can't go into details, other than to say he is definitely our serial killer."

I looked at Alistair; neither of us could believe what he'd just said.

"Obviously this man is extremely dangerous, we are advising the public if they see him, not too approach him, but call the nearest police station or 999. There will be a television appearance later today by the Chief Constable appealing for information to identify his whereabouts. In view of your previous history I would advise you to be on your guard. I'm sorry, I have to go into a strategy meeting now, but we'll keep you posted, goodbye."

"Thank you Inspector, I can't believe what you've just

told me, this guy is pure evil I've suffered first hand and seen what he's capable of, I'm sure the police in Rochdale will be stunned when they discover he's still alive."

"So they have evidence that links him directly to the other murders, I wonder what they've found?"

"Don't know, Carter, but I'll make enquiries with my contact at the station, could be prints or DNA or maybe they found the ring and matched it to the victims."

Alistair and I just sat there in complete and utter shock at this news, "This confirms he's the bastard that tried to kill Bob and me driving through the Peak District, did he kill Cleo, I would bet almost certainly? All along I suspected this swine was behind it. Earlier, when the police reported he'd been found dead in a fire in strange circumstances, I didn't believe it, just seemed too bloody convenient, almost like the trail ends here so don't bother looking for me."

"I think you're right Carter, the fact the police ended their investigation early and then decided to destroy the drugs because there would be no trial seemed to me at the time to be a bit previous."

"Yes, I agree but, I wonder did they know some of it was switched before it was due to be incinerated? Maybe, Fat Albert, or his cohorts were still pulling the strings."

"What puzzles me Carter, if he was responsible for killing Cleo, he went to great lengths to set it up. Arranging a fake booking for you, just so he could get at Cleo."

"I think I was the target, not Cleo, it was probably a spur of the moment thing when I left the sunroom, he took his chance thinking she would be an easy target, not realising she was well capable of looking after herself then it all went pear-shaped."

"You're probably right."

"Don't forget, Alistair, before his supposed demise he

was a wanted man, couldn't be seen in public, or the myth would be busted, what better than to arrange a meeting at night, well away from civilisation. It's his style, the only thing that's doesn't add up was the blood found at the scene didn't match his DNA."

"Do you know what, we need to get onto DS Lofthouse immediately get them to re-check the DNA from the blood found at the Willows in Doncaster? It's bloody obvious he engineered that fiasco in Belgium, substituting a body from some poor unfortunate, then faking his death to throw people off the trail. We know he's a slippery bastard, maybe somehow the blood tests were tampered with, in view of what's happened I think it's imperative they are re-tested."

"I agree Alistair, it's hard to believe he's still alive plus he's obviously gunning for me after the incident in the Peak District. We need to move on this, no time like the present, I'm gonna call him now."

I tried the number for DS Lofthouse but as usual, I was told he wasn't available I was put through to the desk sergeant.

"This is Carter Dean,... again, I'm trying to get in touch with DS Lofthouse but as usual I'm not having much luck, however, this is important. I'm ringing in connection with an incident several months ago when my fiancée was shot then just left to die. At the time my driver was shot and seriously injured, the culprit then shot dead another chap then hijacked his van."

"Yes sir, I remember it well."

"The DNA results didn't provide a match at the time to anyone in the police database, the blood samples need be re-checked because they may provide a match for Albert Bonetti who is wanted by several police forces in the north. Please convey this message to Lofthouse, if he can find the time from his busy schedule to ring me because this is important."

"Very good sir, I'll pass your message on."

I had my doubts if he would pass the message on, even if he did that anything would be done about it.

"Well, what's the story I gather he's not there?"

"He's probably there alright, but as usual just won't take my call."

"Maybe he needs to be confronted in person."

"Do you know what Alistair, I think you're right, I'm going to take a drive over there because I don't think even if he gets the message he'll act on it."

"I'll come with you there's more strength in numbers, plus I've nothing very important scheduled for this afternoon."

After paying our lunch bill, we hot footed it over to the Watervale station in Doncaster and presented ourselves at reception.

"I'm Carter Dean, I spoke with the desk sergeant earlier."

"Yes sir, you spoke with me, I passed your message on to DS Lofthouse."

"Good, let's hope he did something about it."

"He is under a lot of pressure but I'm sure it's on his to do list."

"Or maybe, not to do list."

"It's in hand."

"It's what's in his hand that worries me."

"I'm sure it will receive his attention in due course."

"Look this is very urgent something critical has just come to light can we possibly see him?"

The sergeant had that pissed off look on his face; you'd think I'd asked to borrow a fiver off him.

"Moment sir, I'll just see if he's available."

After making a quick call he directed us to the end of the corridor. His office door was open, he didn't stand, didn't even look up from his desk, obviously I was becoming an utter pain in the arse. We walked in and closed the door behind us.

"Dean, I got your message, what do you want?"

"Well, there's a nice warm welcome and it's lovely to see you too. Anyway, enough of these pleasantries, seeing as you won't answer my calls I decided to come and see you in person."

"Now you've seen me, I suggest you bugger off, I'm busy."

This guy was really starting to piss me off. "Listen you arsehole, my fiancée was murdered. You've done fuck all to convince me you are doing everything in your power to apprehend whoever was responsible. You won't answer my calls, I've had no feedback for months, plus this morning I got word that Bonetti, a suspect in at least eight murders was in fact not dead as previously thought, but alive and kicking after faking his own death on the continent, and is almost certainly connected to the incident at the Willows."

"And how does that effect me?"

"Oh I'm sure it will when you find yourself visiting the job centre."

"Is that a threat?"

"Not at all, I'm just stating the obvious, because that's where you'll be heading unless you get your finger out and start cooperating with us. Derbyshire CID at St Mary's Wharf, confirmed he's still alive, he may well be responsible for the attack at the Willows when my fiancée was murdered."

"We've no evidence of that, blood found at the scene didn't match anyone on the police national database."

"That's why we want you to get the blood samples re-tested, this is my lawyer Alistair Bracken you may recall meeting him that night."

"Inspector, in light of this recent discovery we feel the blood samples taken from the incident that night should be re-tested."

"I don't see much point in doing that, the lab we use are highly efficient, we've never had a problem with them before."

"No, but you've never dealt with anyone like Albert Bonetti before. Responsible for a number of deaths, including his own, before he miraculously rose up and it's not even Easter. He tried to kill myself and my driver on our way home through the Peak District just a couple of weeks ago, ran us off the road deliberately. His fingerprints and DNA were found in a vehicle he'd hijacked, after killing the driver he's wanted by the police for a whole list of crimes, I'm sure you've been notified."

Lofthouse was unmoved; he didn't acknowledge what I said, just carried on filling out forms or whatever he was pretending to do.

"Look, only a short time ago I received a call from the investigating officer that Bonetti was responsible. Here's the number for DI Wilson from Derbyshire CID he's handling the investigation into the hijacking and murder."

I placed a slip of paper with his details on his desk; he wasn't interested he just glared at me. I know I was pissing him off, I expected any second to be told to get out, but I was going nowhere without a satisfactory outcome.

"If you are not prepared to go down that route, can we have the blood samples and we'll get our own DNA analysis done?"

Lofthouse glared at me, steam was coming out of his ears. "I'm sorry," he spluttered, "we don't work that way here, the tests have already been done by an accredited laboratory, used on numerous occasions we're happy with the results, you seem to be inferring we have in some way tampered with them."

"Nobody is suggesting you did that, but this guy Bonetti is ruthless, how do you know he didn't get at the people in the lab?"

"Your grasping at straws suggesting somehow the results have been tampered with, it puts a cloud over everyone involved and I'm not prepared to sully their reputations."

"You're worried about a cloud, well let me tell you, this cloud will become a shit storm if you continue to be obstructive? My fiancée has been murdered, this fucking bloke has killed at least eight people that we know of."

Then Alistair interjected, "I can apply to the courts for an order for the release of the blood samples if you want to go that route. I can tell you as a lawyer, the courts would almost certainly grant this application, I can't see why you would want us to take that action, you are only frustrating your colleagues in other stations around the country. It seems like you are deliberately obstructing the investigation, you don't know how dangerous this man is."

Lofthouse stood up. He was totally pissed off. He stormed across to the door and opened it.

"I think we are done."

As I walked up to him I stood inches from his face, the kind only a mother could love, I was so close I could smell his disgusting breath. "You've not heard the last of this, and by the way I think a visit to your dental hygienist is long overdue."

Then Alistair stood directly in front of him, he gave him an intense stare before he said, "See you in court."

As we walked away from his office, Lofthouse called out, "Very well, you've made your point I'll get the samples re-tested and I'll take great pleasure in telling you the results will be the same as before."

We turned and walked back to face him. "I'll be surprised if they are," said Alistair.

"I'm confident the result will be the same, now get out, I've things to do."

Alistair stood in front of him. "Let me say this, as a lawyer, I've dealt with many senior officers in my day to day work, however, I can't remember meeting anyone as obstructive and objectionable as yourself. You need some serious re-training in dealing with the general public, you can rest assured the Chief Constable will be getting a memo from me."

"Do as you see fit."

"Oh, don't worry I will, here's my card, I would appreciate a copy of the report from the lab as soon as it's available, please email or fax it through to my office, good day."

As the two of us left his office, the door was slammed shut with such force; it almost came off its hinges, "That's a bit childish, guess we upset him, but loved it Alistair when you said about applying to the courts, that didn't go down at all well, he looked like he was ready to punch you."

"He was just being an obstructive little shit but, I don't know why he should be, every cop in the country is on the lookout for this guy and its like he's determined to frustrate the investigation."

"Probably thinks we're interfering, but I've been getting nowhere with him not taking or returning any of my calls."

"I think we put a rocket up his rear, it will be interesting to see how he performs from here on, but I think we should also contact DI Wilson and put him in the picture, the more pressure we put on him the better."

Two days later, just after ten in the morning, the concierge at my apartment block called me to say DS Lofthouse was in reception requesting an audience, I asked him to send him up. Fortunately Alistair was with me. "I wonder what he wants?"

"Probably selling tickets to the policeman's ball, either that or it's an invite to his retirement party."

"If it is, it's not before time."

I walked over and opened the door. Lofthouse stood there with a sheepish look on his face.

"Come on in."

"Gentlemen, sorry to arrive unannounced, but I have the results of the DNA retest. You were right; they do belong to Albert Bonetti.

"The person, who did the original tests and report, no longer works at this lab. They disappeared soon after and haven't been since; no one at the lab has any idea where she went. The manager has been taken in for questioning because this shouldn't have happened. It's not clear at this stage if it was a deliberate attempt to mislead us and pervert the course of justice or, it was just an honest mistake, and the lab assistant realising she'd made an error decided to for want of a better term, do a runner.

"However, our investigation is continuing because this shouldn't have happened. It places us in a very difficult position because we don't know if any other DNA results have been compromised. This lab has been placed off limits whilst our enquiries continue. Please accept my apologies, I've been under a considerable amount stress lately. After the two murders on our patch, my department was under the hammer to provide results, especially after it was revealed we let the killer pass through a checkpoint unchallenged.

"From a personal standpoint, it wasn't that I didn't want to take your calls I just didn't have the time or have anything new to tell you. I realise now I was wrong and should have been more understanding, you suffered a huge loss and I'm extremely sorry I wasn't more co-operative."

What a complete turnaround, he'd gone from being uncooperative to apologetic.

"Thank you I accept your apology, this guy gets under the skin and is responsible for more heartache than is imaginable, he has to be caught."

"The Chief Superintendent and members of my team will be making a television broadcast later today, we will be advising the public to be on their guard and not to approach him directly, but to report any sightings to the police. It seems hard to imagine that someone with such a distinctive appearance seems able to move around with impunity, without being spotted. Anyway, I'm due back at the station to prepare for the broadcast, I just thought I would deliver the results so that I could apologise to you personally, once again I'm very sorry, good day."

"Thanks, I appreciate it."

Lofthouse shook our hands and left the apartment,

"My my, Alistair, what a transformation, I almost felt sorry for the guy."

"He's obviously had a bollocking from on high, especially after my note to the Chief Constable, but he was being an awkward so and so, who'd be a copper hey?"

For the rest of the morning we discussed this latest twist in what was becoming purely unbelievable. If it was the script for a movie, you wouldn't believe it, neither of us could come to terms with the latest revelation. For me it was more distressing as I had been associated with this evil man for years, why didn't I know what he was like, there must have been some signs, but try as I could, nothing stood out in his character? That is, until his temper got the better of him about breaking our contract, that was my first indication, all was not as it seemed.

It's one thing losing you temper, but what makes a person like Bonetti into a ruthless murderer, what was it that tipped him over the edge? He started by killing male singers, why, what was it that caused him to do this? Someone suggested it was because he was a failed singer and was jealous but that's ridiculous and I doubt if this was the reason. Obviously, human life meant very little to him, seeing as he'd become one of Britain's most prolific serial killers. But, when he took the life of Cleo it became more than personal, I wouldn't rest until this evil bastard was on the receiving end of the kind of treatment he'd been dishing out the past number of years.

I brought Bob up to date with the latest revelations, he had already been on the receiving end of two attempts on his life, I told him if he wanted to resign I fully understood, however he refused point blank to even consider this. He would stick with me until this madman was caught.

Next, I gathered all my staff together and stressed to them to be on their guard at all times and to let me know if any of them saw or became aware of anything out of the ordinary. It might seem over the top, but I felt I owed it too them to protect them from this lunatic until he was no longer a threat. Some questioned me, some thought I was being ridiculous, but we needed to be on our guard. Then Alistair told me he'd been able to establish from his contact at the station, Bonetti's fingerprints had been found on the leather jacket of one of his victims. His house was raided and his gold ring had been found hidden along with several kilos of cocaine concealed under a floorboard in a bedroom. The ring matched exactly the impressions left in the neck of his victims. There was now no doubt he was the serial killer who had wreaked fear and havoc amongst the entertainment sector.

Fat Albert was now Europe's most wanted. All air and seaports were on high alert for him, several pictures of him were released on TV and in the press. Some were mocked up, showing him in various disguises on how he might look with an array of hair and skin colour, some with spectacles some without. A number of possible sightings in various counties had been reported, but none had resulted in him being apprehended. With all the police activity it was thought it was only a matter of time before he was found.

Chapter Seventeen

In view of the fact that Fat Albert was still on the loose, I thought that I needed to get in some more basic training in self defence. I had gone with Cleo a couple of times, but because of the pressure of work I hadn't completed the course. It was probably only a matter of time before he came after me again and it was best to be ready. I was reasonably fit, not what you'd call overweight and had always considered I had a balanced diet and ate the right kind of healthy foods, apart from when I indulged in one of my mother's Lancashire hotpots.

After Cleo was murdered, the first thing I did when I started to come out of my state of depression, was to start running. It was a form of therapy and certainly helped me to overcome my demons. I wasn't at marathon standards yet, but could manage 10 kilometres runs quite easily two or three times a week, so my basic level of fitness was good. However, I needed some training in unarmed combat to be prepared, the kind were I could inflict a killer blow to the throat or beat him senseless with my handbag. Of course, to be able to shoot the bastard would be my preferred option, starting at his ankles and working my way up until I could see his eyes pleading for mercy. Alistair still had contacts in the Marines; the thought crossed my mind about asking him to see if he could acquire a firearm for me. Then decided against it, I had drawn him into my situation more than I should have and I would be jeopardising not only his career, but also his freedom.

I suggested to Bob if he felt up to it that he should get some training in self-defence and he agreed. So I signed us both up for one night a week over a twelve-week course at DiMaggio's, a gymnasium on Rochdale road.

Get a Proper Job

Week one, there were about twenty in the class, mostly they were women and it was all pretty basic stuff as the instructor explained his version of martial arts. His was a combination of, Karate, and Taekwondo, with a bit of Kick Boxing thrown in for good measure. What you would call, his own hybrid style, and not for the purist. That didn't worry me; I just wanted to be able to defend myself in the most effective manner.

By the third week the numbers had dwindled to eight, I could see why you had to pay up front for the twelve-week course. Our instructor was a fellow called Bart Turnbull, a brute of a man, an ex-marine built like a brick outhouse. He looked like the Jaws character in the James Bond movies. He would challenge us to attack him from the front, or from behind, but it usually ended up in failure with us being flat on the mat, wondering how the hell had we got there?

By week eight, we had improved dramatically and could deal with an assailant armed with a number of different weapons from a full frontal attack to one from behind. We could also inflict the deadliest of injuries on an attacker, his life size rubber model was the ideal way for delivering a lethal Karate chop to the throat, or an upward strike to the base of the nose, or a roundhouse kick to the head. Basically, we could strike and kill our assailant, with a variety of kicks and punches, in short, we were lethal.

After the twelve-week course was finished, we received a diploma stating we had completed the course in self-defence; it would go on my lounge wall next to my certificate for flower arranging.

As for Fat Albert, there was still no sign of him, he had reportedly been seen in Scotland, but that turned out to be false. There had been several sightings in the south of France in Lyon and Marseille, but this turned out to be a Polish lookalike, and they say lightening never strikes twice.

We were still on full alert and every day I would stress to my team to keep their wits about them. It was reported in the press the UK police applied to get ex-detective Porter extradited from Spain to help with their drug enquiries, but as usual, this was proving far from straight forward. An enquiry had been started in Lancashire to investigate the exploits of Porter and his former associates, and as such, he needed to be interviewed.

Eventually, Porter was extradited from Spain and held in Strangeways prison until his trial on drugs offences. He was denied bail because he was considered a flight risk, however, he was probably safer where he was than being free. It was thought he was sure to give evidence against former colleagues to save his own skin. Alistair was under the impression, speaking to his contacts this wouldn't go down well, and there may be an attempt to shut him up. Fat Albert would probably be the first in line to provide this service, come to think of it; Porter could well be used as bait.

Life at my agency was good and we had a steady stream of bookings for our acts. Several new clubs came on stream and it was thought the strength of the economy was the reason why, that's if you believe the propaganda politicians who never missed a chance to spout out about. Personally, I never believe what they say, I don't trust them, and I think they are only in it for their own ends. Anyway, that's enough soapbox crap.

Every year in Ireland, there is a comedy festival held in Kilkenny in the month of June that lasts a few days. Comedians, from all over the world have performed there, and it has grown in popularity year by year since its inception. One of the last things that Fat Albert did, before we parted company, was to arrange for me to participate. I had thought about cancelling, but contractually it could be problematic, so I decided the best thing was to go ahead and perform. Having never been to Ireland as the time drew near I was quite looking forward to it. I had a reservation for four nights, the only downside was it was outside of the city and would mean a commute. I tried to reserve more suitable accommodation but every place was fully booked for this period so I would just have to make do with what I had. Bob agreed to take care of things during my spell away and I was confident he would do a good job.

My flight arrived into Dublin airport just after six pm, once I had cleared immigration and customs; I made my way to the Hertz desk in the main terminal to pickup the paperwork for my chariot. After leaving the airport, I headed south on the M50 then exited at junction 9 onto the N7 eventually getting onto the M9 exiting at junction 8 for a straight run to Kilkenny. My sat-nav told me the journey would take 1 hour and 25 minutes. I hadn't been able to locate any meaningful information on the Internet regarding my hotel; Fat Albert had always booked the cheapest of accommodation if I had an overnight stay. As I pulled in front of Mrs. Murphy's Guesthouse, he hadn't disappointed me. The house was badly in need of painting, a sign just visible above the undergrowth indicated it was a Bord Failte the Irish tourist board approved hostelry, however, it looked a dump.

As I walked up the driveway, a huge lady in a pink overall opened the door. As I got closer I could see she had large hairy wart on her chin and was so grotesque, she looked like a Disney character.

Then the beast opened her mouth, "What do you want, if it's a room you're after, we're fully booked."

Now there's a warm Irish welcome for you, come into the parlour, my arse.

"My name's Dean, you should have a reservation for me for four nights."

"Don't think so."

"This is Mrs. Murphy's Guesthouse, or have I come to

the wrong hovel?"
"What?"
"Sorry, hotel."
"I'm Gloria Murphy and we're full, it's the festival, been booked for months, try Sea View on the Dublin road about a ten minute drive. She'll probably have a room, but keep your bedroom door locked, the landlady and her daughter are prone to sleepwalking."

With that, she walked back inside and slammed the door shut. Jesus Christ, what just happened, that was unbelievable? I took a quick photo with my iPhone, as I would be contacting the tourist board about this shoddy treatment. This is no way to treat people coming to perform at the comedy festival, or anyone else for that matter. Although, I suppose in her favour she had mentioned an alternative, but, Sea View, don't take the piss; we have to be about seventy kilometres from the bloody coast. Surely they could think of something more original, like "Cows Arse View' or 'Pigshit Villa'. Anyway, it was getting late and seeing as this old bag wasn't prepared to put me up for the night, it was time to find somewhere that would. I punched in Sea View into my sat-nav and the seductive voice of Hilda Ogden directed me along the Dublin road, until I came to a small whitewashed cottage with a red painted corrugated tin roof... Oh what joy!

By now it was after nine o'clock, my chances of finding anywhere locally were diminishing by the minute. A poorly hand-painted sign in the front garden, indicated this was indeed, 'Sea View' somebody obviously had a sense of humour; maybe they were appearing at the festival. With my options limited, I approached and gave the brass knocker a couple of taps. The door was opened by a tall, slim beautifully looking young woman in her late teens early twenties; I'm definitely not locking my door. She had long blond hair tied in a ponytail and lovely blue eyes. I was greeted with lovely big smile that showed her perfectly formed gleaming white teeth. I was in love.

"Hi I wondered would you have a room for four nights, I'm appearing at the comedy festival?" I thought this information might help my case.

"You're a comedian then?"

"It's been alleged."

"Just hang on a minute, I'll ask me Ma."

I stood waiting at the door, not sure whether to cut and run for the airport and sod the festival. Then mummy appeared. She looked to be in her fifties, quite tall with a fresh complexion with blond hair, and was wearing a pale green overall.

"I'm Vera Donohugh, you need a room?"

"Yes, if you have one, my name's Carter Dean."

"You do know it's festival week?"

"Yes I know, I had a booking confirmed with Mrs. Murphy's Guesthouse, but when I arrived she denied I had a reservation, so she sent me along here."

"You won't find any place within a twenty mile radius because of the festival. The only room I have is a small box room that I wouldn't normally rent out, but seeing as you're desperate, I'm prepared to offer it to you at a reduced rate of fifty Euro. But I warn you, it is pretty basic, plus, you'll have to share a bathroom with my daughter. The rate includes a full Irish breakfast, do you want it?"

That's not a bad deal, a room, the daughter, and full breakfast for fifty Euros.

"Great, I'll take it."

"Come on in, Sophie will show you your room."

I followed her daughter along a narrow corridor that had an abundance of religious pictures adorning the walls. At the end of the corridor was a door with an old style latch, the kind were you press your thumb then pull a trigger like handle that opened the door. She reached her hand inside and switched on the light.

"This is your room, you should be comfortable, bathroom is there on the right, hot water takes a bit of time but it will get there eventually."

"Thank you Miss, sorry I didn't catch you name."

"It's Sophie, breakfast is from seven, if there's anything else you need, I'm just next door?"

Not sure if this was an invite or what, "Thank you Sophie, I think I'm OK, I'll be glad to get my head down, it's been a long day."

I closed the door and looked around the room, it was hell. Wallpaper was peeling away from the walls, and there was an acute smell of dampness. I tried to open a window but several dozen layers of paint held it firmly glued shut. Obviously, this landlady had never heard of duvets or comforters, because there was a seriously dated candlewick bedspread on an old wrought iron bed. There was a mismatch of furniture in the room, on the floor a couple of different coloured carpets were pieced together, on the walls religious pictures added to my discomfort. There was a sideboard with a mirror that had a huge crack in it. Could I really spend a night in this shithole, what was I thinking? I sat on an old wicker bound chair whilst I contemplated my situation. There was no way I was prepared to spend four nights in this Hilton from Hell, and if I survived the wanderings of the landlady, I would be leaving at first light.

I made myself as comfortable as possible and climbed into bed, it felt like I was lying on a bed of street cobbles, each one finding a spot on my back like a vintage Shiatsu machine but without the massage. Every move I made, the bed protested as the springs creaked and groaned. Then, after about thirty minutes as I lay there in acute discomfort, I heard the most horrendous noise, it sounded to be coming from the roof, like a thousand drummers, beating out some call to battle. I had to investigate, when I looked out of the window I could see it was raining heavily, obviously this beating down on the tin roof was the reason for all the noise.

Getting a decent nights sleep looked pretty remote, but eventually I dropped off, I suppose through sheer exhaustion, that is, until I awoke around two thirty when I heard the metallic click as the door latch was pressed. I had been warned the landlady was prone to wandering, I sat bolt upright in the bed. The door was then opened slightly; in the gloom I strained my eyes to see who my visitor was. Suddenly, the door closed and my visitor for whatever reason, decided not to come in. This unnerved me, who was it?

I must have lain there for another hour before I fell asleep. Then I woke when I heard the door latch again, this time I got out of bed, determined to investigate, as I walked across the floor the door was flung open. In the gloom I could make out a tall figure as they raced into the room, their arm was raised, and they struck at me with what I assumed was a large knife. I used my recent training to parry the blow with my left arm, at the same time deliver a strike to the throat with my clenched fist as hard as I could. The knife fell to the floor, my attacker coughed as I delivered another chop to the side of his head. He staggered back into the corner of the room, picked up the small wicker chair and flung it at me before he raced out of the room. I tried to avoid the chair but it caught me midriff and I tripped and fell over it. By the time I'd gathered my thoughts and chased out of the room he was gone. At the end of the corridor I was met by the landlady in curlers and housecoat, a real vision of beauty, what I would call a passion killer.

"Jesus, Mary and Joseph, what the hell's going on, you've woken up the whole feckin house?"

"Somebody just tried to stab me, is that normally the way you treat your guests?"

"I'm calling the Guards."

"Good, because someone just tried to kill me."

By now, bedroom doors started to open as other

guests came out to investigate what all the commotion was about. Her daughter, Sophie, dressed in what I would term a baby doll nightdress sprinted down the corridor to the kitchen, then raced back and breathlessly announced, "Ma the front doors been broken open. I heard something about an hour ago but when the dog didn't bark I thought I'd imagined it. That feckin dog is about as useful as a chocolate fireguard. He's as deaf as a post, he needs some lead in his ear."

"Will that help him?" her mother asked.

"It will if it's from a gun."

If this wasn't so serious it would have been mildly funny, but I was still shaking after this encounter, I was trying to come to terms with what had just happened. Why would someone break into my room and try to knife me? Who was it? My mind went into overdrive. Bonetti, it had to be, he's the only person that would do such a thing. If it were a robbery or a mugging, they wouldn't charge in wielding a knife. Plus, he knew I would be in Kilkenny, because he made the original booking, albeit at another guesthouse.

Not long after, Ireland's finest arrived to investigate. We retired to the kitchen, and got down to the serious business as the Sergeant was given the obligatory cup of tea and biscuits. He was a huge man with a neck like a bull; the uniform struggled to cover his massive bulk, buttons looked ready to pop. His hair was ginger, what else would you expect, he spoke with a thick accent that was proving difficult to understand, as he and Mrs. Donohugh discussed the weather and the price of sliced bread.

Then he turned his attention to me, "I'm Sergeant Mick Byrne, and this is Guard Donal O'Connor. Tell me exactly what happened Mr. Doran."

"It's Dean, Carter Dean. I was in bed when some nutter burst into the room and tried to stab me. Fortunately, I've had training in martial arts and self-defence so I was able to disarm him with punch to the throat. He dropped the knife; I think it's still on the bedroom floor. He raced out of the room but he was too quick for me."

"Would you be able to identify him?"

"Not positively, it was too dark, all I can tell you is he was very tall."

The Sergeant indicated to his associate to go and bag the knife, Sophie lead the Guard down the corridor, purposely flicking her nightdress up as she skipped along revealing momentary flashes of her bare white arse, no doubt scarring this poor sod for life.

"I gather from your accent, you're English?"

"Got it in one Sherlock, bet nothing much gets past you?" he smiled I think he took this as a compliment, either that or he knew I was taking the piss.

"Why are you in Kilkenny?"

"I'm appearing tomorrow at the Comedy Cat Laughs festival, although after this I think I'll be bowing out."

"Would you have any idea why someone would want to kill you, if that was what it was?"

"What else would you call it, someone breaks into your bedroom in the middle of the night and tries to stab you, or is this a typical Kilkenny welcome?"

"There is always an increase in crime during the festival, usually pickpockets and petty theft, with the odd vehicle break-in that kind of thing, but never attempted murder."

"Well, there you go then, there's always a first."

"What made you choose this hotel?"

"Did you say hotel, you need to get out more? I think it's stretching it a bit to even call it a guest house."

"Whatever...why did you choose this one?"

"I had a reservation at Mrs. Murphy's Guesthouse, but when I got there she told me they were full and had no record of my booking so she sent me here."

"Consider yourself lucky, that place doesn't have a

good reputation."

"Bet they don't get many stabbings."

At this point the landlady who'd just come back into the room interjected, "This has never happened before, if you don't like it you know what you can do."

"That's great, first attempted murder, then eviction in the space of a couple of hours, is this what you call comedy? I think you need to advertise it a bit more you know, organise killer weekends I'm sure there's a market for it, although, you probably wouldn't get many repeat visitors."

"Don't talk to me Ma like that, it's not her fault."

"Sorry, that was a bit rude of me, but I have been through a frightening experience."

After another ten minutes of futile questions, the sergeant folded his notebook.

"Mr. Dean, I think that's all I need, I gather you'll be around for a few more days?"

"That's debatable, I'm booked for a number of shows starting tomorrow night, but I don't know if I'm up for it. What will you do with the knife?"

"We'll get it checked for prints, see if we can identify who it was."

"Will this take long?"

"No, just as soon as I get back to the station I'll get my detective on it when he starts his shift."

"Can I give you the telephone number of a police station in Derby, they have prints on file of a criminal called Bonetti, wanted in connection for at least eight murders?"

"Do you think this is connected?"

"It could be, he attempted to kill me a few months ago and he's responsible for murdering my fiancée."

The sergeant looked shocked, probably never had anything more serious to deal with than the odd drunk, wife beater or sheep shagger. I wrote the name and number of DI Wilson on a slip of paper and handed it to him. "This is the detective who is handling the case, also here is my card with my mobile number on it, if you get any information as to who this chap was, will you ring me immediately?"

"Just as soon as we process the knife for prints, assuming there are some and he wasn't wearing gloves. After this we'll check with Pulse our national database to see if we have a match then we'll get in touch with your man in Derby."

"Thank you sergeant, I appreciate it. Should you establish it was Bonetti a word of warning, he is highly dangerous, wanted by Interpol for murder, kidnapping and dealing in drugs."

Chapter Eighteen

By now it was daylight as I made my way back to my room, I sat down on the bed whilst I studied my options. I couldn't stay here; it wasn't safe, apart from the room being no better than a slum dwelling. The security such as it was, consisted of a deaf dog and doors that could be opened without the command, 'Open Sesame.' Whoever my attacker was, they may well come back. I was fairly certain that Mrs. Donohugh wasn't responsible; she seemed more shocked than I was. Then I started to think about the first guesthouse where I had been so rudely turned away. Was this deliberately done by Murphy, this needed to be investigated. Then there was a knock on the door, the latch was pressed, and Sophie walked straight in.

"Mr. Dean, I'm very sorry for what happened, me Ma is terrified you're going to report her to Bord Failte. They don't like getting complaints from tourists and it's her only means of income."

"Tell her not too worry, I won't do that, but I can't stay here anymore, you can understand why. This bloody nut job may come back."

"Nothing like this has ever happened before, me Ma's devastated, one of the guests has already told her he's checking out. She's been taking in guests since the festival started twenty odd years ago, before I was born."

"I'm sorry Sophie, but if the attacker turns out to be who I think it might be, you need to be on your guard. I'm not trying to frighten you but this chap is very dangerous."

"Don't you worry about me, I've got a shotgun, and I'm not afraid to use it. I've been clay pigeon shooting since I was a kid. Won loads of prizes all over the country so I'm well used to a gun."

"That's good to know, if he comes back, make sure you shoot him in the ankles then work your way up his body."

"You're not a fan of him then?"

"Most definitely not, killed my fiancée and at least eight other people that we know of. He's also made two attempts on my life; the man is Interpol's most wanted. Tell me this, is Sergeant Byrne up to the job?"

"Oh, you mean Podgy, that's his nickname, has the hots for me Ma. He's all right; they say he's never booked anyone for any crime, more likely to give em a thump behind the ear than have to do any paperwork. Since me Da died four years ago he's a regular in me Ma's kitchen, sticks his head around the door for a cup of tea and a natter, but I'm sure he'll do whatever he can."

"That's good to know although I wouldn't advise him giving Bonetti a thump around the ear."

"Anyway, breakfast will be ready now, it will set you up for the day."

I thanked her, and disappeared into the bathroom to freshen up, afterwards I made my way along the corridor to the dining room. There were four other people already having breakfast, and judging by their conversation, were also attending the festival.

"Morning, were you responsible for all the bloody noise in the middle of the night?" said one bearded individual.

"Who me, didn't hear a thing?" I said sarcastically, "slept like a log."

The bloke looked at me, he wasn't sure what to say next. "Sorry, I thought it was you."

"Well, you know what thought did?"

"What?" he said with a smirk on his face.

"Followed a muck cart and thought it was a

wedding." I had to go back to my childhood to dig that one out. Stunned silence followed, and for the rest of the time very little was said. But I wasn't in the mood for smart arsed comments after my ordeal. After breakfast, I made my way back to my room to collect my things then check out. As I was just about to leave, Sophie came into the room.

"I know you want to check out, but me Ma says she can put you in the Green room if you like, one guy has already left after what happened. It's a lovely bedroom with an en suite and you can have it at the same rate."

"Thanks for the offer, but that nutter could return, I might not be so fortunate the next time."

"Look Mr. Dean I don't think there's much chance he'll come back, sounds like he got second prize. Plus, I've got a double barrelled twelve bore and I'm not afraid to use it if he breaks in again."

"You mean you're offering to ride shotgun for me?"

With a smile on her face she said, "If that's what it takes, I can even stay in the room with you if that would make you feel comfortable."

What was she saying, she was a lovely looking girl offering to keep watch over me. In my youth I would have taken her up on her offer. However, I was sure she was only joking. This now presented me with a dilemma, if I intended to perform at the opening gala at the Kilkenny Hotel later that day, I would have to find alternative accommodation, but this would mean having to stay well outside Kilkenny and travel in each evening. This didn't appeal to me, of course, but neither did getting attacked again. Although, with little Annie Oakley, keeping watch over me, it was unlikely.

"Just follow me, I want to show you the room."

What could I do? I followed her, halfway down the corridor we made a sharp right turn down the T shaped layout. The room was at the end of this corridor. Sophie opened the door and invited me in.

"Here we are, it's a lovely room, this is a king size bed, feel, it's nice and firm," she said as she patted it, then she walked across the deep pile carpet, "in here is your en suite with both shower and bath. For entertainment, you've got free Internet also satellite TV with all the sports channels. You'd be very comfortable in here, what do you think?"

"It's a massive improvement on last night."

"To be honest, I'm amazed you took that room, place should be condemned. Me Da used to store all his old crap in there, then Ma decided to earmark it as another bedroom but we never got around to furnishing it. Let's just say it's on her to do list."

"I have to say it was the worst room I've ever had to stay in, but I didn't have much option."

As I looked around there was an absence of religious artefacts. "This is a lovely room alright, you may have just persuaded me to change my mind."

"That's great, I'm delighted I'll be right next door in Ma's room, just dump your stuff here and we'll go and tell her you're staying."

I followed Sophie down to the kitchen, my eyes fixed on her long slim legs as she walked along like a model on the catwalk.

"Mrs. Donohugh, I've decided to accept your offer and stay in the Green room, I don't have time to move especially as I'm on stage at the gala opening tonight."

Sophie interjected, "I'm really looking forward to it, already got tickets for the show."

"Good, I hope you enjoy, I'm on at eight then other acts will take over. Not too sure at this stage who else is on the bill, I heard a couple of people had pulled out for family reasons."

"I'm delighted you're staying, once again I'm sorry about last night," said Mrs. Donohugh.

"I think we all got a bloody shock, hopefully Sergeant Byrne will be able to find out who the culprit was."

"I know he doesn't come across as Columbo, but he's not as dumb as he looks."

"Let's hope you're right."

"If you'll excuse me, I want to take a drive into the city centre to the ticket office and also to see where I'm appearing tonight."

"If you want I'll show you the way," said Sophie.

"If it's not putting you out."

"Not at all, just need you to stop at Clancy's for a couple of minutes, got to pick up my dress, it's on the way."

I knew there was a catch. We headed into the town and eventually found a parking spot, we walked miles around this historic old city, Sophie, gave a running commentary on the places of interest. We ventured into the Kilkenny Hotel, the venue for my first appearance. Afterwards, we visited the ticket office I took the opportunity to grab a program covering the three days, at least I would know who was on the same bill. Satisfied I'd seen enough of this beautiful old city, we made our way back to Sea View. We had just parked, when Sergeant Byrne drove in and parked his Garda car beside us.

"Mr. Dean, I have some news, we managed to find a couple of prints on the knife. Detective O'Sullivan ran them through Pulse the national database and he immediately got a match, a real villain called Pauric Mallon a prison escapee originally from Northern Ireland. He's wanted for a number of crimes in the Republic, murder, drug dealing and armed robbery. He was being taken from Portlaoise prison to court in Dublin last month, when he overpowered two security guards and escaped in their van. He overpowered and broke the neck of one officer then bit the nose off another when he tried to intervene. Apparently, he ate it. Can you believe it? The security guard is having reconstructive surgery to build him a new nose. He used

Get a Proper Job

the prison van to make good his escape, they found it abandoned in the Dublin Mountains. He's evaded capture ever since, despite a nationwide search. I've been in touch with Garda Headquarters in Dublin, advising them of the attack on you last night, there is already a squad on its way here. We've set up a number of roadblocks to monitor traffic, although by now he's probably long gone. He's known as the 'Fox' a real slippery and vicious individual. Anyway, you can breathe a sigh of relief, it's not your man Bonetti."

"I doubt I can do that, you're telling me the guy I thumped last night is a cannibal on your most wanted list."

The sergeant smiled, just then he got a call on his radio.

"The station tell me the first coach has arrived with backup, they will be here shortly. Afraid they will want to check the room where you were attacked, it will be treated as a crime scene, but hopefully it won't be for too long. The good thing is you'll have plenty of protection, you should be able sleep easy in your beds, that's assuming your still staying here."

"Yes, that was my intention but I don't feel that comfortable, not after what you've just told me"

The sergeant went inside to break the news to Mrs. Donohugh, not an ideal thing when you're trying to run a guesthouse. I wasn't sure if I was relieved or not, somebody tried to kill me who it turns out is as bad as Bonetti. I still couldn't get it out of my head that there may be a connection, after all he was in cahoots with a lot of nasty and dangerous people, but maybe I was grasping at straws linking the two of them. But why pick on me? Was it purely a random thing? Then I cast my mind back to Murphy's Guesthouse, this needed to be looked at further. I searched out Sergeant Byrne and told him I had concerns about the way I was dealt with, maybe she had something to do with it, and he agreed he would follow it up.

After showering and putting on my best bib and tucker, never really understood what that meant I assumed it referred to clothing, in any event I scrubbed up well, or so Sophie thought. She asked me for a lift, so I obliged, there was just one thing, we needed to stop on route to pick up two of her friends who were also attending the gala opening. With a full load we drove into the city centre and parked in my assigned spot. The girls wished me well then they headed into the nearest pub, I made my way into the hotel. I met a number of comedians I'd appeared with who were attending the festival, not all of them were performing on the opening night. I nervously waiting for my introduction, I just hoped I didn't seize up like I did for the TV broadcast.

"Good evening ladies and gentlemen, it's lovely to be here in Kilkenny. It's my first time in Ireland and I've had a killer welcome," if only they knew, "walked around the city this afternoon, saw some of the sites. I was standing by the river and there was a woman on the other bank so I called across, "How do I get on the other side."

"She looked a bit confused and shouted back."

"You are on the other side."

"When I was near the castle this blonde was walking towards me with her blouse open and I couldn't help but notice her left breast was hanging out. I thought I should tell her.

"Excuse me dear, I hope you don't mind me telling you, but you could be prosecuted for indecent exposure."

"Why."

"Your left breast is hanging out."

She looked down and screamed, "Oh my God, I left the baby on the bus again."

"I arrived into Ireland last night and I left my hotel for a short walk and a breath of fresh air. I noticed two

Get a Proper Job

drunks staggering towards one another. One says to the other in a slurred drunken voice pointing up into the sky, "Escuse me, is that the sun or the moon?"

The other guy replied, "Don't ask me, I don't live round here."

"I have ten kids, five of each, my wife said that was enough she didn't want anymore. I decided to get a vasectomy so she wouldn't get pregnant, but it doesn't work, all it does is change the colour of the baby.

"My wife was out the other day when her car suddenly just stopped, luckily she was just entering the forecourt to a garage and was able to push it the rest of the way. She told the mechanic it had died. He worked on it for about ten minutes.

"What's the story?" she asked.

"Just crap in the carburettor."

"How often do I have to do that?"

"She's not the best driver, has a very short attention span. She got caught for speeding. When the cop pulled alongside side her, she was knitting. He couldn't believe his eyes. He banged on her window. "Pull over, pull over." He shouted.

"No, it's a scarf."

"Two years ago she got stopped for speeding, the cop asked her for her licence.

"I wish you guys would get your bloody act together, yesterday you took my licence away and now you expect me to show it to you.

"I'm not a full time comedian, some of you might think I'm not a comedian at all, just thought I'd throw that in before any of you commented. Anyway, I work in the post office and last Christmas I found a letter addressed to God so, knowing it couldn't be delivered I opened it and I was so touched by what it said."

"Dear God

I am an eighty-three-year-old widow, living on a very small pension. Yesterday someone stole my purse it had

one hundred pounds in it. This was all the money I had until my next pension payment. Next Sunday is Christmas, and I had invited two friends over for dinner. Without that money I have nothing to buy food with. I have no family to turn to, you are my only hope.
Sincerely
Edna

"I felt so bad for this poor lady I organised a whip-round in the sorting office to see if we could help. By the time the envelope came back to me, there was ninety-six pounds in it so I sealed the envelope and sent it on to Edna. Just after Christmas, another letter arrived addressed to God, so I opened it and we all gathered round to read it.

"Dear God
How can I ever thank you for what you did for me? Because of your wonderful gift I was able to buy food and make a lovely dinner for my friends. By the way, there was four pounds missing, it's probably those thieving bastards in the post office.
Sincerely
Edna

After several more gags my twenty minutes were up, "Thank you very much Kilkenny, you've been a wonderful audience."

I introduced Dermot Wallace the next act and walked off to a great round of applause. I headed into the bar for a quick orange juice. Shortly afterwards, Sophie and her friends arrived.

"I thought there was no interval?"
"There isn't, but we needed a drop of gargle."
"Let me buy you girls a drink, what would you like?"
"Three pints of Harpic will do the trick," said Sophie.
"Harpic," I asked enquiringly.

Get a Proper Job

"Harp, you know the lager."

"Oh, now I see."

"You were brilliant, never laughed so much, that one about the two drunks is my favourite. Absolute classic I almost peed my pants, where are you on stage tomorrow?"

"The Kilford Arms."

"Got that girls, me Ma has six tickets courtesy of Sergeant Byrne so we can all go."

The girls demolished their pints and headed back into the show. "See you later alligator." then they all fell around laughing. I went back into show, from the rear watched some of the acts strut their stuff, there was quite a variety of performers, one guy in particular caught my eye, a young fellow called Maverick I assumed it was his stage name. If he wasn't already signed up, I would be interested in talking to him. I waited around until I got the opportunity to speak to him.

"Can I have a word, do I call you Maverick, or is that just your stage name?"

"Actually, my name is Billy Maverick, I just cut the Billy when I'm performing."

"Are you contracted to anyone?"

"No, I wish I was, bookings are hard to get I only got this gig because one guy pulled out at the last minute."

"Where are you from?"

"Bradford in Yorkshire, you?"

"Bury in Lancashire."

"I know it well, my sister married a chap from Bury has a plumbing business in Ramsbottom."

"Jesus, it's a small world, I'm from that neck of the woods. I have an agency in Bury; have over forty different acts on my books from singers to comedians to magicians. Look after them all get plenty of bookings, particularly lately with the upturn in the economy. If you're interested in talking about it further, come and see me I'll be back in Bury early next week, here's my card."

"Thanks, I'll definitely do that I've been looking for a while and seen a couple of people but they weren't interested."

"I can see with a bit of coaching you could be in demand, come and see me and we'll talk further."

"Thanks, I will you've made my day."

With that he raced off to tell some old dear I assumed was his mother. Shortly afterwards Sophie and her two friends spotted me.

"Carter, we're just going to Morrison's night club, you coming?"

"Not sure I should, I don't want you mother accusing me of keeping you out all night."

"I am twenty one you know."

"Actually I didn't, but I'll come with you for one, I don't want to be driving back to your place drunk."

Morrison's was as the girls put it, 'heaving' even getting served was no mean feat but the girls seemed quite well known, and within a couple of minutes were clasping their pints of as they called it, Harpic. In between swilling down drinks they spent time on the dance floor as the resident DJ belted out eardrum-shattering music. Sophie dragged me on the floor for a couple of dances, but I soon got tired and left them to it.

Just after two am the nightclub finished, sweaty and exhausted, we made our way back to my car. I dropped her two friends off on route, as we got near to Sea View up ahead I could see the blue flashing lights indicating there was a checkpoint. The Guard put his hand up for me to stop.

"Shit, what now I've been drinking, that's all I need."
"You haven't had that much."
"Enough."
"Don't worry, if it's a local you'll be ok."
I wound the window down. The Guard shone his

torch directly onto our faces.

"Good evening sir, can you tell me where you coming from?"

"Yes, I've been performing at the Comedy Cat Laughs festival."

"Where are you going to?"

"Back to my hotel Sea View to get some rest." I heard Sophie mutter under her breath, "hotel?"

"Do you own this vehicle?"

"No, it's a rental from Hertz at Dublin airport."

He walked around the car checking the tyres and the bodywork.

"Have you been drinking?"

"You kidding, I've been performing we're not allowed to drink?"

"Very well, on you go. Drive safely."

Breathing a sigh of relief, I pulled away.

"Fucking maggot, do you own this vehicle, did he think you'd stolen the fucking thing?"

"I suppose, Sophie, he was only doing his job."

"Typical redneck Dub asking anal questions, probably because every second car up there is nicked."

"I suppose he's on the lookout for this guy Mallon."

"He's definitely not a local, swallowed what you said about not drinking though, you fibber."

"Swallowed being the operative word."

Not long afterwards we pulled in front of Sea View, there was no evidence of police presence, Sophie took out her key to open the front door.

"Come down to the kitchen, I'll make us a cup of tea."

"Are you sure, I'd rather us get to bed."

"Easy tiger, let me have me caffeine first."

"Oh, Jesus, that came out all wrong, I didn't mean us going to bed, I meant me."

Sophie looked kind of hurt. "Would that be such a bad thing, us getting into bed?"

This was getting awkward I wasn't sure how to

handle the situation, "Look Sophie, you are a beautiful looking woman, but I'm years older than you it wouldn't be right."

"That's nonsense, this age thing is a load of bollocks, do you find me attractive?"

"Of course I'd be mad not to do, it's just." I paused. Before I said anything else she said, "Very well, no further discussion needed, sup your tea and hold onto your hat cowboy."

Chapter Nineteen

Just after six thirty I woke up, when I looked at the empty pillow beside me, I began to think I'd dreamt the previous night. Then I remembered, Sophie had to rise early to help her mother prepare breakfast for the other guests. I started to feel guilty, I hadn't been with a woman since Cleo and had the feeling I'd betrayed her. The next thing the door opened.

"Brought you a cup of tea, tiger, thought after last night you need some sustenance."

She sat down on the edge of the bed and looked at me, "How long is it since you were with a woman?"

I started to feel uncomfortable, even more guilty now. "Why did it show?"

"You kidding, you were a wonderfully energetic lover, never experienced anything quite like it, but I've only had one boyfriend and he buggered off as soon as he got what he wanted."

"Was that long ago?"

"Over a year, I've been celibate since then."

"That is until last night, what made you choose me?"

"Afraid I was drunk as well as desperate." she said with a sad look on her face.

"Thanks a bunch Sophie, that really does my ego a power of good."

"I'm only joking, you're so easy to wind up. But the reason is, the minute I saw you I got the feeling there was a spark between us, and don't tell me you didn't feel the same."

"I have to admit I liked what I saw, but it's going a little bit too fast don't you think."

"At your age Carter, I think you need to move more quickly, you don't know how long you've got."

"I know, got my bus pass last month, although I haven't used it yet."

"Really."

"Now who's so easy to wind up?"

"Well, can we carry on seeing one another, what do you say?"

"Look, Sophie, last night was wonderful what I remember of it, what's your mother going to say?"

"Don't worry about her, she's very broad minded."

"Even so, I'm so much older than you. I do find you very attractive and you have a lovely personality."

"Why do I have the feeling there's a but coming?"

"We've only just met, I feel I've taken advantage of you, it's not right."

"I think it was me who took advantage of you. Look Carter, don't beat yourself up over last night, if you feel outside of your comfort zone, I understand, we can take it slowly, but I really would like to keep seeing you."

"And how's this going to work, if we keep seeing one another, I'm in the UK and you're over here, plus your mother needs you."

"I'm experienced in office work, typing, computers, book keeping I could work in your office. Failing that, you could sign me up as a performer, I'm a champion Irish dancer as well as being a crack shot with a twelve bore."

I had to admire her enthusiasm. "Are you really a champion dancer?"

"I'll show you my medals if you want, I think I've got over sixty from all over the country, put those with my trophies from trap shooting, I have to be the most decorated woman in Ireland."

This girl was so different and refreshing, the only person of the opposite sex since Cleo that I was remotely attracted to, and yet, totally opposite in character.

"Don't take too long to make your mind up, Carter,

boys are queuing around the block to get into my pants."

At this point I just broke down laughing. "Oh, Sophie, you're such a character, you should be on the stage."

"Does that mean your going to sign me up?"

"I don't know about that, but taking everything into consideration, I think I'd like to get to know you better."

"Good, I'm fucking delighted, if you'll excuse the expression, we'll work out the fine details later. Better get back to the kitchen, Mr. Paulson will be wanting his sausage, I've already had mine," she said, giving me a wink.

I think I'm in love again; this girl is such a beautiful refreshing person with the looks and personality to go with it. I've never heard a woman use such colourful language before, the last thing you'd expect to come out of this angelic mouth; she made the word bollocks sound sensual. Even so, there were problems in taking it further, not least her mother who I wasn't looking forward to meeting at breakfast.

Sergeant Byrne had been doing some investigating at Mrs. Murphy's Guesthouse, what he discovered was highly significant and warranted further discussion so she was taken down to the station for more talks.

"Morning Mr. Dean, full Irish OK? Sophie tells me you were great last night, one hell of a performer."

Jesus, what do I say to that, I looked over at Sophie and she was doubled up laughing?

"Yes it went very well, hope I perform as well tonight."

At this point, the two of them were in hysterics; the other diners were probably wondering what the hell we'd been drinking. Shortly after I finished breakfast, Sergeant Mick Byrne arrived at the guesthouse.

"Morning Mr. Dean, can we have a chat?"

"Sure, what's on your mind?" Mrs. Donohugh guided

us into the privacy of the kitchen where the sergeant sat down and was given the mandatory cup of tea.

"I had a talk with Mrs. Murphy, an old friend of ours, we've had her in before because of her Republican connections. Anyway, when I broached the subject of your booking, she initially said it was just an honest mistake. However, when I pressed her further, she eventually admitted, the guy who made the original booking, Albert Bonetti, had cancelled it. Your old friend, I believe. He told her you wouldn't need the room; she wasn't concerned as there was a huge demand with over thirty thousand looking for accommodation in the county. She's still in custody because we discovered a family link between her and Pauric Mallon."

Jesus, this is just unbelievable, I half suspected Bonetti was behind the cancellation, but I never thought we'd prove it. Was Mallon instructed to kill me; there's no doubt in my mind he was? When will this bastard ever give up, obviously not until I was dead?

"We still have her in custody because of her association with Mallon, we believe she was responsible for sending him down here. At this stage we don't know if it was at the behest of your friend or, something else."

"Oh, there's no doubt in my mind he was behind it."

"We can't be one hundred percent sure at this stage, but we're working on it."

"Why not just honour the original booking and eliminate me there?"

"Probably wanted to avoid the bad publicity it would bring."

"It's already in the press, Mrs. Donohugh says two reporters were here and spent a good portion of yesterday trying to find out exactly what happened the night before."

Sergeant Byrne looked at Mrs. Donohugh. "Vera, I'd appreciate it if you'd try and avoid giving the press any details, it might just compromise our search for Mallon."

"We never told them feckers anything, whatever's in the papers it probably came from your lot, or the guys sent down from Dublin, I saw them in discussion for quite a while, but it certainly didn't come from us."

Vera looked annoyed at the suggestion she was responsible.

"Thanks, Vera, I know I can count on you, we don't need any added complications because it's developing into something a lot more complex than first appeared. We've still got Murphy in custody, I know I can tell you in confidence; it appears this lady has been dealing in drugs. One of her suppliers is her wait for it her brother in-law Mallon. We had no idea they were connected by marriage. Hard to imagine isn't it, this old lady dispensing pills like sweets? We got a search warrant and we've found loads of the stuff, they're still searching her premises and could be there a while."

This was becoming surreal; Bonetti's reach was long and unrelenting. I never thought when I set off for Ireland, I'd be viciously attacked, but there was no doubt in my mind it came as a direct order from Bonetti.

After this briefing, the sergeant left but promised to keep us updated. To be honest, I couldn't wait to get back to Bury; I was well outside my normal routine and feeling vulnerable. The only good thing about this trip was meeting Sophie but I wasn't sure how that was going to work out, if at all.

"I just can't believe Gloria Murphy has been dealing in drugs, her husband must be turning in his grave, he was the sacristan in St Mary's for twenty years, he'd be horrified," said Vera.

"I'm afraid they're everywhere, it's at epidemic proportions, certainly in the UK. This guy Bonetti is a major player, connected to some really bad people."

"You're still going to perform tonight at the Kilford Arms tonight aren't you?" asked Sophie.

"Yes, I am, unless something else crops up."

Then my mobile rang and I could see it was Bob.

"Morning Bob, everything OK?"

"Afraid not, hope you're sitting down?"

I wasn't looking forward to what was coming next.

"Somebody set fire to the offices in the early hours of this morning, there's a massive amount of damage. I got a call just after two to say smoke was seen coming out at the back of the building. By the time I got in, the building was well on fire with three appliances in attendance. It appears a guy was seen pouring what they think was petrol on the back door near to the kitchen; he lit it and ran off. The building is almost totally gutted so I'm afraid we'll need to look for other premises."

I was stunned, "Jesus, what next, has to be Bonetti again, what about our records?"

"Fortunately, I have everything on computer at my apartment from when I was working from home, there might be the odd document missing but nothing that will compromise running the business."

"That's great, a stroke of luck you did that."

"How's the festival going?"

"I'll tell you all about when I get home, I'm going to get the first flight back to Manchester."

"Is the festival over?"

"No, but I can't leave you to sort out the mess."

"You can't do an awful lot here, I'll contact all the staff and bring them up to date. Obviously, the office telephones are out of action but I've been able to get all the calls directed to my cell. I can carry on working from my apartment until we find somewhere. Why don't you stay over there until the festival is finished I can look for alternative accommodation? I've already been onto the Royal Hotel about renting a suite or a room and they're due to get back to me, but they didn't turn it down flat."

"Are you sure, I don't like leaving you and Denya to deal with this by yourselves?"

"Look, Carter, it's not a problem, all the bookings for the next week are taken care of, everyone knows where they're appearing plus we can deal with new enquiries from my home, Denya is very capable so we will be fine."

"OK, if you're sure, but if you need me holler and I'll be on the first flight back."

"Roger, now carry on and don't worry."

"Is there a problem?" asked Sophie.

"You could say that, somebody set fire to our offices during the early hours, totally destroyed them, there is no doubt Bonetti is behind it. We only rented the building so we have to find somewhere else in a hurry. I was going to return home to deal with it."

"Please don't do that Carter," said Sophie, "we're all coming to see you tonight."

"Don't worry I'm staying, Bob my manager says he will take care of things, so I've decided to remain on here for the rest of the week."

"That's great, this morning after I've finished helping me Ma, I want to take a drive with you and I'll show you the sights."

"OK, I'll be in my room I just need to go over my routine for tonight, can't repeat any gags from last night."

About mid morning, Sophie, and I left the guest-house and set off on our excursion. We drove for a while, chatted about all kinds of things, from her early childhood and education, and how her father had always encouraged her in Irish dancing. He showed her how to use a shotgun, she became an expert at clay pigeon shooting winning many competitions, at one stage was considered for the Irish Olympic team. She talked about the heartache when he passed away suddenly, never been ill a day in his life then one morning just dropped dead with a massive heart attack. He had been her rock and she missed him terribly.

Eventually, we parked the car and went for a walk in the Castlemorris grounds; it was a nice warm day as we walked hand in hand for what seemed hours. I told her about my childhood, my desire to become a comedian, some of the experiences I'd encountered as I tried to fill my dream. I didn't dwell on Fat Albert; I wanted this to be a fun day. We laughed a lot, kissed a lot by the time we got back to the car, I knew this girl was something special. She was extremely intelligent, with a wicked sense of humour; above all she was stunning looking.

"Tell me this Sophie, how come you're still single, I can't believe you haven't been snapped up before now?"

"If you've been hurt like I was, you don't want to repeat the exercise. When I first met Tommy Fitzpatrick, I thought he was the one, tall, blond good looking, and a great Irish dancer. We kept bumping into one another as we both competed around the country; slowly we got to know one another. We became very close and the relationship developed. Anyway, he told me he loved me, one thing led to another and I lost my virginity to him. Then after a few months he cleared off, just used me for what he could get. I gave in to him, something I vowed I'd never do until I got married. As a result there hasn't been any serious relationship since, nor have I had any desire for one, that is until I met you."

"You mean I had that much of an impact on you."

"Well, you are a bit of a looker aren't you?"

"Nobody's ever called me a looker before, sure you've not been on the sauce?"

"When you first came to the door, I liked what I saw, tall blond haired guys always appealed to me."

"I think it's more grey than blond."

"Then there's the deep blue eyes, and square jaw, want me to go on?"

"Stop Sophie, you're beginning to embarrass me."

"So now you know what I like about you, what are my good points?"

Get a Proper Job

"Still trying to find some, but not having much luck."

"Well, you can feckoff back to England, you Limey toss pot."

"Oh, Sophie, you are such a colourful character, but an absolute vision of beauty. Apart from your obvious stunning good looks and your colourful language you're such fun to be with. I know we've only known one another a short time but you're really having an effect on me, in a good way. What am I going to do when it comes time to leave?"

"I'm hoping you'll stay, surely you could run your business from over here."

"It wouldn't work, all the bookings are in the UK, all my entertainers are based there, it would be much easier if you came over to me."

"And do what precisely?"

"Come and work with me, you say you've office experience, or there could well be work as an Irish dancer."

"Then what, if I made that commitment, what's in the future for me?"

"Nobody can predict the future, Sophie, but I won't take advantage of you, it's not my style. All I can say is I made the commitment to marry someone once before, but it was cruelly taken away. I'm not proposing marriage, that would be absolutely insane at this stage, but if you mean what you say we could give it a try and see how things go. However, one thing that bothers me is your mother, how would she cope on her own?"

"She'd be OK, Florence her friend could take over from me she's done it before, I was only helping Ma temporarily in between jobs, it wasn't a permanent thing."

"I'll be returning to the UK after the festival is over, give it plenty of thought and if you want to come over and give it a try, I will look after you. I've got a lovely new apartment in Bury and you would be well paid for whatever job you do. I'm sure there would be a demand for a dancer in some of the Irish clubs that I'm connected with. I could profile you as a champion Irish dancer and I'm sure you'd get plenty of bookings plus you'd be getting well paid, that's if you want to do. Anyway, let's go and get some lunch I'm starving."

We drove to the Foodworks Brasserie and had a lovely lunch, after this we did a very interesting tour of the Smithwick's Brewery, and sampled their lovely ale, this left just enough time to get back to the guest-house and have a short rest before the show at the Kilford Arms. The next two venues were a hit, and I thoroughly enjoyed performing in this beautiful historic city, why wouldn't I, after all I had my own fan club? The audiences were fantastic and I met a number of fresh young comedians, some of them I asked to get in touch with me back in the UK.

Sophie and I and continued to get to know one another, each hour we spent together we seemed to be cementing our relationship stronger. Sergeant Byrne had nothing further to report; apart from Gloria Murphy had been charged with possession of drugs. She was still being held in custody because of her reported connection to Pauric Mallon. No link to Bonetti was established, but deep down I knew there was one.

Chapter Twenty

It was time to return home to the UK and I really wasn't looking forward to it, apart from leaving Sophie behind, there was the task of finding new offices. Bob had been in touch saying the owners of the building intended to rebuild it, just as soon as was possible. The police had established it was a deliberate act of arson but as yet, no one had been apprehended for it. Not having seen the building up close, only a clip from Bob's mobile phone, it wouldn't be a straightforward task. Units on either side had also been affected, they would probably need stabilising, in short, it could take weeks for removing the debris, shoring up either side before they could even think about rebuilding. I wasn't sure how we were fixed contractually with our existing lease, or the insurance implications but we're only required to insure our contents not the building. Maybe the owners wouldn't want us to continue, for the risk of a repeat fire, time would tell.

After breakfast, I gathered my bag and went to pay my bill and leave Sea View, never did ask why or who christened it that.

"Thank very much for everything, Mrs. Donohugh."

"It's Vera, after all, you're almost family now," she said with a smile on her face.

"I'm sure we'll be meeting again, and Sophie what can I say, it been an absolute pleasure meeting you?"

"You're not getting rid of me that quick, I'm coming to the airport to see you off."

"There's no need to do that, how are you going to get back?"

"I'll walk."

"You can't, that's crazy."

"As if, ... there are such things as buses you know."

"Even so, it's putting you out."

"Nonsense, I want to come, see you later Ma."

With that, she grabbed hold of my arm and escorted me to the car. The journey to the airport was a mixture of sadness and laughter, as we talked endlessly, neither one of us wanting the journey to end. As we approached the airport I followed the signs and returned the car to the Hertz parking lot, then we caught the shuttle bus to the airport.

"Guess this is where we say goodbye, I'll call you every day I promise."

"If you don't there'll be trouble."

"As soon as we've sorted our office problem out and things get back to normal, I'll send you a ticket to come over then you'll have my undivided attention."

"Promise."

"Of course I do, can't envisage life without you now, it's been an amazing few days."

At this point, Sophie broke, down floods of tears ran down her angelic face,

"Look what you've done you Limey bastard, no man has ever made me do that before."

"Come on Sophie, don't cry you're making me feel bad."

"Sorry, they're just crocodile tears, can't wait to see the back of you."

"That's better, that's more like you."

We had one last long embrace, and then I headed in through security, feeling bad that I'd left this poor girl to make the two and a half hour bus journey back home.

I arrived back in Manchester just after lunch, after retrieving my car from the parking lot I made my way to Bury. The first thing I did when I got there, was to take a drive over to our offices, it was utter devastation. Workers were just in the process of erecting braces to support the existing walls. As I walked around the building there was still a strong smell from the fire, there was nothing identifiable in the rubble, apart from a couple of metal filing cabinets bent and broken minus their contents. It was a gut-wrenching scene, it made my blood boil. If I get my hands on the little retard that did this I'll tear him limb from limb. As soon as I got back to my apartment, I contacted Bob and asked him to come over.

"Hi, Bob, come on in, how are you?"

"Great, had some success looking for office space. I've found a two-story building on Manchester road, newly decorated and fitted our as offices. They are prepared to offer it as a six or twelve month rental, the guy I spoke with said if they got the right offer they'd be prepared to sell. I think you'll like it, for an added bonus there is a security guard there looking after the area it's in a gated community, so they don't left any riffraff in. How did things go in Ireland?"

"Very well, apart from nearly getting stabbed to death on the first night it was great."

"Jesus, what happened?"

"Bonetti was behind it, he cancelled my booking at the guesthouse and I was diverted to another place, then this head-case stormed into my bedroom in the early hours with a bloody massive knife and tried to stab me. It was a setup so this guy could get at me. But, the training we had came in handy, I was able to disarm him, unfortunately he got away. Prints on the knife showed it was a guy called Pauric Mallon. The Irish police were able to establish he was connected to Murphy's guesthouse and was supplying drugs to this landlady. The guy is Ireland's most wanted, a real villain, murder, drugs you name it, this bloke's done it. Fat Albert was probably supplying him so you can see he spread his net far and wide.

"My God, what next, the sooner someone puts a bullet through Bonetti's head the better. It's unbelievable how far this guy will go."

"Apart from this diversion, the comedy festival was brilliant, saw some great talent and asked a couple of people to get in touch with a view to signing them up. Also met a lovely young lady called Sophie, she will be coming over just as soon as we get organised, she's a champion Irish dancer."

"Good, we don't have anyone like that on our books, we keep being asked for Riverdance style acts. Anyway, regarding the fire, the insurance company's assessor was out first thing this morning and he's happy enough with my figure for the loss of contents destroyed in the fire. Said we should have a cheque within a couple of weeks. It was just fortunate I had all the records on my PC at home so I think we'll be fine. Things like the cheque book and print outs were destroyed along with your certificates and plaques on the wall, but the records can be reprinted out sadly, your comedy awards are a charred relic of their former glory."

"When could we take possession of the offices?"

"Straight away if you like, we could take a look first thing in the morning, if you're in agreement we can stop by their office and sign the contract."

The following morning, we took a drive over to the new office and I was pleasantly surprised with what I saw. With very little effort we could be up and running almost immediately. The location was only five kilometres from our old office it consisted of six offices including a boardroom more space than we would ever need, also a fully fitted kitchen and toilets spread over two floors. I decided to take the plunge, so we signed the contract for six months then arranged to wire three months rent in advance. There was an option to lease for a further six months, but I wasn't sure how contractually we were fixed on our current agreement.

"Come on, Bob, I'll buy you lunch by way of a celebration, you can then bring me up to speed on

Get a Proper Job

whatever else has been happening."

Later that day as promised, I rang Sophie again. She was missing me already. We talked for hours as we discussed our plans for the future.

Sergeant Byrne and his team had found a huge stash of drugs in the grounds of Mrs. Murphy's guesthouse. In stables at the rear, they discovered two thousand ecstasy pills, twenty-five kilos of pure cocaine plus about twenty kilos of heroine. Her son was arrested trying to leave the property; they caught him in possession of a large quantity of cocaine. The search was ongoing and it was expected to yield significantly more drugs in other outbuildings. The two of them were still in custody as they were considered a flight risk.

Mallon was still at large but the net was closing in, then word came in that he'd hijacked a high performance sports car from outside the Shelbourne Hotel in Dublin. A tracking device fitted to the vehicle indicated he was racing towards the border into Northern Ireland. This man was a killer, every effort had to be made to stop him. Armed police were dispatched to intercept him. He was injured when two Gardai opened fire at him when he refused to stop at a roadblock just outside of Dundalk. He rammed their squad car injuring one of the Guards seriously, before he sped away.

Police on both sides of the Irish border were now in the hunt for him. Shortly after 11:00pm he was intercepted just over the border into Northern Ireland outside of the town of Newry. The tyres on the stolen sports car were shot out in an effort to bring the vehicle to a stop, but it raced along for several hundred metres, showers of sparks coming off the bare metal rims like four giant Catherine wheels. Eventually, the car spluttered to a stop and Mallon jumped out, he then retrieved a Kalashnikov rifle from the car and opened fire on police officers. However, superior returning firepower coming from several sources on either side of the road meant his run was over. He died in a hail of gunfire; police on the island of Ireland would breathe a sigh of relief that this man was no longer a threat.

I contacted Alistair and brought him up to date on everything that had happened on my trip to Ireland. Bob had already told him about the fire, sadly he couldn't believe about the attack and the drug connection, but was delighted when I told him about Sophie and that it appeared I was moving on with my life.

After a couple of weeks, we were firmly installed in our new offices; Denya and Bob quickly had systems in place to ensure things ran smoothly. We were all very conscious that Fat Albert still posed a huge threat, he seemed to have a charmed life evading capture both in the UK and on the continent. All bookings were scrutinised to make absolutely sure they were genuine; we didn't want a repeat performance of the Willows incident. Nobody was allowed into the office complex without an appointment, all visitors had to produce ID before the security guard allowed them in. This might seem over the top to some, but in view of past incidents I was happy this arrangement was in place. I was in daily contact with Sophie, she was desperate to come to England, but after speaking with Alistair I asked her to delay it for a short while. He advised me that she could well be a target, nothing could be ruled out until this madman was apprehended. Convincing her however, was another matter, assuring her I was concerned for her safety and not just having a change of mind about our relationship.

It was mid August when the trial of Porter commenced at Manchester Crown Court, it soon became apparent that he was only one of a large group who'd been

Get a Proper Job

peddling their misery. He'd been offered a deal of a lighter sentence for his full cooperation and disclosure of those involved. A lot of people would be quaking in their shoes not knowing what he would reveal.

Day four of the trial, Porter was in a security van being driven from Strangeways Prison on route to court, when a large Volvo tipper truck raced out of a side street ramming the prison van with such force it turned it on its side.

Three men jumped out of the Volvo, two of them armed with cutting equipment that consisted of a chain saw and an industrial angle grinder, they climbed on top of the van, and proceeded to cut the doors. The third man raced to the cab, he fired several shots from a high-powered rifle through the toughened glass. Eventually, the glass gave way; the driver and his associate were hit in the chest. Within a few minutes, the inner cell door that housed Porter was cut through, he thought he was being released but his joy was short lived because they fired at least twenty shots into his body. Then they climbed out of the van and the three of them jumped into a waiting Mercedes that was driven off at high speed. The whole operation lasted only minutes and was witnessed by dozens of shocked early morning onlookers, not something they normally see on their way to work. By the time the police and ambulance arrived, the attackers were long gone. They took statements from several people who had witnessed the incident. No doubt a large number of people, some in the police force, would be breathing a huge sigh of relief.

I was in our new offices when Alistair rang me, "Hi Carter, it's just been announced that Porter has been assassinated on his way to court."

"Jesus, I don't know whether to laugh or cry, how did it happen?"

"Prison van was ambushed after leaving Strangeways

prison and he was shot dead, along with two officers."

"Unbelievable, in a supposedly civilised society that this can be allowed to happen, it's get more like Kabul every day."

"Talking to colleagues, revelations that have come out so far in the trial have fingered a load of people, some in the police service, two judges and a politician so there was no doubt this was done to silence him. Of course he'd also implicated Fat Albert as the source of the drugs, no love lost there. But it's evident a number of people wanted him silenced. It's endless, one thing after another but it seems like a lot of the major players have been rounded up apart from Fat Albert that is."

"Will he ever be caught? I ask myself that question all the time, each revelation that comes out makes it more and more difficult for me to relate to the bloke I once knew, just goes to show how wrong you can be about people."

"I don't think there's any doubt he will eventually be caught Carter, no man can keep getting away the way he has, sooner or later his luck will run out."

"I admire your optimism Alistair, but this guy doesn't operate on luck he's the Devil's disciple."

The death of Porter was a major talking point, politicians in parliament were asking serious questions about the security services that this assassination had been allowed to happen, as a result security was stepped up on the transfer of prisoners to and from court.

The revelation that a senior labour politician had been arrested for his involvement in drugs added to the frenzy sweeping parliament. Then came the breaking news, that prints found on the prison escort van belonged to Albert Bonetti, other prints confirmed that Victor Noble and Glen Todd well known to the authorities for their involvement in a range of crimes took part in this audacious assassination. It was imperative that these criminals were hunted down; as a result, a number of properties associated with these people were raided. Pressure was the watchword, hound them until they make a slip or other underworld characters get so fed up with the constant harassment it impacted on their ability to do business to the point they'd tip the police off as to their whereabouts, that was the hope. Early morning raids occurred daily, as police continued this policy of harassment. It worked, three weeks after the assassination of Porter; police received a tipoff that Bonetti, Todd, and Noble were lying low in a cottage near Brighton. Heavily armed police were dispatched to the location and surrounded the building; a loud hailer was used advising of an armed police presence. They refused to come out; eventually teargas was fired in through the windows to flush them out. A violent gun battle ensued, before first Noble was shot dead as he ran from the building, then Todd was shot dead as he raced upstairs into an attic. Room by room, the building was searched but there was no sign of Bonetti.

The fact that Mallon had been caught and eliminated was of great satisfaction to me, one by one associates of Fat Albert were being rounded up. By mid October I thought it was time that Sophie came over, against the advice of Alistair I might add. She was delighted of course. I collected her from Manchester airport then moved her into my apartment in Bury. Over the coming weeks we were inseparable, she came into the office every day and familiarised herself with the artists and bookings. At night we resumed our love making, losing several kilos of weight in the process. I chaperoned her everywhere, never let her out of my sight. After two months I knew she was the one for me so asked her to marry me, thankfully, she said yes. Alistair agreed to be my best man, the wedding would be held in Ireland at St. Mary's church in Kilkenny early in the New Year.

Sophie became more and more involved with the running of the business and eventually secured a booking to perform her dancing skills at the Portland in Wigan, an up-market club.

The night of her first performance in the UK was upon us; Sophie was really looking forward to it. She had a beautifully ornate dress with intricate Celtic designs embroidered on it. She also had with her several pairs of shoes for the various step dances she would be doing like jigs and reels. The music to accompany her dancing was provided by a group called The Blarney Gold, they consisted of a fiddle player, a bodhran player a kind of drum, a tin whistle player and a lady playing the uilleann pipes, a form of bagpipe. The club was packed to capacity; they all seemed to be enjoying the different acts that had been booked for their entertainment.

Just after nine, Sophie appeared on stage looking majestic, as soon as the music started she went into her routine, the hairs on the back of my neck stood up, I'd never seen or heard anything like it. As the hard tips and heels on her shoes hit the stage, they made a loud percussion noise, the movement of her feet was mesmerising straight out of Riverdance. It seemed effortless for her as she skipped and danced around the stage, she was amazing.

She wowed the audience with an array of different dances, pausing only for a brief second whilst she changed into her soft shoes to complete a series of jigs and reels. When she eventually finished, the audience got to their feet and gave her standing ovation. This girl was good; the audience loved her shouting for more and Sophie duly obliged performing two more dances.

I met her backstage. "You were simply amazing, and the audience loved you, what an ovation you got."

"Afraid I was a bit rusty, haven't danced for a while, if my Da was alive he'd have been very critical."

"Nonsense, you were simply fantastic, bet they've never seen anything like that before. What did you think of your backing group?"

"Yes, I thought they were good, why?"

"They don't have a manager so I've asked them to come in and see me, I think the two of you could be good, one compliments the other."

"Yes, I think you're right, it was like we'd been performing together for years."

After she'd changed her clothes, we left the club, but not before the manager heaped high praise on her and made a booking for St.Patrick's day the following year. Then we headed for home after a job well done, when we got outside the weather was particularly nasty with heavy rain and poor visibility.

As we approached the outskirts of Bury, a black four by four overtook my Mercedes on a blind bend, and then suddenly it pulled directly in front of me and braked hard. This was deliberate; as I stamped on the brakes I lost control of the car on the wet surface and went into a skid, slamming into the rear of the Range Rover. This activated the airbags; I couldn't see where I was going until we came to a stop about a hundred metres further on. Several seconds passed as I gathered my thoughts.

"Are you OK, Sophie?"

"I think so but my ankle hurts, are you OK, what was that idiot thinking it seemed he did that on purpose?"

"Yes I'm fine, but you're right that was no accident."

"You stay here while I go and investigate."

When I got out of the car and looked back, the Range Rover was embedded in a wall, the rear was sticking out into the road with one of the hazard light flashing, steam was coming from the engine that appeared to be still running. Pieces of plastic and metal were strewn around the road, glass was everywhere, but as I got close I could see there was no one in the vehicle.

By now cars were stopping to investigate, I called the police and ambulance because whoever was in the Range Rover had to be injured. I walked around looking for the driver but they were nowhere to be found, then as I approached a row of bushes a tall figure stood up from behind them and staggered towards me, at that point I realised it was that bastard Bonetti, I should have known!

He had a gun in his hand; he raised the pistol and fired two shots. Thankfully they missed me, he pressed the trigger again, but it appeared the gun had jammed. Before he could fire again, I raced towards him, striking him as hard as I could in the throat with my fist. He stood upright coughing and gasping for breath, then I brought the flat of my hand up striking him at the base of his nose tearing it from his face. I gave him two more hard punches to his throat, each one in revenge for the terrible things he'd inflicted on Cleo.

I repeatedly hit him until he dropped to his knees. I got hold of his head and gave it a sharp twist until I heard his neck crack. I let go of his lifeless body and he slumped to the ground. At last I had avenged every evil thing he had done to Cleo and myself. I don't know whether I was relieved or not, I've never taken a life before but at least my nightmare was finally over.

As I turned and walked back to my car, people were attending to someone on the ground. Then as I got closer I realised it was Sophie. Oh, sweet Jesus, what's happened, I had told her to stay in the car, I didn't realise she'd followed me? As I raced up to her, a lady was attending to her.

"I'm a nurse, she's been shot in the chest, her pulse is very week, and she's bleeding quite heavily. Do you know her?"

"Yes, it's Sophie she's my fiancée." I knelt down beside her and held her hand, "It's OK Sophie, you're going to be alright." She was unconscious and looked terrible, it was all my fault, I should have listened to Alistair. Even till the very end Fat Albert had been able to inflict the worst possible trauma. She must have been standing directly behind me when Bonetti fired. I cradled her head in my arms, talking to her, telling her she was going to be fine but deep down I knew she wasn't.

Within five minutes the police and ambulance arrived, Sophie was placed on a stretcher and once they got her into the ambulance they started to work on her to monitor her vital signs. They inserted a drip into her arm to replace some of the fluid she was losing, hooked her up to a heart monitor, and placed an oxygen mask on her. Eventually, when she was stable they closed the doors and got ready to take her to Fairfield Hospital, I wanted to go with her but the police insisted I answer some questions. I was in shock this was so cruel, what would I tell her mother?

"I'm Sergeant Dave Hilton of the traffic police, are you OK?"

"A bit shaken, other than that lucky to be alive."

"What's your name?"

"It's Carter Dean."

"Can you tell me exactly what happened, Mr. Dean?"

"I'll try, I was driving home with my fiancée Sophie Donohugh, when the Range Rover that's embedded in the wall overtook us on that bend, then he pulled straight in front of me and slammed his anchors on deliberately. I braked hard but on the wet surface I couldn't stop even with ABS. I skidded and ran in the back of him, that's my Mercedes up the road. When I walked back to investigate, and find out what the hell he was playing at, the driver had got out of the car and was hiding in bushes. He then came out and fired two shots at me, I didn't realise my fiancée was standing behind me and she was hit in the chest. Anyway, I know this chap, he's called Bonetti wanted for at least twelve murders and responsible for the recent attack on the prison van leaving Strangeways."

"Where is he now?"

"In Hell I hope, he's lying near those bushes, after he'd fired two shots at me I wasn't prepared to stand there and get shot at again, so I hit him, several times in fact. Don't know if he's dead or not, to be honest I don't give a flying fuck. It doesn't look like my fiancée will make it thanks to this evil swine."

"Have you been drinking?"

"No, but right now I could do with one."

"I'm required by law to ask you to take a breath test, are you OK with that?"

"Of course."

The sergeant got his kit from the car and I was asked to blow on the tube, the device didn't detect any alcohol.

"That's fine, it's negative."

"Can you just sit in that police car whilst I investigate this further?"

"No problem." The sergeant and another officer went back to where Bonetti was lying and retrieved the firearm. Within minutes four more police cars and a scenes of crimes van arrived and the road was sealed off to all other traffic. Large arc lights were positioned around the site, a tent was erected over the body then the area was taped off and treated as a secure crime scene. Two separate witnesses, who'd waited patiently to speak with the police, confirmed that the Range Rover had driven in a dangerous and erratic manner, it had caused the accident deliberately. They saw Bonetti emerge from the bushes shooting at me, striking Sophie in the chest, that I had acted in self-defence when I disarmed him. I was grateful that these witnesses had been able to corroborate my version of events.

"Mr. Dean, I gather you are concerned about your fiancée and would like to get to Fairfield Hospital, we

Get a Proper Job

will want to speak to you again of course, but for the moment you are free to go."

"Thank you, do you have any idea how my fiancée is?"

"I'm sorry I don't."

"I don't suppose there's any chance of a lift is there, I would assume my car has to remain where it is for the time being, although looking at the front of it it's hardly driveable?"

"Thompson, can you give this gentleman a lift to Fairfield hospital?"

The officer acknowledged the request.

"That's very kind of you."

"Not a problem, he's going back to the station and it's on his route."

I immediately phoned Alistair and brought him up to date with the demise of Bonetti but that he had shot Sophie as a parting gesture, he said he'd meet me at the hospital...again.

"What can I say, Carter, that's shocking bad luck, is there any word on her condition?"

"They've removed the two bullets one from her chest the other from her upper arm, she's out of theatre but still in a bad way, they've moved her into intensive care whilst they monitor her, but they don't put her recovery rate at any better than fifty-fifty."

"I've a feeling she'll make it, seemed a feisty young woman to me."

"I hope you're right, we'd made such plans for our future after losing Cleo I never thought I'd find another person until I met Sophie."

"So, Bonetti is dead, it's hard to believe after everything that's happened?"

"Yes, at last, he came at me firing a pistol, missed me but hit Sophie. I punched him in the throat several times, they tell me I severed his windpipe; broke his nose then snapped his neck. Don't know whether that constitutes self defence, but too be honest, I don't give a fuck after the pain he's inflicted on others and myself. Thankfully, there were two witnesses who saw the whole thing and they have given their statements to the police."

"I don't think I'd worry too much about that, Carter, I don't think CPS will even think there's a case to answer, it was self defence in my book. This lunatic has been causing havoc for years, you've done the nation a huge favour getting rid of him."

"Not sure what to do about her mother though, do you think I should call her now and let her know?"

"Maybe you should wait until morning, she can't do anything before then and you might have better news."

Every few minutes I checked with nurse's station but there was no change in her condition, then, just after 5:00am all hell broke loose, people were scurrying around doctors coming and going into intensive care. At 6:00am a doctor came out to see me. I knew this wasn't good news.

"Mr. Dean I'm afraid your fiancée suffered a setback. We had successfully removed the bullet from her upper arm and the one deep inside her chest. We were happy with what we'd achieved and she seamed quite stable, when suddenly, and unexpectedly she went into cardiac arrest. We were eventually able to restart her heart, unfortunately, because of the length of time this took; her brain would have been starved of oxygen. As a result we don't know at this time if there will be any permanent damage. She is stable now and she will be closely monitored, all we can do is to hope that she will regain consciousness and have suffered no ill effects as a result. You can go in and see her for a short while."

"Thank you doctor."

As I walked into intensive care I was numb, when I saw her my heart sank, she was ashen faced, breathing through a ventilator, various drips, and pipes were attached to her body and machines monitored her vital functions. What had I done, Alistair was right when he advised me to leave it until Bonetti was caught, but I wouldn't listen? I was allowed to hold her hand, she felt cold.

"Sophie, it's me, Carter, you're going to pull through, you can't disappoint them on St Patrick's day, keep fighting love I know you'll make it. I'm just outside I'm going nowhere until I know your OK."

A nod from the nurse indicated it was time for me to go. I went outside and sat with Alistair.

"How was she?"

"She looks terrible, breathing on a ventilator I don't think she's going to make it."

"It's early days, Carter, you'll have to be patient."

Hour after hour I sat there, by 11:00 am Alistair had to leave for a previous court appointment. It was 9:00pm when a nurse came out and summoned one of the doctors. I was convinced she'd died, after a further thirty minutes he came out to see me.

"Mr. Dean, I'm delighted to tell you your fiancée has regained consciousness, initial tests don't indicate any permanent brain damage, she will have to be assessed further of course, but early indications are good. You can go and see her if you like."

"Thank you doctor." She was awake and I got a half smile when she saw me.

"How are feeling?"

"Lousy, my chest hurts and I'm a bit woozy although that's probably the morphine and other stuff, not sure what's in these other drips."

"Do you remember what happened?"

"I was following you when I saw a flash then got the most horrendous pain in upper arm almost immediately I got hit in my chest. It knocked me off my feet, don't remember anything after that until I woke up in here."

"Where are you from?"

"You know where I'm from, Kilkenny in Ireland."

"What's your mother called?"

"Have you been drinking?"

"Look Sophie, you suffered a cardiac arrest and it took them a while to get your heart started, they said there was a possibility you may have suffered brain damage, through lack of oxygen. I'm just trying to see if that's the case so I'm going to ask you a few questions, OK?"

"Fire away."

"What's your mother's name?"

"Vera."

"What does your mother do for a living?"

"She runs a guesthouse."

"What's the name of the sergeant who calls to your house?"

"Mick Byrne."

"What's his nickname?"

"Podgy."

"What sort of medals have you won?"

"Over sixty for Irish dancing and at least eighty for trap shooting, you see, I'm OK."

"One last question, what does your boyfriend do for a living?"

She thought about it for several seconds, "He's a pimp."

"Really?"

"No, only joking, he's a fat rustler in a corned-beef factory."

"Now I know you're OK."

Made in the USA
Middletown, DE
26 November 2017